ANTONY COYNE

Shadows of the Past

Copyright © 2025 by Antony Coyne

All rights reserved. No part of this publication may be reproduced, stored or transmitted in any form or by any means, electronic, mechanical, photocopying, recording, scanning, or otherwise without written permission from the publisher. It is illegal to copy this book, post it to a website, or distribute it by any other means without permission.

This novel is entirely a work of fiction. The names, characters and incidents portrayed in it are the work of the author's imagination. Any resemblance to actual persons, living or dead, events or localities is entirely coincidental.

Antony Coyne asserts the moral right to be identified as the author of this work.

First edition

This book was professionally typeset on Reedsy. Find out more at reedsy.com

Contents

1	Chapter 1 – Ghosts of the past	1
2	Chapter 2 – Blood in the blue	7
3	Chapter 3 – Descent into darkness	11
4	Chapter 4 – Shadows on the playground	18
5	Chapter 5 – Shadows in the rear-view mirror	24
6	Chapter 6 – The reckoning begins	31
7	Chapter 7 – Fragile hopes	34
8	Chapter 8 – The breaking point	38
9	Chapter 9 – Ghosts and Allies	42
10	Chapter 10 – Echoes of laughter	46
11	Chapter 11 – Rage and regret	50
12	Chapter 12 – Into the abyss	54
13	Chapter 13 – Shattered hope	57
14	Chapter 14 – A line crossed	61
15	Chapter 15 – Tick Tock	65
16	Chapter 16 – The weight of it all	69
17	Chapter 17 – A summer's day	72
18	Chapter 18 – The puppet master's game	76
19	Chapter 19 – Vendetta	79
20	Chapter 20 – Shadows of doubt	83
21	Chapter 21 – Spiraling into shadows	88
22	Chapter 22 – In the dark	92
23	Chapter 23 – New directions	96
24	Chapter 24 – Behind closed doors	102

25	Chapter 25 – Pieces of the puzzle	106
26	Chapter 26 – Close quarters	110
27	Chapter 27 – Fractured loyalties	117
28	Chapter 28 – The waiting game	121
29	Chapter 29 – Hanging by a thread	127
30	Chapter 30 – In the shadow of the badge	131
31	Chapter 31 – In the grip of doubt	135
32	Chapter 32 – Threads of deception	138
33	Chapter 33 – Alison's solitude	142
34	Chapter 34 – Worst fears	147
35	Chapter 35 – Beneath the silence	153
36	Chapter 36 – The call	156
37	Chapter 37 – Unmasking the past	160
38	Chapter 38 - The Bridge Between	163
39	Chapter 39 – Silent doubts	166
40	Chapter 40 – Crossroads	172
41	Chapter 41 – Raising the Stakes	177
42	Chapter 42 – Megan's Fear	180
43	Chapter 43 – Shotguns and silencers	182
44	Chapter 44 – Game of Nerves	185
45	Chapter 45 – Echoes of the Past	188
46	Chapter 46 - No Safe Place	192
47	Chapter 47 - Focused Fury	196
48	Chapter 48 – Bound by grief	201
49	Chapter 49 - The Whistling Shadow	204
50	Chapter 50 – Reaching out	207
51	Chapter 51 – Lines of deception	210
52	Chapter 52 - Old Faces, Dead Ends	212
53	Chapter 53 – Riverside reckoning	216
54	Chapter 54 – Marshall's fate	220
55	Chapter 55 – Boundless evil	225

56	Chapter 56 – Burden of truth	228
57	Chapter 57 – Brother in doubt	234
58	Chapter 58 – Broken bonds	238
59	Chapter 59 – On the hook	242
60	Chapter 60 – Let's be Frank	246
61	Chapter 61 – Game changer	251
62	Chapter 62 – Mending bridges	254
63	Chapter 63 – False hope	257
64	Chapter 64 – Frank's trap	260
65	Chapter 65 – In the cross-hairs	265
66	Chapter 66 – Checkpoint one	268
67	Chapter 67 – Silent breach	272
68	Chapter 68 – A father's promise	275
69	Chapter 69 – The face off	279
70	Chapter 70 – Megan's cry	286
71	Chapter 71 – Final breath	289
72	Chapter 72 – A tribute	292

1

Chapter 1 – Ghosts of the past

The Broken Bottle. This depressing hole of a bar has been my second home for almost two years now. It was the first place I stumbled into after they booted me from the department, back when I still had the energy to feel anything.

The name had called out to me; it was quite fitting, The Broken Bottle. Here I was, a broken man, looking for a bottle. I wanted to drown out the reality of what had become of my life.

This place had practically beckoned me inside, welcomed me with open arms. The dim lighting and cheap whiskey a bonus.

It is the kind of place where people come to escape, forget about everything on the other side of the exit door. Relieve themselves of the weight of their own sins. No one has bothered to fix the broken jukebox for months. The only sounds are the groans of more drinks orders and glasses slamming down on the bar when they are empty.

The place stinks of stale beer. The walls bear stains from old cigarette smoke, dating back to before the smoking ban. It's a place for ghosts, people who've lost their way and are waiting for the end to come, one drink at a time.

I'm one of them now.

"Same as always, Ray?" Jimmy, the bartender, doesn't even wait for me to nod. He's pouring two fingers of cheap whiskey before I've even settled on the stool. He's seen me come in here every day like clockwork, and he's probably heard every sob story under the sun. I don't bother adding mine to the pile.

The whiskey burns on the way down, but it doesn't do much to numb the ache anymore. Still, it's part of the ritual, and I need rituals. They keep the chaos in my head from spilling out onto the floor. So, I sit here, day after day, pretending that if I drink enough, I can forget everything that's gone before.

But it never works.

I reach into my jacket pocket and pull out a crumpled photograph. A picture of Megan, my daughter. I stare at it every night. She is smiling that beautiful smile of hers. She was five when this photo was taken. Five, and still full of trust and love for her old man. That was before everything went to hell. Before I was forced to walk away from everything that mattered.

I hold the picture too tightly, almost as if I can somehow reach her through it. The paper is soft and worn from too much handling. We talk on the phone from time to time, but I honestly don't remember the last time I saw her in person. I miss her. Christ, I miss her more than anything.

This isn't how it was meant to be. I should be with her, watching her grow, holding her, not some damn picture.

My name's Ray Gordon. I used to be a cop. A good one, or at least I thought so. Now I'm just a lazy drunk who spends his days in a bar that smells like regret. A disgraced ex-cop, let go by idiots who wouldn't know good police work if it slapped them across the face. That's what I tell myself, anyway. But

CHAPTER 1 – GHOSTS OF THE PAST

deep down, I know I made mistakes. Maybe I was just doing my job, perhaps things just got out of hand. It doesn't matter anymore, not to them, not to Alison. Once you're branded guilty, people stop caring about the details.

It was two years ago when everything fell apart. Alison, my wife, well, ex-wife now, never stuck around to hear my side of the story. I should have known. She was always good at seeing through the bullshit, even mine. "A man doesn't end up dead on your watch unless you wanted it that way," she said as she packed her bags. She didn't even raise her voice, not once. That's what stung the most, I think, the cold, flat certainty in her words. She looked at me like I was a stranger. Someone she didn't recognize. Perhaps she was right.

She packed her things with a sense of eerie calm, folding each garment as if it were just another daily chore. I could only stand around, helpless to stop her from leaving. There was no use in begging or pleading; she had made up her mind and there was no going back. Nothing I said would change the fact that I had become the villain in her story.

What broke me wasn't her leaving, though that was bad enough. No, it was the way Megan's small suitcase was the first thing Alison packed. Our little girls' toys, her books, all ripped from the shelves, leaving them empty. Megan was six then. She was old enough to know something was wrong, but too young to understand it.

I remember standing at the foot of the stairs, watching Alison move through the house, imaging my life when she was done, how empty the house would feel. Megan was sitting on the couch, gripping her teddy bear tightly. She was staring up at me, huge sad eyes, wet with tears.

"Daddy," she whispered, "why is Mummy angry at you?"

I wanted to reassure her, to tell her everything was going to be okay. But I couldn't find any words. I was just as upset as she was. Any attempt to explain this would likely see me breaking down.

"Sometimes mummy's and daddy's fight sweetheart," I said, as calm as I could manage. "But it is all going to be OK, I promise."

She nodded, gave me a sweet smile, but a look of confusion remained etched across her face. I wanted to ease her confusion, but the truth was I hardly understood it myself.

"Is Mummy really taking me away?" Megan asked, her voice so quiet I almost didn't hear her.

That question shattered me. It took everything in me not to break down right there in front of her. My little girl was my last shot at redemption. My life was otherwise miserable. Now, I was powerless to stop her from being taken away.

I couldn't speak. I just nodded, held back my emotions as best I could. I had to leave; I didn't want to lose control and do something I couldn't take back. Alison had the right to her decision, no matter how devastating it may be.

So, I walked out the front door, head bowed low with shame, and I kept walking. I wandered the streets for hours. I needed to distract myself from the heart-wrenching reality of what was happening at home. When I finally returned, they were gone, all their belongings gone with them. I knew right there and then that I had a dark future ahead of me.

But even now, after two long years of drowning my sorrows, the memories are still raw. No matter how much whiskey I drink, it won't numb my pain. It won't remove the face of the man I killed on the night that changed everything. The night Alison could never let go of. But I was just doing my job....

wasn't I? Either way, what I wanted never mattered then and it sure as hell doesn't matter now.

I slide the photograph of Megan back into my jacket, feeling the familiar sting of guilt settle in. I haven't been the father she deserves, not by a long shot. Calls on birthdays, awkward visits where we both pretend things are normal, although it has been too long since the last, it's not enough. Nothing will ever be enough.

The bar door flings open. A chilly wind rushes in, along with a group of college kids, all laughter and energy. Their whole lives are ahead of them. I feel a flash of annoyance and quickly down another shot of whiskey. Let them have their fun. It won't be long before they are coming here to drown their own sorrows.

As I finish yet another drink, I pull out my phone to check for any messages. Probably nothing but bills or spam, but the moment the screen lights up, I see it, a text from Alison. My heart jumps in my chest, suddenly filled with mixed emotions of both dread and hope.

I open it, not knowing what quite to expect, probably more snide comments or another legal notice about custody. But it's much, much worse than that. There are just three words.

Megan is missing.

I drop my glass, and it smashes into pieces on the bar right in front of me, but I barely notice it. The bar falls silent around me as I block out all the noise and read those words over and over again.

Megan is missing.

And just like that, everything changes.

I pushed back from the bar. If I'd looked around, I would have seen all the deadbeats staring at me. But, I had more important things on my mind. So, I threw on my coat and headed for the exit. My entire body was shaking at the news. All that whiskey failing to dull the panic that's setting in. I fumble with the phone, trying to dial Alison's number, but my fingers feel clumsy, uncooperative.

She picks up on the first ring, her voice tight with fear. "Ray," she says, and I can hear the tears in her voice. "Ray, oh god Ray, she's gone. Megan, our little girl, I don't know what to do..."

"What happened?" my voice is harsher than I mean it to be. "Where is she?"

"I don't know!" Alison cries. "I...I just turned around for a minute, and she was gone. Ray, please, help me, please!"

I've spent the last two years trying to forget, trying to stay out of Alison's life as much as possible. But none of that matters now. Megan is missing. My little girl is out there somewhere, and God help whoever took her.

Because they do not know what kind of man I really am.

2

Chapter 2 – Blood in the blue

Being a cop in Chicago is an extremely dangerous job. I think the danger always lured me to it. That, and my father was a cop. Seeing him dressed in the glorious blue of a Chicago beat cop always made me happy as a kid. Even now, the city is in my blood. It breathes through the cracks in the streets, spills into the alleys, and echoes in the sound of a siren tearing through the night. It always has.

My father, Officer Robert Gordon, was a legend in his own right. The stories about him are still told around precincts to this day, passed like ghost stories around a campfire. Some were true; most were embellished. They called him "Rocky" because he was unbreakable. At least, that's how I remember him. His uniform fit him perfectly, and it earned him respect. Fear, too. But fear and respect go hand in hand in this job.

When I was just a boy, I would sit on the stoop of our apartment building, excited, waiting for him to come home. I would see him walking toward me with his broad shoulders and his head held high. He was the absolute picture of authority. He was larger than life. Other kids looked up to superheroes; I looked up to Officer Gordon. I wanted to be just like him. To wield that power, to have people look at me the way they looked at him, with a mix of awe and terror.

There is something about the uniform, the power, the authority over others. I have always enjoyed feeling like I am in charge, making men bend the knee. It is like a drug. The badge represents that power. When I step into a room, knowing that I am the law, that what I say goes. Most people understand that. Most people know their place when I walk in, when I speak.

But not everyone. And those who don't...well, they learn.

The first time I tasted proper authority, I was just a rookie, just a year on the force. My father had pulled some strings to get me assigned to the South Side, the rough territory, where respect was bought in blood and broken bones. I remember the rush; the electricity running through me the first time I stepped out of a patrol car there. It wasn't like the watered down, training-ground scenarios at the academy. This was the real deal. This is what I had been waiting for. Chicago at its bloodiest.

I remember a call we got about a domestic disturbance. Nothing new, nothing interesting. Just another case of someone getting too drunk and their spouse being on the receiving end of it. But when we pulled up, I knew right away this one was different. It was the middle of July; the heat clinging to everything, making tempers flare like the sun itself. The guy, big, wiry, face full of anger and whiskey, was already outside, yelling at his wife who stood in the doorway, clutching a crying kid.

I stepped out of the car, my hand on my belt, feeling my baton for reassurance, the cool grip of my service weapon just inches away. I was calm, composed. My partner was a few steps behind me, but I didn't need him.

"Sir," I said, in my most commanding cop voice, "you need to calm down."

He turned and looked right through me, his eyes wild and bloodshot. The stench of alcohol was unbearable. "And who the fuck are you?" he growled. "You think you're a big man cause you got a badge?"

The way he said it, along with the way he looked at me, no hint of fear or respect. I could feel the rage burning on the inside, but I maintained a calm manner. My father always taught me the importance of maintaining control. But he also taught me not to back down, that respect wasn't a given; it was earned. Or, if needed, taken.

I stepped closer, getting in his face. I made myself as big as I could. "Right now, you got two choices," I said, low and steady. "Either you shut up and go inside, or I put you down right here, right now."

He didn't move. Didn't even blink. Instead, he spat at my feet. And that was it. I saw red.

Before I knew it, I had thrown a punch right into his gut, knocking the wind out of him. He staggered back, wheezing, and then I had him against the wall, my forearm pressing against his throat. My partner yelled something, but it was just noise. My heart pounding in my ears. This was the rush I loved. I was looking directly into his eyes. I wanted him to see mine. I wanted him to know that I was in charge here, that he wasn't dealing with some rookie who he could push around. I wanted him to fear me.

When I let him go, he crumpled to the floor, trying desperately to get his breath. His wife was screaming hysterically, and the kid kept crying, but I didn't care. That rush of power was everything to me. I looked down at him and said, "Next time, you won't get back up."

My partner wrote it up as a standard arrest; no one batted an eye. Not in Chicago. Not back then. Unbreakable Officer Gordon would have been proud.

But not everyone who wears the badge would understand. Some of these new guys they think it's about protecting and serving. They don't get that sometimes you have to break a few rules to get respect, to keep the peace. And sometimes, keeping the peace means making people fear stepping out of line.

The city demands it. Chicago demands it. This is not a place for weakness. Cops need to be tougher than anyone else, and I plan to be one tough son of a bitch.

Some days I wonder if that makes me a good cop or just another piece of this city's machinery, grinding and chewing everything in its path. But that's not a question for today. Today, all I know is that I need to be harder than this city, harder than everyone in it. Because that's what it means to wear the blue in Chicago.

And God help anyone who doesn't respect that....

3

Chapter 3 – Descent into darkness

"I'm on my way," I say and hang up the phone.

Alison had been so full of panic that her voice was almost unrecognizable. This time she wasn't furious with me; she was terrified, and she needed me.

I fumble for the keys, nearly dropping them in my haste as I break into a sprint toward my truck. My body is sluggish from too much whiskey, but nothing is going to stop me from getting to Alison and finding out what the hell is going on. I shouldn't be driving, not after the amount I've had, but none of that matters now. Megan matters. Every second counts. My little girl is out there somewhere, with God knows who, and every dark possibility claws at my mind.

I put my foot down, wanting to get there as quick as I can, the tires screeching against the road as they spin beneath me. A complete stranger has taken my daughter. It's a thought I cannot begin to comprehend. A mix of the adrenaline and the booze sending my head spinning. It feels as though my heart is being ripped from my chest.

Each time I think I have hit rock bottom, something worse

comes along and drags me down further.

I thought I had suffered enough punishment. But no, the universe isn't done with me yet. And this... this was the pinnacle. The one thing that could utterly break me. But it won't. No. It'll do the opposite. They've made the worst mistake of their lives. Whoever they are, they've brought me into their world now, and they do not know what kind of hell I can bring. They've set something in motion they can't control, and I'm going to make them sorry they ever laid a finger on Megan.

The drive to Alison's is long. She didn't stick around after the divorce, moved far enough away that I wouldn't be able to just show up whenever I felt like it. Typical Alison, always wanting control, even over the distance between us. Now it feels like those ninety minutes stretch into a goddamn eternity. My mind races with possibilities, trying to figure out who did this and why.

The self-loathing, the guilt, has already started. This is all my fault, of course it is. I have a list of enemies longer than I care to consider. Criminals who could crawl out from under their rocks at any time to punish me now that I am no longer a cop. Hell, some of my former colleagues would probably like to take a stab at me. I didn't join the force to make friends. But when I was being forced out, the other cops turned their backs on me. They wanted no connection to the dirty cop.

But who... who could hate me so much that they would do this? Why not just put a bullet in my fucking head and be done with it? Why take my little girl? She doesn't deserve this. She's innocent in all this. Leave her out of it.

And then there's that memory, the one that keeps replaying in my mind, the night everything went to hell. That night two years ago, the night that started my almighty fall from grace. My partner, Joey and I had gotten the call, a suspect in a missing child case, Leroy Jenkins. We already knew him well, and so did the whole force. He was a lowlife, in and out of the system all his life. He was a scumbag, but we had never picked him up for anything like this. It was a reminder that you just never truly know what these street rats are up to. It was pouring down with rain that night, the kind of night you wished for paperwork at your warm desk.

We tracked Leroy to an abandoned crack house, typical for scum like him. The sighting came from some neighbor who'd probably seen more than they wanted to. I remember the look Joey gave me when we pulled up, both of us soaked to the bone, headlights off to keep the element of surprise. He was nervous. So was I, though I'd never admit it. Leroy was a big guy, dangerous, and desperate. I told Joey to go around the back while I took the front.

Everything happened so fast after that. One minute, I'm kicking in the door, the next, Leroy's on the ground, blood pooling around him, eyes wide open but seeing nothing. And there I was, standing over him with a gun in my hand. Joey came running in just as Leroy took his last breath.

It is a memory that never leaves me, no matter how much whiskey I drink. I am brought out of my daydream by a huge 18-wheeler heading straight for me, its horn blaring and lights flashing. I swerve just managing to avoid being hit. Just then, it hits me that this could be revenge for what happened that night. Someone connected to Leroy could be doing this.

I quickly pull the truck over to the side of the road; I take big, slow, deliberate breaths as I try to calm myself down. I slap myself hard across the face, forcing myself to focus. I'm no good to Megan if I'm dead before I even start looking for her.

I roll down the window and let the frosty night air slap me awake. The rain's picked up again, drenching the road ahead, but it helps. It keeps me grounded. Keeps me sharp.

No more daydreaming. No more distractions. Nothing but complete focus now. Whoever took Megan was going to pay. They're going to pay in ways they can't even imagine. I'll make sure of that.

I pull back onto the road, determination hardening inside me like steel. I will bring her home no matter what it takes.

When I got to Alison's house, she was out the front door before I had brought the truck to a stop. She came running toward me, looking drawn and white as a ghost. I thought back to when we first met. She had bright blonde hair, with blue eyes that stood out from across the room. Her looks would stop men in their tracks as they would take her in. I couldn't believe I was looking at the same woman right now. Grief was a terrible thing. She had clearly been crying. She looked as though she hadn't slept for a week, like she was drowning in grief. It broke my heart to see her this way.

Slowly, Evan stepped out behind her, dragging his feet like he didn't know whether to follow or stay hidden. The new man in her life. My replacement. He was a small, unremarkable guy, wearing his usual tank top and glasses that screamed "safety first." I guess after me, the rough cop with baggage, she wanted stability. A dowdy professor with soft hands and soft words. Yeah, he was safe. But safe didn't find Megan. Safe didn't protect her.

I hated him on principle alone. Not just because he was filling a role that used to be mine, but because I didn't trust a man who thought reading books could save the world. This world?

CHAPTER 3 - DESCENT INTO DARKNESS

It chewed you up and spit you out if you weren't ready to fight back. And he clearly wasn't.

I had barely opened my truck door when Alison started screaming at me. "This is connected to you, Ray. I know it! This is because of something you did, something you couldn't keep in the past! You did this! You got our girl taken away from us!"

Her words hit me hard. As much as I wanted to fight back, as much as I wished I could tell her that wasn't true, I couldn't. I just stood there and took the blame, let her put all the guilt on me. I couldn't deny it, not really. I'd been thinking the same thing the entire drive over. My enemies had always come after me, but I never thought they'd sink so low as to come for my little girl.

But now wasn't the time to place blame. We needed to focus. I needed to stay clear-headed, even though everything inside me screamed to unleash the anger boiling in my veins. No. Megan was what mattered now. I had to push everything else aside.

"Alison," I said, trying to stay calm even as my voice cracked, "I need you to tell me what happened. Start from the beginning. Where were you when she went missing?"

Her face twisted into something darker, something colder. "Don't you dare tell me to calm down, Ray! Not after what you've done. Not after you brought this down on us." and then she allowed herself to cry.

I remained calm, trying to maintain my composure. We needed to be rational. "I'm sorry," I mumbled, trying to keep my tone even, "but for me to look for Megan, I need to know everything. Every little detail. Please."

She took her time, looking at me as she breathed in and out

heavily. I could see the tension in her shoulders shifting, her body relaxing slightly. She knew as well as I did I was her best shot at finding our daughter. Whether she liked it didn't matter right now. She wiped away her tears and tried hard to compose herself.

Evan came up beside her, wrapped his arm around her shoulders, trying to comfort her. I had to push away my anger at the sight of it. What right did he have to offer comfort when he was the one that had failed them both?

But I bit my tongue. This wasn't about him.

"We were at the park," Alison began, her voice small and tired. "The one on Regent Street. Megan was on the swings, like she always is. She loves that park, Ray." She put her hand to her mouth, trying to keep herself from crying. "I looked away for a second. Just a second."

"We?" I asked, my voice sharp. "Who was with you?"

Evan stepped forward, his voice shaking. "It was all of us. The three of us. We go to the park together; Megan always enjoys it." He looked at me, pleading with his eyes like that would somehow make me go easy on him. "Ray, I am so sorry this happened. We.... she was just there, and then...."

His words hit me like a hammer. He was there. He was supposed to protect her. That was his job, his responsibility now. My composure left me, replaced with seething anger. Before I knew it, I was moving toward him, fists clenched.

"You son of a bitch!" I roared. "How could you let this happen? How could you take your eyes off her, even for a second?"

Evan recoiled, retreating behind Alison like the coward I always knew he was. He looked up at me, fear evident all over his face, "I.... I'm so sorry," he stammered. "I didn't mean...."

CHAPTER 3 – DESCENT INTO DARKNESS

But Alison wasn't having it. She got into my face, protecting Evan, shoving me back as hard as she could manage. "How dare you!" she screamed, her voice raw and furious. "How dare you come here and blame him! This isn't on him, Ray! This is on you! If you weren't such a disgrace, if every lowlife did not hate you in this city, this wouldn't be happening! You did this, Ray! You brought this down on us all!"

Her words stung, cutting deep. I couldn't argue with her. I couldn't even defend myself. She was right, this was on me. My every instinct told me that whoever took Megan was connected to my past. And now, I had to fix it. I had to make this right.

I looked at Alison and made a promise. "I am going to do everything I can to bring our girl home."

Alison said nothing. She didn't need to. The look in her eyes said everything. She hated this situation. Hated that she had to rely on me after everything that had happened. But she knew, just like I did, deep down, she knew I was her best chance at getting Megan back. She didn't have to like it. Hell, she didn't have to trust me, but right now, I was the only hope she had.

And when I found her... whoever was responsible was going to regret ever crossing me.

4

Chapter 4 – Shadows on the playground

I drove away from Alison's house in pain. Her words, echoing thoughts I'd had a thousand times myself, stung like a fresh wound. Coming from the woman I once loved, the woman I had brought up my daughter with, it was a special kind of personal. The kind that doesn't heal.

But I couldn't afford to dwell on it now. That kind of self-pity would only slow me down. The only thing that mattered was finding Megan and doing so quickly. Ex-cop or not, disgraced or not, I still had instincts. I was still a damn good cop when I had to be. So, I needed to think like one again. This wasn't just another case; this was personal.

Regent Street Park. That was where it all happened. I needed to see it for myself. Sure, the place would be crawling with cops, and they wouldn't let me within ten feet of the scene, but that didn't matter. If there were clues to be found, if there were any scraps of evidence those idiots might miss, I was going to find them. I had to.

When I got there, my worst fears solidified into reality. Police

CHAPTER 4 – SHADOWS ON THE PLAYGROUND

had cordoned off the entire playground, wrapping it in yellow tape. A police cruiser sat parked just outside the swings where Megan had been playing. Seeing that yellow tape, knowing it was there because my daughter was part of an active crime scene, it sent a shiver right through me. I could feel the panic setting in all over again, as if I were finding this out for the first time right here, right now.

But this also meant I would not be allowed near the park. The police didn't like me much before, and now I was just a civilian, an outsider. No way they'd let me poke around their crime scene, no matter how personal it was for me. But I had to try.

I got out of my truck and strolled over to the cruiser. Two cops were inside. Neither of them looked particularly sharp. One of them, a kid, really, rolled down his window when he saw me approach.

"Can I help you?" he asked.

The officer looked fresh, probably straight out of the academy. The job hadn't yet worn him down. He still looked at people like they could be trusted.

"I hope so," I said, keeping my voice steady. "My name's Ray. I'm Megan Gordon's father."

The young officer's face fell. "Oh, man... I'm sorry, Ray. This whole thing, it's awful."

"Yeah, thanks," I said. "I need to get in there. I need to look around. I need to know what happened here so I can give myself a chance to find her."

The kid hesitated. It was clear he wanted to help me out, but he didn't have the authority here. Before he could speak, his partner in the other seat spoke up.

It was an officer called Clayton.

I knew him. He was one of the many who'd turned their back on me when things went south. One of those cops who had a long memory and a short fuse. The kind of guy who didn't forget a grudge.

"Well, well, well," Clayton sneered, leaning over to get a better look at me. "If it isn't former officer Ray fucking Gordon. What the hell are you doing out here, Gordon? Got lost on your way to the bottle?"

I ignored the jibe "Clayton," I said, trying to maintain my calm. "You know this is my daughter they've taken. You know I need to find her."

Clayton's face remained stone cold. He just sat back, made himself comfortable, and shook his head slowly. "You're not a cop anymore, Gordon. You don't need to do shit. Leave this to the professionals. I don't need you going rogue and taking out anyone who might have looked sideways at your girl."

It hadn't taken long for this son of a bitch to get under my skin. I had to fight hard to control my anger. I could see myself dragging Clayton out of that cruiser, slamming his smug face into the pavement. But if I did that, and ended up in jail, Megan would be lost forever.

I swallowed the anger, forcing it back down. I took a breath; it took everything I had to not sink back into my old patterns when it came to be disrespected.

"Come on, Clayton," I said, my voice tight with restraint. "What would you do if it were your kid out there? Huh?"

Clayton just laughed. A cold, hollow sound. "I wouldn't be in this situation, Gordon. I don't have a list of enemies waiting to come after me and mine. But you? That's a different story."

I stared at him, my vision narrowing into a tunnel of pure hate. He would not help me. I knew that. Clayton would not

CHAPTER 4 – SHADOWS ON THE PLAYGROUND

let me near the scene, and trying to force it would only make things worse.

I stepped back, forcing myself to look around the park from the distance. My eyes scanned for anything I could use. CCTV cameras. Witnesses. Anything. But from where I stood, all I saw was emptiness. The park looked like any other park in the rain, lonely, bleak, and without answers. The frustration mounted, threatening to pull me under again.

But I wouldn't let it. Not now. Not with Megan on the line.

I forced myself to turn away, the urge to head straight for The Broken Bottle gnawing at me like an old addiction. But I couldn't go back there. Not yet. I had to regroup, clear my head. I wasn't done. I wasn't giving up. I'd find my daughter, no matter what it took.

I headed back to my truck, my mind racing with anger and doubt. As much as I hated the self-righteous bastard, he was right. I had enemies, enemies of my own making. Hearing him say it had only added to the frustration I was already feeling. I got back in my truck and forced myself to forget about Clayton, focus on Megan, try to understand what happened here. And why?

The rain was falling hard now, the wipers on my truck barely able to keep up with the torrent of water, blinding my view of the road. Most people had the good sense to stay indoors, away from the weather and other dangers that lurked out here. I didn't have that luxury. My daughter was out here somewhere, with God knows who, and it terrified me.

As I hit the highway, my view of the road became even more hazardous. I could barely see the road, and oncoming headlights blurred my vision even more. The sound of the rain and wipers moving side to side was not enough to drown out my thoughts.

I thought back to the days when I would take Megan to the park. She loved when I brought her to that park. I would push her on those swings for what felt like hours. She would laugh and laugh, beg me to push higher, higher daddy. I could still hear her laughter clear as day right now.

The sound of my phone buzzing broke the memory. I glanced at it, hoping to see Alison's name, hoping it would say everything was OK. She is back home now. But it was just a message from an old contact, a private investigator I used to know from back in the day. He had heard about Megan. The message was brief, but it was enough to increase my heart rate.

"Need to talk. I have something."

I gripped the wheel tighter. It could be nothing. It could be a dead end. Or it could be the break I needed. Either way, it was something. And right now, I was desperate enough to chase down any lead, no matter how thin.

I shot back a quick reply, setting up a meeting. At least it gave me something to hold on to. The drive home didn't feel as endless now. I had a direction, a purpose again.

But I couldn't help but doubt myself, doubt if I was up to this. Was I too broken to save Megan? I didn't have any of my old advantages. No badge, no uniform. My authority was gone. What chance did I stand?

My mind kept drifting back to that night two years ago. To the man I killed. The way everything fell apart afterward. Someone out there knew something about that night, and now they were making me pay for it. But what if they weren't done? What if they were just getting started with me?

A set of lights behind me had caught my eye. This same car had been behind me for miles, and now it was getting closer.

CHAPTER 4 – SHADOWS ON THE PLAYGROUND

I focused in on the mirror, trying to see what I could of the vehicle. The road was nearly empty. Why were they tailing me?

My pulse quickened. Was it paranoia? Or was someone really following me? I couldn't be sure either way, so I put my foot down, the truck speeding up way past the speed limit. The car behind me matched my pace, keeping its distance but not backing off.

I made a quick turn onto a side road, my heart hammering in my chest. The rain made the roads slick, and my tires skidded slightly as I straightened out. I watched the rear-view mirror, waiting, my breath caught in my throat.

But the car didn't follow. It sped past the intersection, continuing down the highway, and I let out a breath I hadn't realized I was holding.

I shook my head, gripping the wheel tighter. Maybe it was nothing. Just another car on the road. But the paranoia was creeping in now, threading its way into my mind like a poison.

I had to stay sharp. I couldn't let this get to me. Megan was out there, and I couldn't afford to lose my focus, not now.

I turned back onto the main road, the rain still hammering down as I drove. I headed to my meeting with the private investigator.

5

Chapter 5 – Shadows in the rear-view mirror

I parked out front of the small diner where I had agreed to meet him. The rain had finally relented, leaving behind that damp air smell. I could see him, Frank Mulligan, Private Investigator, sitting in a booth near the window. He had ordered himself coffee. It had been a long time since I last saw him, but he hadn't changed much, still grizzled, and unshaven.

Frank nodded as I approached. "Ray. Sit down. You look like shit."

I didn't respond. I just sat down across from him, waiting. He had a scar on his neck, sort of shaped like a hook. I had noticed it every time I met him, never cared enough to ask how he got it.

Frank sipped his coffee, dragging out the silence, making me wait longer than I needed to. "I heard about Megan," Frank said finally. "It's a damn shame. Kid didn't deserve this."

I clenched my jaw. "You said you had something."

Frank leaned back in his seat, pulling out his phone. "I might have something. Could be nothing, but you never know with these things." He swiped a few times on the screen before turning it toward me. "Look."

On the screen was a grainy image of a dark SUV parked a few blocks from the playground. It looked like many cars that might have passed through the area, but it was something just enough to spark a shred of hope.

"A security camera a couple of streets down from the park recorded that. The car remained parked there for over an hour during Megan's disappearance. No plates, nothing identifying. But I figured you'd want to see it."

I stared at the image, my mind racing. Could it be connected? Or was this just a coincidence, another dead end?

"That's it?" I asked, my voice tight. "A car?"

Frank smirked, leaning forward. "It's a lead, Ray. Granted, it's not much to go off on its own, but it's more than you've got right now. And with a little digging, well, who knows? I've got some friends who can find out more, but they don't work for free."

My eyes narrowed. "How much?"

Frank tapped his fingers on the table, considering. "Five grand up front. More if they have to dig deep. These people don't come cheap."

A familiar feeling as my anger was building again. Five grand. For a blurry photo of a car that could belong to anyone. It was a joke. Frank, this absolute low life, was trying to exploit my desperation for an easy payday.

"I'm not made of money, Frank," I said, my voice low. "And this," I jabbed a finger at the phone, "this could be nothing."

"Could be," Frank agreed, with a touch of smugness, "Or it could be something. How much are you willing to risk not finding out?"

I stood, towering over him as he remained seated. "You're a real piece of work, Frank. Trying to make a buck off my kid's disappearance."

Frank didn't even flinch. He just shrugged. "I'm a businessman, Ray. And business is good."

I felt my fists clench again, that familiar rage boiling over. I wanted to punch Frank in the face, to throw him through the window. But what good would it do? Frank was just another bottom-feeder, another parasite trying to profit off my misery. I couldn't afford to waste time or money on false hope.

I said nothing else; I simply shook my head, turned, and left the diner. I could feel Frank's eyes on me as I left, but I would not allow him to waste anymore of my time.

As I climbed back into my truck, the frustration welled up inside me. Another dead end. Another waste of time. I smashed the palms of my hands against the steering wheel, shouting at nothing and no one.

I took some time to compose myself, taking deep breaths in and out.

Frank's blurry photo might have been useless, but it served as a cold reminder. Someone out there had Megan, and they were hiding her. Someone took her for a reason connected to me. I just knew it.

A thought nagged me; how did Frank find out so quickly? How did he already have pictures of CCTV in the area? Was he in on this? Was he doing this to me? I could feel the anger again. It never really leaves me, but this was getting to me.

I waited for Frank to leave, to tail him. Maybe if I followed him, I could get my baby girl back. I watched the slimy bastard as he sat sipping his coffee like he didn't have a care in the world. Willing him to get up and leave. Willing him to take

CHAPTER 5 – SHADOWS IN THE REAR-VIEW MIRROR

me to where I could find answers. I was fidgeting nervously, hands and legs in constant motion. I was impatient.

I knew Frank well enough, too well, in fact. The slimy grin he wore when he flashed that CCTV image was still burning in my brain. He was too damn comfortable with it, like he was enjoying having the opportunity to show me it. It just felt like he knew more than he was saying.

I sat impatiently, taking deep breaths in and out as I tried to compose myself, thoughts flashing through my mind. But mainly, I was thinking back to how I met Frank. It was apparent right away that he wasn't to be trusted.

It must have been about 10 years ago; I was called to the scene of an assault. The suspect was already in cuffs as another patrol arrived first at the scene. Frank was also there before me; he was all too familiar with the suspect in cuffs. There was almost a nudge and a wink between them, as if to say, 'I got your back.'

The suspect had beaten another man half to death with his bare hands. It was a brutal scene, the man's face so badly swollen his own mother wouldn't have been able to identify him. Story went that the guy on the floor, currently gurgling his own blood, had been sleeping with the suspect's wife. Someone hired Frank to investigate the affair.

Being the slimy weasel that he is, Frank, upon confirming the affair, saw an opportunity to make more money. He confirmed the affair with the suspect and was kind enough to offer the exact location of his wife's lover, for an extra £2k, of course.

Frank led our suspect right to this man, to this mangled, bleeding heap on the ground. And then he sat back and watched as the suspect broke the poor bastard's face in. I imagine Frank watched with a sleazy grin on his face, too. The sick fuck. He never intervened, never called for help. He just watched, probably thinking of all the ways he could spin this to his advantage later. That's how he operates. He's always got an angle.

I never liked him, never trusted him, but he proved useful, had good contacts, and sometimes, useful information. As a cop, you keep a guy like that close. But now, all those memories felt like red flags I should've noticed sooner. Now, I couldn't help but wonder if Frank had been playing me all along.

Back in the present, I kept my eyes on Frank. As much as I wanted to go back inside and grab him by the throat, shake the truth out of him, I knew it wasn't the smart move. If I stay patient, he may just lead me to somewhere useful.

Frank finally made a move, getting up and leaving his booth. I stayed in the shadows, out of sight, watching as Frank gave that sleazy grin to a waitress as he paid his bill. His smirk alone was enough to make me boil. He swaggered out of the diner like a man who had achieved what he came here for.

I watched him through the rear-view mirror as he headed for his car. I was certain he did not know I was still there. He paused for a moment to light up a cigarette. The light from the flame highlighting that hooked scar on his neck. He took a long drag on the cigarette, then jumped in his car. He had parked just a few spaces behind me.

He started his engine, pulled the window down, took another long drag of his cigarette before discarding it out of the open window. I hunched down in my seat so he wouldn't see me as he drove by. His lights illuminated my truck into full view as he pulled out of his space, but he didn't notice, or care, that I was there.

I waited a few moments but setting off in pursuit, the darkened streets working to my advantage, giving me cover. I

CHAPTER 5 – SHADOWS IN THE REAR-VIEW MIRROR

kept my distance, but never let him out of my sight.

I knew these roads well, the same roads I'd patrolled for years as a cop.

Frank took a few casual turns, winding his way through back streets. Maybe he was just heading home, or he was just on his way to meet someone. It didn't matter. All I knew was that I had to stick to him like glue.

The anger still bubbled beneath the surface, coiling tighter in my chest with every passing minute. My fingers flexed on the steering wheel, the rubber groaning under the pressure. I couldn't get that nagging thought out of my head: How had Frank gotten that CCTV footage so damn fast?

He wasn't stupid. Shady, and always working an angle, but not stupid. Something didn't sit right. A guy like Frank didn't just stumble into a case like mine without there being something in it for him. So, what was it? What was his angle this time?

My headlights caught a glimpse of him as he turned right onto a quieter street. I slowed down, watching his taillights disappear for a moment behind the curve before I made the turn myself. Up ahead, I saw him flick on his blinker, pulling into a gas station.

I slowed down even further, driving past as if I had no interest in stopping. My eyes locked on his reflection in the station's glass windows. He pulled up to the pump, stepped out, and casually walked inside.

I drove around the block once, circling back like a shark. I parked a little way down, staying out of sight, but with a clear view of the station.

What the hell are you up to, Frank?

I watched his every move as he slithered around the station

aisles, picking up some gum and a bottle of water.

He could well be on a routine drive home, but I couldn't shake the thought that he was holding out on me.

I felt my foot tapping nervously on the floor-mat, my mind racing through scenarios, every one of them darker than the last. What if he was meeting someone? What if he was involved? What if he were just dangling bait in front of me, leading me in circles while my daughter, God, I couldn't finish that thought?

The door jingled as Frank stepped back out, and I tightened my grip on the steering wheel, ready to continue the chase. He hopped back into his car, started it up, and rolled out of the station with the same casual ease as before.

I waited a beat, then followed. He made a left, heading toward the outskirts of town. The road stretched out, quiet and desolate. If you needed to get away from it all, this was the place to go.

I adjusted myself in my seat more comfortably. I was on high alert now, ready for any possibility. Whatever Frank was involved in, I was about to find out. And if he had any part in taking Megan... well, he was going to wish he'd stayed under that rock he crawled out from.

For now, I just had to wait. Wait and follow. Wherever this bastard was going, I was right behind him. And he wasn't getting away from me this time.

I kept pace with him, careful not to make too much noise. Wherever he was going, I was going to be right there behind him. I was going to get answers.

6

Chapter 6 – The reckoning begins

I have her now. The moment I've waited for, the moment Ray Gordon finally pays for what he did to me. That bastard ruined my life, tore it apart at the seams, and now it's my turn to return the favor. Every second of my plan has been years in the making, every detail carefully plotted out, and it went as smoothly as I knew it would. Snatch and grab, easy as pie. Almost too easy.

I can picture him now, sitting somewhere, stewing in his anger, thinking that rage will somehow be enough to solve everything. Thinking that he's still the sharp cop he used to be, like he still has it in him to fix this.

Not anymore, Ray. Those days are long gone. Now you're nothing but a washed-up booze hound with trembling hands and bloodshot eyes. You can't solve this. You can't even come close. Not this time.

But I'm going to let you think you can. Oh, I'm going to let you stew in it, let you run yourself ragged trying to play detective again. I want you chasing your own tail until your legs give out beneath you. You'll think you're getting closer.

Maybe you'll feel one step away from finding her. But you'll realize you've been running in circles the whole time.

Because this, this is going to take time. This is going to torture you in ways you never saw coming. I want you to suffer, Ray. I want you to hurt. The way I hurt. I want you to feel your hope slipping through your fingers, piece by piece, until there's nothing left but despair.

And when that happens, when you're completely broken, I'll be there. And you'll watch. You'll watch as I decide her fate. Maybe I'll even let you look her in the eye before I do it. Wouldn't that be poetic? Your failure staring back at you while you beg, while you bargain, while you crumble.

You won't be able to forgive me, Ray. And why should you? I have never forgiven you, no fucking chance of that happening.

Even steven, right? It's about damn time.

The smile creeps across my face, and I let it sit there for a moment, savoring the feeling of being in control. He doesn't even know what's coming. He doesn't have a clue that this is all just the beginning.

And that's what makes it so perfect.

The last year of my life has been leading to this. The long nights of planning, the weeks of watching, waiting for the right moment. The satisfaction of watching everything fall into place, just as I knew it would.

It's almost funny. For all his tough-guy cop instincts, for all his years of experience, Ray never saw it coming. He never even thought to look behind him, never suspected the danger was right under his nose the entire time.

But he will. Soon enough, he will. And by then, it'll be too late.

This is my show now, Ray. And you? You're just the audience.

CHAPTER 6 – THE RECKONING BEGINS

Let the games begin.

7

Chapter 7 – Fragile hopes

Alison sat at the kitchen table, holding onto a cold cup of tea she had made hours ago but forgotten to drink. The house was painfully quiet without Megan's laughter. She remembered her little girl, full of joy, running through the house. The only sound was Evan's footsteps above as he paced up and down, not knowing what to do with himself. The whole thing was unbearable.

Her phone was on the table in front of her, but it was as silent as the house. No messages, no news, no hope to cling to. With every passing minute, she felt more helpless.

She told herself it was too soon, that Ray needed time, but the uncertainty gnawed at her. She squeezed her hands together; her knuckles white. She hadn't realized just how much she was shaking.

She looked up when she heard the soft creak of the stairs. Evan was standing in the doorway. He looked exhausted. He was full of guilt. He looked as worn out by this as she felt.

"Any word?" he asked quietly, his voice full of hope that she might have some update, anything, to cling to.

CHAPTER 7 – FRAGILE HOPES

"No," Alison whispered, shaking her head. Her voice was hollow. She watched as Evan sank into the chair across from her. His hands fidgeted on the table, tapping lightly, restless.

"Maybe we should have just left it to the police," he said after a few moments of silence. His words were cautious, as though he was tiptoeing around something they'd both been thinking but were too afraid to say aloud.

Alison winced at the suggestion, though it was a thought that had crossed her mind a thousand times since she had contacted Ray. The police followed protocols and procedures; They weren't clouded by personal feelings or haunted by demons from the past. Ray... Ray was nothing but personal feelings and demons.

"Perhaps," Alison admitted. She glanced at Evan. "But... you know how they work. How long it takes to get anything done? Megan..." she took a moment to regain control. The mere mention of her name made her ache. "Megan doesn't have time for bureaucratic red tape."

Evan rubbed his hands over his face, sighing deeply. "I get that. I just... I don't know if Ray is the right one for this. He's... he's not exactly stable, Al. He could do more harm than good. You've seen the way he acts now."

"I know," she replied. She could understand his concerns. "Believe me, I know better than anyone. But Ray will do whatever it takes. He won't stop until he finds her."

"Or until he finds the bottom of another bottle," Evan muttered under his breath.

Alison's anger took over. She snapped, "You don't know him like I do. Ray may have his issues. But, for our Megan, he'll go to hell and back to bring her home. No matter what it costs him."

Evan raised an eyebrow. "But that's the problem, Al. What will it cost him? And what if he gets so wrapped up in this that he..." he hesitated, searching for the right words, "that he screws things up? We can't afford that. We can't afford to lose her because Ray lost control.... again."

She slumped back in her chair, staring at her phone again. What Evan was saying was true, but she simply didn't want to hear it right now. Ray had a way of spiraling when things got too intense, pushing boundaries, crossing lines. She'd seen it in their marriage, seen it in the way he'd obsess over cases until they consumed him. And when he broke, it was chaos. It would impact on their lives for months on end.

But this was different. Megan was different. Ray loved their daughter more than anything in the world, and despite everything they had gone through, Alison knew that deep down. She knew he would do anything to bring her home, and that was the only thing keeping her from falling apart completely.

But she couldn't stop the doubts from gnawing away at the back of her mind. What if.... what if Ray lets her down again?

Evan was still there, waiting for her to say something. "Do you regret bringing him into this?" he asked softly.

Alison took a deep breath, her chest tight. She shook her head slowly. "No. I don't. Because Ray he's... relentless. Possibly even reckless, but I know he won't stop." She looked up, meeting Evan's gaze. "He'll get her back, Evan. I know he will."

Evan studied her for a long moment, biting his lip as if he didn't want to say anything. "I hope you're right," he hissed. "I pray to God he doesn't let you down again."

Alison felt the weight of those words. She understood why Evan felt the need to say them. She couldn't handle another betrayal from Ray. Not after everything they had been through. But she just had to believe that with their daughter's life was on the line, Ray would do this the right way.

"He won't," she said, more to herself than to Evan. "He can't."

The house returned silence, unbearable and deafening. They both drifted back into their own thoughts, the tension in the air so thick it was almost tangible.

Alison felt the familiar ache in her chest, the fear that had been gnawing at her since Megan had disappeared. She pressed her hands against the table, grounding herself, willing herself to hold on to the last shred of hope she had. For Megan. For Ray. For all of them.

The phone didn't ring, but Alison held onto her belief. Ray would stop at nothing. Ray would bring Megan home.

8

Chapter 8 – The breaking point

I watched from a safe distance as Frank got out of his car, the man I once scarcely gave a second thought to, now potentially the key to finding Megan. He strolled across the driveway and headed inside the house like nothing was wrong. Was this his home? I never cared enough to know where he lived. Men like Frank were always better kept at arm's length, useful only when needed, never to be trusted.

But what if this was it? What if my little girl was inside, tied up in some grim basement while Frank was out here, trying to squeeze money from me? My mind flashed with images of Megan blindfolded, her voice trembling as she called out for me in the dark. It was too much. I couldn't take it. The rage bubbled over, pushing logic to the back of my mind. I had convinced myself Frank was involved. There was no way I was walking away now.

I slammed the door of my truck and marched across the yard. My whole body tensing up as the anger surged through me. The weight of every worst-case scenario pushed me forward. I felt the urge to rip this whole situation apart with every step.

CHAPTER 8 – THE BREAKING POINT

I pounded on the door, the sound like a judge's gavel in the dead of night. No answer. I banged again, harder. Finally, the door creaked open, and there stood Frank, looking bewildered, with a dopey grin still lingering on his face.

"Ray? What the f—"

Before he could finish, I lunged. My hand gripped his throat, shoving him back into the house with the door slamming shut behind us. His back hit the wall with a thud as I tightened my grip, cutting off his air. The power in my hand surprised me. I could feel his larynx compressing under my thumb, and yet I stayed calm. That kind of calm that only comes from a darkness deep inside. My voice came out low and steady, like a frigid wind across a grave.

"Where is she?" I asked.

Frank's eyes bulged as he gurgled, clawing at my arm, trying to pry my hand away. He rasped out one word: "Who?"

"Don't fuck with me!" I snapped, my voice rising, venom coursing through every syllable. "Megan! Where is she? Tell me, or I'll crush your goddamn windpipe right here."

Frank was shaking now, his legs giving out as his face turned a sickly shade of purple. I could see that he was close to passing out, so I let go and then threw him across the room. He hit the floor hard. He was wheezing, struggling to get air back into his lungs. He had a look in his eyes. It wasn't fear; it was a look I was all too familiar with; it was rage. Frank wanted to kill me almost as much as I wanted to kill him.

I doubted myself. Was he actually clueless? Or was this just a master class in deception? Despite my uncertainty, I refused to relent. I stepped closer to him and drove my fist into his face, forcing him into a bloodied heap on the floor.

Then I heard a sound, a tiny whimper. Not from Frank, but

from across the room. I turned to see his wife and two terrified children watching, staring in disbelief at this violent monster who had just invaded their lives.

My heart sank. But I wasn't done. Not yet.

"MEGAN!" I shouted, tearing through the house. "Megan! It's Daddy! Where are you, baby? I'm coming for you!" I steamrolled my way through the house, from room to room, like a madman. Barging through every door, into every closet. I headed for the basement, practically falling down the steps as I rushed to see what was down there, who was down there. But there was nothing there, nobody there. I found no sign that anyone had been held prisoner down there.

There was no sign of Megan.

I felt the floor beneath me spin. The blood drained from my face, replaced by a sickening void in my chest. I had been so sure.

Climbing back up, I saw Frank standing in the hallway, a gun now in his shaking hands. He had the barrel aimed at my head. Blood dripped from his swollen, bloodied face onto his shirt. He was furious, wheezing, his eyes blazing with fury.

"You're a crazy bastard, Ray," he spat through gritted teeth. "You really think I'd take your daughter? Why the fuck would I help you then? Face to face? Think, Ray! I was offering you a lead, not screwing you over!"

His words pierced the fog of rage in my mind. Reality started creeping back in. The doubt. The guilt. But mostly confusion. Why had I jumped to this? What was happening to me?

I had nothing I could say that would make any sense.

Frank took a deep breath, his gun still trained on me. "I could kill you right now," he said, his voice cold. "And believe me, I should. But I'm not like you. I don't let my emotions run me off a cliff. Now get the fuck out of my house before I change my mind."

I didn't argue. I just turned and walked past him, my steps heavy, my mind blank. Out the door and back to my truck, where the realization hit me: I had no plan. I had no leads. And worse, I had alienated one of the few people who had offered to help.

Back to square one. And Megan... still out there.

I got into my truck, stared at the steering wheel, and felt the weight of it all pressing down on me.

9

Chapter 9 – Ghosts and Allies

As I drove aimlessly through the streets, trying to plan my next move, any move, really, my thoughts drifted to whiskey. Could I think better at The Broken Bottle? Could drowning my thoughts help me sort them out?

I shake my head hard, push the thought of drink away. Don't be so fucking stupid, Ray. Focus.

There was still one person I could turn to, someone I hadn't bothered to keep in touch with, but an old friend, Joey. We were partners once, back when the job meant something. He may not be as emotionally invested in this nightmare as I am. Maybe he can go at this with a straight head, keep me on the right path.

I pulled over to the side of the road, wanting to slow everything down. I didn't feel I had enough focus to drive and talk to Joey at the same time. Hell, I didn't even know if he'd want to hear from me after the way I'd ghosted him. Months of missed calls and ignored texts. If you weren't whiskey, I didn't give you my time.

I scrolled to his number and dialed. The phone rang again

CHAPTER 9 – GHOSTS AND ALLIES

and again. I almost hung up, but then his voice came through on the other end.

"Well, well. If it isn't the ghost of Ray fucking Gordon," Joey said. "Finally paid your phone bill?"

"Hey, Joey," I replied, trying to keep my voice steady. "Sorry, it's been a while."

"A while?" he scoffed. "Understatement of the year. Haven't seen you since we left the force. And I think it's been over a year since you bothered to pick up a call."

I didn't have time for the guilt trip. Not now. Not with Megan on the line.

"Listen, Joey," I said, my voice low. "I need your help."

"Oh, now you need my help?" He was laying it on thick, and I could hear the smug grin through the phone. "Well, I got no money to lend you, Ray."

"Shut the fuck up," I snapped. "This is serious. Meet me at the place. One hour." I didn't wait for a reply, didn't need his confirmation. He'd show.

The place was an old diner we always ended up at after closing a case, without even thinking. It was run-down and dirty on the outskirts of town. It was a place for locals who didn't mind the smell of stale coffee and grease. It felt timeless. The same faces seemed frozen in the same booths year after year. But the coffee was good. And it was quiet, dark enough that no one paid attention to you unless you wanted them to.

I parked the truck and walked inside. The bell over the door jingled as I slid into the same booth we always used, back when we were partners, when the world made more sense. The smell of burned coffee brought it all rushing back. The hours spent here decompressing, after interrogations, long stakeouts, or worse. This was where we always ended up, including that night.

Two years ago.

After the incident that changed everything.

We had just come out of hours of questioning. Two cops dragged through the wringer. We were tired, strung out, and still trying to wrap our heads around what had happened. Only, this wasn't just another case closed. We were both under investigation. And all because of me. A man lay dead, and I was the one who pulled the trigger. The chiefs didn't see a good reason for it. Neither did Joey.

That night, we ended up here, at this booth, our usual large black coffees in front of us, steaming in the thick tension that hung between us.

Joey broke the silence first. "What the fuck happened back there, Ray?"

"I took scum off the streets," I replied, voice cold, detached.

"No, Ray," he shot back, leaning in closer. "You executed someone. And you didn't bother to use your fucking brain when you did it!"

"Lower your voice, you dumb son of a bitch," I growled. But the damage was done. He had already seen it, seen the darkness inside me that even I was trying to ignore.

We didn't speak after that. Not a word. Joey finished his coffee in silence, then got up and left. I didn't stop him.

Now

Back in the present, I sat in the same booth, my eyes on the door as Joey walked in. He looked a hell of a lot better than me, handling unemployment. Or perhaps he was simply better at faking it.

"Wow, Ray," he said, sliding into the booth across from me. "You look like shit."

CHAPTER 9 - GHOSTS AND ALLIES

He wasn't wrong. "Good to see you, Joey. Been a long time."

He studied me for a beat, eyes narrowing, his usual cocky grin fading. "What's going on, Ray? This isn't just a catch-up call."

"It's Megan," I said, hardly above a whisper. "Someone has taken her."

He blinked, a look of confusion taking over his face. "What the fuck are you talking about? Taken? Like, kidnapped?"

I nodded, swallowing hard. "Yeah. I'm lost, Joey. I don't know where to start. I don't even know who's got her."

Joey leaned back, letting out a slow breath as he ran a hand through his hair. "Shit, Ray... Who would do this? And why?"

"You know as well as I do," I said. "I've made enemies, Joey. Enough to fill this whole damn diner. Could be any of them. I just don't know which sick bastard it is. But I need your help."

Joey leaned forward again, his expression serious now, all the teasing gone. "How can I help?"

"I need you to think like a cop," I said, feeling the weight of my words. "Because I can't. My head's not clear, and I don't have time to waste. I need someone who isn't drowning in whiskey and rage to think straight."

Joey nodded slowly; his eyes locked on mine. "Alright, Ray. Let's figure this out."

For the first since this began, I felt a flicker of hope. If anyone could help me piece this mess together, it was Joey.

But deep down, I wondered if even he could pull me back from the edge.

10

Chapter 10 – Echoes of laughter

Four Years Ago

As Megan hid beneath the covers, her playful scream carried throughout the house. It was the greatest sound in the world, so full of laughter, full of joy and innocence. My heart ached for her to stay this way forever.

She was happy. She was safe. She was with me.

I lumbered after her; the floor creaking under my weight as I slowed down, pretending to search for her like a bumbling monster. "Rawwwwr," I growled, deepening my voice, "I'm coming to get you, little girl! The tickle monster is huuuungry for belly buttons!"

Beneath the covers, I could hear her stifled giggles, the muffled sound of her trying so hard to keep quiet but failing miserably. I grinned to myself and kept the act going.

"Where did she go?" I said in exaggerated confusion, standing by the bed. "Is she under here?" I peeked under the bed and shook my head. "No, not there..."

She was giggling uncontrollably now. It had me giggling, too. The blankets were shaking as she tried to hold still.

CHAPTER 10 – ECHOES OF LAUGHTER

"She's not in the closet..." I said with a sly smile, dragging out the suspense. The more I feigned confusion, the more the covers shook with her barely contained laughter.

And then, without warning, I pounced onto the bed, grabbing her and the blankets in one swift move. "Got you!" I roared, wrapping her up and tickling her belly through the blankets. Megan's laughter burst out in fits, high-pitched and wild, the kind of laughter that makes you feel invincible. I couldn't help but laugh too, my heart soaring. Her tiny body wriggled in my arms as she tried to escape my relentless tickles, but I held on tight.

"Daddy! Stop!" she gasped between giggles, her little hands pushing weakly at mine. "You're too strong!"

"I am the strongest monster there ever was!" I said, roaring again for good measure. "No little girl can escape the tickle monster's clutches!"

She squirmed free of the covers, her flushed face shining with joy. "You found me, Daddy!"

"I sure did, baby," I said, my voice softening. I pulled her close and squeezed her into the tightest hug, feeling her tiny body against my chest. She still smelled brand new, like that new baby smell. I never wanted her to lose that. I kissed the top of her head and put her in bed. "Now, let's get you all tucked in tight."

"Not too tight, Daddy," she whispered with a sleepy smile. "I need room for my cuddle."

I smiled at her and pulled her into one last cuddle. Her tiny arms wrapped around my neck, squeezing like she didn't want to let me go. I watched as she settled into sleep. She looked so peaceful, so safe.

I just sat there for a while longer, just watching her sleep. I just couldn't believe how something so perfect could be part of me. Her small hand rested on my arm, fingers curled like she was still holding on, even in her dreams.

I love you, baby girl. I'll always protect you.

I leaned in, careful not to wake her, and kissed her chubby little cheek, then quietly slipped out of the room. Before closing the door behind me, I took one last look and smiled with pride. She is my world. As I stood there in the hallway, I already missed her.

I'll always protect you. Those words replayed in my head as I walked away from her door. They weren't just a promise; they were my vow to her. I didn't know at the time that I would fail her. I never intended to break my promise. I didn't know how powerless I could be.

Back to Reality

Joey snapped his fingers in my face, jerking me out of my blissful memory and back into the present. The smells of the diner: stale coffee, grease, more than enough to bring back to reality.

"Ray!" Joey leaned forward. "Where did you go? You disappeared for a while there."

I blinked, taking a moment. The booth felt too tight, too small. Megan's laughter still echoed faintly in my ears, which was making the guilt feel heavier. It hurt knowing I couldn't reach out and touch her.

"I was just... thinking," I muttered, rubbing a hand over my face. I felt as though I could still feel her little arms around my neck, her chubby cheek against my lips.

Joey stared at me, concern in his eyes. "You okay, Ray?"

"Not really," I admitted. "I promised her I'd always protect her, Joey." My voice faltered. "And look where we are now.

She's gone, and I don't even know where to start. I've failed her."

He said nothing for a moment, just kept his gaze on me, letting the weight of my words hang between us.

Finally, Joey sighed and leaned back in the booth, his expression softening. "You haven't failed her yet, Ray," he said. "You're still here. We're still here. We can get her back."

I clenched my fists under the table, nodding slowly. Joey was right. As long as I was still breathing, there was a chance.

11

Chapter 11 – Rage and regret

Having regained some composure, Joey and I talked things through. Trying to figure out why this was happening. Who could be behind this?

"This won't be easy, Ray. You pissed off a lot of people."

"A long list is still a list, Joe. Gives me something to work with."

Joey nodded, sat back, and just looked at me. I didn't know what he was thinking. Was he doubting I could do this? He'd always tried to pull me back, stop me from letting the rage take over. The whole time we were partners, he worked to prevent me from going over the edge. He always told me to use my brain. I wonder if a small part of him blames himself for what happened that night.

"So, what do we know for sure?" Joey asked, breaking the silence.

"Not a lot," I replied, the frustration seeping into my voice. "Megan was at the park, playing on the swings, and then she was gone."

"No witnesses?"

CHAPTER 11 - RAGE AND REGRET

"Not that I'm aware of. The cops at the scene weren't exactly ready to share information with old Ray Gordon. But that maggot Frank Mulligan has been in touch, with 'information.'"

This piqued Joey's interest. He sat forward, his voice lowering to a near whisper. "What information?"

"Just a dumb grainy image of a truck parked near the scene. Couldn't get anything from it if I tried."

"Well, let's go see Frank," Joey said, almost jumping out of his seat. "He might have more information."

"Not a chance," I replied bleakly. "I was at his house beating the shit out of him an hour ago. No way he helps me now."

"What the fuck, Ray! Why did you do that?"

How did I answer that without showing just how far I've fallen? I didn't want Joey, my old partner, to see the depths of my desperation, the unraveling of the man I used to be. But the truth was the only answer I had.

"I couldn't get over how he had the image so quickly," I said, my voice tinged with regret. "I convinced myself he was involved, that he was the one responsible for all of this. I followed him home. I beat him, all for no reason. He was just being his usual selfish bastard self, trying to make money from the misery of others."

Joey shook his head, lowering it so I couldn't see his face, but his disappointment was clear in his voice. "Shit, Ray, you're making this harder already."

He was right. I hadn't taken a forward step yet. And it was torture.

Joey sighed deeply, his hands resting on the table as he leaned forward. "Look, Ray, I get it. You're spiraling, man. But if we're going to find Megan, we can't do this your way. The rage, the impulse, it's going to lead you straight into a wall. We need to think, plan, not just react."

I nodded. I knew he was right, but the anger never went away. It would always be there, my cross to bear. "So, what do we do now? Frank's out of the picture, and the cops aren't exactly lining up to help."

"We need to retrace our steps," Joey said, his voice firm but calm. "If Frank's got that image, there might be more. Something he hadn't shared or something he didn't even know he had. We need to get back into his good graces, or at least find a way to get that information."

I stared at Joey, unsure if he realized how impossible that sounded. "You really think Frank's going to hand over anything after what I did to him?"

Joey shrugged, a smirk playing on his lips. "Not if you ask him. But me? I might have a shot. You keep your distance, stay out of sight. Let me work on Frank."

It wasn't how I wanted to do things, but I had nothing better right now. "Alright," I agreed through gritted teeth. "But what about the truck? The image?"

"I'll do some digging," Joey replied. "I know it's a long shot, but it is possible someone around the park saw something that day. A truck like that doesn't just go unnoticed."

"Okay," I agreed, trying to push down the gnawing doubt in my gut. "I'll try to keep a low profile. No more beating up suspects."

"Good," Joey said, standing up. "We'll get through this, Ray. But you've got to keep it together."

I watched him walk out of the diner, feeling the weight of his words settle on my shoulders. Keeping it together. It sounded so simple, but in the chaos that had become my life, it felt like an impossible task. But I had to try. For Megan.

CHAPTER 11 – RAGE AND REGRET

I sat there for a moment longer, the memories of her laughter echoing faintly in my mind, pushing me forward. The man I used to be might be slipping away, but the father inside me was still fighting. And as long as there was fight left in me, I'd do whatever it took to bring her home.

12

Chapter 12 – Into the abyss

This is all too easy. It's almost not fun. Almost. But knowing that Ray is suffering? Now, that's something. The thought of him, helpless with rage, searching for his daughter, warms me more than any drink could. With everything that selfish bastard took from me, he's going to pay for it in ways he can't even comprehend.

The old Ray was a force to be reckoned with. I maybe would have been concerned back then. But now? He's a broken man, dulled by guilt, rage, and a bottle of whiskey. If he can't even start looking for her, this game won't be any fun. I need him desperately clawing at every shadow, questioning every move. I need him to feel the weight of his failure crushing down on him, just like I did.

Maybe it's time to up the ante. It's too quiet, too calm. He needs a push, something to make him realize just how deep he's in. Something that stings that really paints the picture. A little something through his letterbox, perhaps. A lock of hair, a piece of that pink dress she was wearing at the park, possibly even a tiny shoe. Something that screams, 'I have your little girl. I am the one in control here.'

I imagine the look on his face when he sees it, the panic, the horror. I can almost hear his voice cracking when he realizes that this is real, that there's nothing he can do but dance to my tune. You're going to be sorry, Ray. You have no idea yet, but you will. You really will.

Megan huddled right into the corner of the cold, dark room. The door scared her, so she stayed as far away from it as she could. She was shivering, a mix of fear and the chill in the room. The blanket he had thrown in the room was more like a sheet and had no effect on the cold.

Her eyes burned from the crying but also from exhaustion, but she was too scared to let them close. What if he came back? What if she fell asleep and never woke up again?

She gently closed her eyes. She didn't want to sleep, but she didn't want to look at this room anymore. She tried desperately to think of something safe, something warm. The memory that came to mind was the last time Daddy was pushing her on the swings at the park. She has laughed so loud as she begged him to push her higher. Higher, Daddy! He'd laughed with her, promising she was safe, always safe. He would catch her if she fell, he'd said. He always did. But here, in this freezing, silent room, there was no one to catch her. No one to stop her from falling.

The room was too quiet, except for the occasional groan of floorboards above her. Each creak made her think the bad man was coming to see her. This thought scared her.

She didn't know the man's name, and she didn't want to, but he had spoken softly, like he was pretending to be kind when he'd brought her here. He'd told her she could go home soon, but only if she listened. Only if she wore the blindfold when he told her to. She hated the blindfold, hated how it plunged her into even deeper darkness, but he'd said she had to. He'd said if she didn't, she'd never go home. She wanted to go home more than anything.

Her chest tightened as questions swirled in her little mind. Why is this happening? What did I do wrong? Why isn't Daddy stopping the bad man? Daddy had always told her to be brave, and she was trying. She really was. But she was so scared. When she cried, she was sure Daddy wouldn't mind.

Her stomach was rumbling all the time now. She realized she hadn't eaten since yesterday. Hungry, cold, and scared, it made her feel so sad that she thought she wouldn't be able to eat any food, anyway. She pulled the blanket tighter around herself, trying to get warmer, but it did nothing. She wishes she could have one of Daddy's cuddles, that would warm her up. He'll come for me. He promised to keep me safe. Daddy always keeps his promises.

But the longer she waited, the harder it was to believe. The fear crept in, slow and icy, wrapping around her thoughts until she couldn't push it away anymore. What if he doesn't find me? What if I never see him again?

The thought brought a small, choking sob to her lips. She slapped her hands over her mouth, terrified the man would hear and he'd come back angry. But he didn't come in. She remained alone, and that was much better than being with him.

As she sat there shaking, wiping away tears from her cheeks, she imagined her nice, warm, comfortable bed back home. But the thought drifted away, taking her bed further away from her. She willed her daddy, 'please come get me.'

13

Chapter 13 – Shattered hope

It was early morning, and daylight was just making its way through the windows of my apartment. The whole apartment reeks of stale whiskey and unwashed clothes.

Another night of no sleep. My bed may as well have been a concrete slab for all the comfort I took from it.

How could I possibly rest? Sleep? My little girl is out there, somewhere, alone. Worse than alone, she was with someone. A crazy someone. I can't bear to imagine what they might have done with her. The thought of it makes me want to throw up. I shake my head and don't allow that thought to settle.

The room reflects the man I've become: filthy, broken, useless. Dirty clothes all over the place, empty bottles on every available surface. I lay there thinking about how far I have fallen, how disgusted others must be in me.

If only I'd bothered to take better care of myself, if I hadn't become so reliant on the drink.... maybe.... Just maybe, none of this would be happening.

I push the thoughts away. I can't wallow in self-pity. I won't. Get up, Ray. Get up and get out there. Get your shit together and show people they are wrong to give up on you.

I pull off the clothes I'm still wearing from the night before, dump them in the pile with the rest of them and step into the shower. The hot, steaming water washes over me, cleaning off the smell of whiskey and, hopefully, the stench of failure. Maybe it can do a job and wash away some of the anger. For a moment, I let myself relax, allowing the heat to soothe me. The steam fogs up the bathroom mirror, blurring the world outside, but it can't cloud what's inside. That constant gnawing fear.

I stay under the water for a long time, enjoying the warmth and accepting the moment's peace.

I finally switch off the show and grab a towel. Even drying myself feels like a chore right now. I wipe the steam away from the mirror. When I look at the reflection staring back at me, I hardly recognize the man I see. He's worn down, almost gray, hair matted, eyes hollow. A man who's given up.

A man who doesn't know the meaning of hope anymore.

I can't bear to look at him any longer. Turning away, I dress quickly, pulling on yesterday's clothes. One task at a time. Keep moving forward. Just keep moving.

The kitchen is barren, no coffee, no food. What the hell did I expect? I can't remember the last time I bought anything but another fucking bottle. Fuck.

Tired and still hungry, I head for the front door. I spot something on the floor. It wasn't there last night. A small parcel. My stomach drops. On the front, written in Megan's handwriting, are the words "Help me, daddy."

I freeze. My heart stops. Holy shit.

The world spins, dragging me around in circles. The walls close in, and I feel my legs give way. Oh God, this can't be real. This cannot be happening. My throat tightens, and before I

CHAPTER 13 – SHATTERED HOPE

can stop it, bile rises. I throw up all over the floor.

I collapse into a nearby chair, clutching the parcel close to my chest. I hold it out and for a long moment, I just stare at it, unable to make myself move. The words burn into my brain: Help me, Daddy. The sick bastard made her write to me, made her plead for her own father's help.

I don't want to open it. I'm terrified of what's inside. But I must. What if there's something, anything, that leads me to her?

Slowly, hands trembling, I rip open the box.

I see what's inside, and everything inside me shatters. My world, already broken, collapses completely.

In the box is a lock of Megan's hair, tied with her little pink bow. I pick it up, my hands shaking uncontrollably. The soft strands slip through my fingers, still smelling faintly of lavender from her bath time wash. My baby girl. My precious, innocent girl.

I hold the hair to my face and inhale deeply. A wave of memories washes over me, her laughter, her bright eyes, her soft, warm hugs. But now, something has tainted those memories. Every thought of her brings pain, brings the sickening reality of what this monster has done.

I break. The tears come hard and fast, and I can't stop them. My whole-body shakes as I sob, huge, gut-wrenching sobs that tear through me. I haven't cried in years, maybe not since I was a child myself. But now, it's as if all the tears I've ever held back are pouring out all at once, and there's no stopping them.

I am broken.

I don't know how long I sit there, cradling her hair in my hands like it's all I have left. I feel like someone ripped my heart out of my chest. There's nothing but emptiness inside me. Just a cold, hollow pit of despair.

Then I spot something else in the box.

It's a piece of paper. I unfold it slowly, my heart already too shattered to break any further, or so I think. It's a drawing, Megan's drawing. A child's scribble of a little girl holding hands with her daddy. Her stick-figure smile seems to mock me. The innocence of it... the cruel irony of it... It's too much. I have no tears left to cry, just an aching numbness that crawls through my veins.

There's something else. Just a small corner of something tucked beneath the paper. I pull it out and examine it. It's the torn corner of a beer mat. I recognize it immediately.

Colton's.

A dive bar from my past. A place linked to Eddie Colton, a son of a bitch who hates me as much as anyone else.

My blood turns cold.

Eddie Colton. A man I really don't want near my daughter!

14

Chapter 14 – A line crossed

I had heard about Eddie Colton. Hell, everyone in the city had. He was the kind of man who thought he owned the whole town just because he owned a dive bar. But until that night, I'd never had to deal with him personally.

That changed when Joey and I were called to a disturbance at Colton's. No names were given, but if the call came from there, it meant Eddie was involved. Nobody else would dare stir trouble in his domain. Eddie wouldn't allow that.

We pulled up to the bar. It was one of those warm summer nights. The streets were full of people making the most of the heat. They drank cocktails, laughed, and got a little rowdy. That's normal. But the closer you got to Colton's, the more the air seemed to change. You could feel it, the energy that only a certain breed of lowlife thrived on. And they all found their way to Eddie's place.

The disturbance involved a woman, which wasn't surprising. Eddie didn't respect anyone, but women? They were tools to him, things he could pick up, use, and discard, however he pleased. Apparently, some poor sap had made the mistake of walking in with a girl on his arm. A girl Eddie had decided was now his.

The guy had more sense than guts. He ran out of there the second Eddie took notice of his date, leaving her to deal with Eddie's unwanted attention. Self-preservation at its finest. At least he called the cops after he left, though that offered little comfort to the girl he abandoned.

When Joey and I walked into the bar, eyes immediately turned to us. Eddie's thugs didn't appreciate cops poking around their territory. But Eddie wasn't stupid enough to let them start anything, not with this many witnesses, no matter how much control he had over them.

We found Eddie leaning against the bar with a woman cowering in a chair behind him. She was strikingly pretty, blonde, with bright blue eyes. I could see why Eddie had taken an interest. But no matter how beautiful she was, no one had the right to claim her as their own, least of all Eddie.

"Got a call about a disturbance," I said, keeping it professional.

Eddie just laughed, an irritating laugh. "No disturbance here, pig. Must've been a mistake."

I look at the woman again; I noticed the marks on her face, what looked to be a nasty black eye. A flash of anger surged inside me. I have zero tolerance for men who lay hands on women. And Eddie? Well, he had just crossed that line.

I turned to him, and he saw it in my eyes. He saw the rage boiling inside me, and he shifted on his feet. He wasn't so cocky now.

"Turn around. Hands on your head," I ordered.

A stunned silence settled over the bar. Eddie's goons exchanged uncertain glances. They didn't know how to react.

CHAPTER 14 - A LINE CROSSED

Eddie was their boss, but I was still a cop. Crossing that line came with dire consequences.

"Right fucking now," I raged at him, the fury taking over.

That's when he made his mistake. He laughed right in my face. "Fuck off, pig. You're in my world now."

You ever heard that saying? "Don't poke the bear"? Well, Eddie had just poked the wrong fucking grizzly.

What happened next was a blur, it was just a blaze of anger. There was Eddie, on the floor, clutching his knee and howling in pain. I had my baton in my hand, but recollection of swinging it. Shame, really, because it was a moment I would have enjoyed.

"You dumb fucking pig," Eddie shouted at me between screams. "You have no idea what you've just done. You're gonna regret this."

I poked my baton into his ribs, twisting it. I knew it would hurt. "Yeah, yeah," I muttered. Then I flipped him onto his stomach and cuffed him. "You're under arrest for assault and resisting arrest."

He writhed beneath me, trying to fight back as I yanked him to his feet. I leaned in close to his ear and whispered coldly, "Give me an excuse, Eddie. I'd love to see just how far I can push this baton into your skull."

He stopped struggling; the fight going out of him like a schoolyard bully who had picked the wrong kid. He knew I had the upper hand, but that didn't mean this was over. Eddie Colton wasn't the type to forget. He'd have something in store for me, eventually. But I didn't care. I was smarter than he was.

As I turned to escort him out, I noticed Joey. He was standing there with his gun drawn, aimed at Eddie's crew, and he looked scared. I wasn't sure if he was afraid of them, or of me.

We dragged Eddie out of there, booked him, and saw to it the woman got home safely. With her testimony, Eddie should have done some serious time. But this is the real world, not some fairy tale. Eddie didn't do time. Not hard time. They released him within hours.

I suppose I'd have to live with the looming shadow of Eddie Colton hanging over my life. But that's fine.

I'm not afraid of shadows.

15

Chapter 15 - Tick Tock

I spring out of the chair too fast. My legs buckle beneath me, sending a wave of nausea up to my chest. Dizzy, swaying, I clutch the table for support, trying to steady my mind, but it's like holding back a hurricane with bare hands. My fists are clenching so hard I don't even notice the crumpled beer mat in my hand until the card tears.

A sudden moment of clarity slices through the fog. "Shit! I'm destroying the only evidence I have."

Evidence? What the hell am I thinking? Evidence doesn't matter. I'm going to take care of this myself, and evidence isn't what's going to put Eddie down.

I gather myself, grab my keys, and head for the door. My hand freezes on the knob. A tiny voice in the back of my mind whispers: 'Is this real? Or is this just another game?'

I don't care. I don't have time to care. I'm going to Colton's.

On the drive over, I doubt myself again. I'm not the man I used to be. No longer a cop, no badge, no backup. I'm already spiraling into alcohol withdrawal, and my emotional state is shaky at best.

I am fueled by adrenaline right now, by anger too, but when that wears off.... I am scared I won't even be able to stand.

I feel a fresh wave of nausea, which forces me to focus even more, holding on tight to the wheel. Can I really take on Eddie in this state? Should I call the cops and tell them what I have so far? I shake my head. No. They'll fuck everything up.

I have to be the one to bring her home.

Joey crosses my mind for a second, but I shove the thought aside. I've let him down too many times before. He'll just try to stop me, maybe even call the cops before I get there. I can't let that happen.

More nausea and for a second, I think I might puke right here in the truck. But the adrenaline is still there, still doing its job. It keeps pushing me, even when every other part of me feels like it's falling apart.

Even if I lost my legs right now, I'd get to Colton's.

When I pull up outside, something's off. It's quiet. Too quiet.

Rain pours down in heavy sheets, a stark contrast to the first time I came here. The place is deserted. No loud music, no crowd of idiots eager to be part of Eddie's world. Somewhere along the way, Eddie lost his shine. Maybe people stopped believing in the power he held over this place. I'd like to think I played a part in that. Watching him crumble that night, human, beaten, might've sown some seeds of doubt.

I step out of the truck. As I head toward the entrance, a thought crosses my mind: I didn't bring a weapon. Dumb fucking move. But there's no going back now.

The doors creak as I push them open, scraping against the floor like they haven't moved in weeks. God knows what I'll find in here.

I step inside, and the stench hits me immediately. It hits

CHAPTER 15 - TICK TOCK

hard. That smell is all-too-familiar, the unmistakable stench of rotten flesh. I gag, covering my nose and mouth as I move further into the bar. No matter how many times you encounter this smell, it never gets easier to breathe through it.

I round the corner toward the bar, and that's when I see it.

Eddie Colton's body lies in a twisted, bloody heap on the floor. Beaten beyond recognition, yet somehow still unmistakably him. For a split second, relief washes over me, a violent wave of satisfaction. Eddie, the bastard, got what was coming.

But the relief dies just as fast. This wasn't justice. This was a message.

Then, beside his mangled corpse, I see the weapon. It's a police baton, stained and slick with blood. Whoever did this, whoever was capable of such violence... I can hardly bring myself to finish the thought, but it's my reality. Whoever this sick fuck is, they have Megan.

I stumble back, shaking my head in disbelief. This wasn't a clue. This was another fucking game. A sick, twisted move in this son of a bitch's game. And I am running around playing to his tune.

I let out a roar of frustration and start smashing everything in sight. Chairs fly through the air, smashing into the mirrors behind the bar. Glasses shatter beneath my feet as I sweep everything off the counter, the bottles exploding on the floor.

For a moment, it feels good to let it all out. But then reality slams back into me.

Sirens. Faint, but unmistakable, growing louder in the distance. I've contaminated the scene. I've left evidence of my presence.

I take a few deep breaths, the dumb fucking exercise that never actually works to calm me down. But I need to do something. I need to think.

I force myself to look back at Eddie's mangled corpse. If it weren't for the situation I was in, I might've smiled. He got what he deserved.

That's when I see it.

The rest of the beer mat, torn but complete. The one that matches the piece sent to me.

I crouch down, and there's a small note scrawled on it. "Not that easy, Ray. Sorry." I can practically hear the bastard's voice dripping with sarcasm.

The note continues, "Dead body. Police on way. Tick Tock, Ray."

I stand up quickly, cursing under my breath. This is the body of a man I hate, a man I wanted dead. And now it's going to look like I'm the one who did it.

The sirens are closer now, wailing through the night, loud and purposeful.

I've lost control. I've lost the game. And I've lost Megan. Whoever this is, they're better than me. I can't win this one.

I don't think I just run. Out the door, into the rain, my feet slipping on the wet pavement as I make a beeline for my truck. I jump in and slam the door, my heart pounding so loud I can barely hear anything else. I hit the gas, tearing away from Colton's as fast as I can.

No plan, no destination, just the instinct to flee. For now, heading in the opposite direction of those sirens seems like the only sensible option.

16

Chapter 16 – The weight of it all

As I drive away from a murder scene, the weight of everything that is happening to me hits like a freight train. I left my fingerprints there, my sweat, maybe even my tears. My mind can't escape the reality that I'm not only chasing a lunatic who's always two steps ahead, but that, soon, I'll have the police on my trail, too.

My vision blurs. The road is an indistinct smear of gray and black ahead of me, and I can't focus on anything. A small beep from the dashboard snaps me out of the fog. Low fuel. Of course. I need to stop, and maybe, in some small way, that'll give me a moment to clear my head.

I pull into the next gas station, the lights of the pumps casting a cold, sterile glow in the rain-soaked night. But instead of getting out immediately, I just sit there. My breathing is heavy. My brain feels like it's firing on empty. No thoughts, no plans, just exhaustion.

I rub my face with both hands, pulling the skin down until my mouth stretches wide, as if I'm about to take a huge bite out of an invisible sandwich. The thought of food reminds me

I haven't eaten in what feels like days. My stomach growls loudly.

I get out of the truck wearily and fill it up, filling the tank to the brim. Who knows when I'll get the luxury of stopping at another gas station? Inside the store, I head straight for the candy aisle. Two king-size chocolate bars. They'll have to be my fuel for the next few hours.

As I'm walking to the counter, I notice two men at the back of the store. They seem…off. Are they watching me? Did they follow me? I can't be sure. Hell, I probably wouldn't have noticed a whole convoy of cop cars behind me in the state I'm in, but now…these two catch my eye. They're standing too still, their eyes flicking toward me too often.

My heart kicks up a notch. Are they just here for gas and snacks like I am? Or are they something more? I slow down deliberately, pretend to be interested in the magazines stacked on a nearby shelf, but all I can focus on is their movements. I can feel my heartbeat pulsing my ears. What if they're out to get me? What if…

As they approach, I ready myself, clenching my fists. I tense up, ready in case of an attack. But as they pass by, deep in their own conversation, they didn't even know I was there.

I exhale slowly, my chest still tight from the tension. Paranoia. It's getting to me. And why wouldn't it? Everyone feels like a threat now.

After paying for my chocolate and fuel, I head quickly back to my truck. Once inside, I realize I'm completely lost, not just physically, but mentally, too. I have no idea where I am. I just drove off in a blind panic, hoping the sirens wouldn't catch up with me.

Worse, I have no plan. No idea what comes next. Should I

CHAPTER 16 – THE WEIGHT OF IT ALL

go see Alison? Tell her everything I've uncovered so far; the package, the games, the hell I've been through? But what good would that do? It'd only upset her further, make her blame me more for everything that's happening. She already thinks this is all my fault, and she's right.

I don't need another guilt trip, but I feel guilty for not telling her. I'm stuck either way.

I rip open one of the chocolate bars and scoff it down right there at the pump. I can feel the sugar rush right away. It's not actual food, but it's something. A car waiting behind me honks, flashing their headlights, annoyed at me for lingering too long.

I hold a hand up in apology and pull away from the gas station, but I still don't know where I'm going. No direction. No clear destination. I just know that, for now, I need to keep moving.

17

Chapter 17 – A summer's day

It was a ridiculously hot summer's day, one of those days when the heat won out and made you feel drowsy. It was one of those days in Chicago where the sun lingered high in the sky, baking everything beneath it. You could hear grasshoppers chirping endlessly as Ray leaned back in the driver's seat of his battered old pickup. They had parked up along the lake shore. He had the windows rolled down, letting in a soft breeze that did little to ease the heat, but felt nice against his sun-warmed skin. Beside him, Alison was rifling through the contents of a small, old cooler, her face set in concentration.

"I Swear to God, Ray, if you forgot the sandwiches again," she said, holding up a small fist mockingly. She was wearing a loose, white summer dress that fluttered whenever the wind picked up, her blonde hair pulled back in a messy bun. Strands escaped to dance around her face, catching the sunlight just right. Ray couldn't help but smile.

"Relax, sweetheart, they're right there. Bottom of the cooler, under the beers," Ray replied, tipping his head towards the cooler with a grin. He was enjoying this, watching her dig

CHAPTER 17 - A SUMMER'S DAY

through the ice, pretending to be annoyed while a smile teased the corners of her lips. "Gotta have priorities, you know."

"Uh-huh. Priorities, my ass," Alison said with a chuckle, pulling out a couple of sandwiches wrapped in film. She set them on the dashboard, then grabbed two cold cans of beer. "Priorities like making sure you get your hands on the last of the IPA."

Ray shrugged, a big smile on his face. "I'm a simple man. A cold beer on a sweltering day, a pretty girl by my side... what more could a guy want?"

Alison laughed, a warm, genuine laugh, which made Ray smile again. She tossed him a can, which he caught in one hand. "Flattery will get you everywhere, Ray."

He watched her open up a cold beer and take a long sip. He could almost see the relaxation kicking in, the tensions of life melting away in front of him. He loved seeing her like this, at ease, happy. They didn't always get a lot of days like this, with him working nights and odd shifts and her putting in long hours at the clinic. But when they did, they liked to get out somewhere like this, somewhere quite different to their every day.

"Remember the first time we came out here?" he asked, tearing open his sandwich. "Back when you still thought I was trouble?"

Alison rolled her eyes, but her smile softened. "Oh, please. I knew you were trouble. Still are. I think it was the scars that gave it away."

Ray laughed. "I got you to come out with me, didn't I? Must've been doing something right."

"Yeah, yeah," she said, leaning back in her seat and staring out at the lake. "You had that whole tortured soul thing going on. 'Bad boy with a heart of gold' I fell for it."

Ray looked over at her, his expression growing more serious. "Well, I meant it, you know? That night. All of it. I still do."

She turned to face him, her eyes locking onto his. It was like time stood still. Ray took in the moment and enjoyed the feeling. Alison always seemed to see right through him, past all his bullshit, all the tough talk, straight to the heart of who he really was. And she loved him anyway.

"I know, Ray," she whispered. "I know."

They just sat for a while, listening to the sounds of the water, of children playing nearby. It felt as though they were in their own little world. They were happy here. He held her hand tight and smiled some more.

"Tell me something," he said. "When did you know? That you wanted to stick around with me, I mean."

Alison smiled, looking down at their joined hands. "It was a couple of months after we had started dating. You took me to that hole-in-the-wall bar...."

"The Rusty Nail," Ray interjected with a grin. "Best jukebox in the city!"

"Exactly," she said, laughing. "And we'd had a few too many, and you got it in your head that you were going to teach me how to dance. And I mean, you were awful, like stepping on my feet and everything. But there was this moment when you were spinning me around, and you just looked so damn happy... I knew right then. I knew I wanted to be with you, no matter what."

Ray chuckled. "So, it was my terrible dancing, huh? That's what sealed the deal?"

"You could say that," she said, as she leaned in and gave him a kiss, then she continued, "It was that, and the way you never let go of my hand. You were so stubborn, even when you had no idea what you were doing."

Ray smiled, his heart feeling a little lighter. "Well, guess I've always been a stubborn son of a bitch."

Alison laughed again, and they sat back in blissful, comfortable silence, still hand in hand. The sun was dipping lower in the sky, long shadows covering the water. Ray was happy, he thought about how he would happily to stay right here with her forever.

"You think we'll still be doing this when we're old and gray?" he asked. "Just us, beer and sandwiches, of course, watching the sun go down?"

"Maybe," Alison said with a small smile, "But I think by then, we'll need something stronger than beer."

Ray laughed, leaning over to press his lips against hers, soft and lingering. When they pulled away, he looked into her eyes and saw his future, one he could actually believe in.

"Then we'll bring whiskey," he said softly, "and we'll keep on dancing."

And for a while, under that golden summer sky, it was enough to believe that they could.

This, of course, was back when life was simpler.

18

Chapter 18 – The puppet master's game

I sit in the shadows, watching, waiting. Ray will come. There's no way he won't head straight here after finding that beer mat. I am a fucking genius.

Is it too much to ask for this rain to piss off, just for a moment, so I can enjoy this fully? The view through the windshield wipers is ruining my fun, blurring the edges of the scene I've so meticulously crafted.

Poor old Ray must be getting slow. I expected him before now. Maybe he sat crying, clutching her hair for a while before he could bring himself to leave. Maybe he's still punching holes in the walls of his apartment. The thought makes me grin.

But waiting is all part of the fun. It makes the reward sweeter.

I sit up in my seat, leaning forward as a familiar truck rounds the corner. Showtime. Here's Ray.

He's moving slower than I expected. His posture is tight, but not reckless. I was expecting him to charge in, guns blazing, like a bull chasing red. Maybe he hasn't completely lost it yet.

CHAPTER 18 - THE PUPPET MASTER'S GAME

Well, I have plenty of moves left to break him.

He disappears inside the bar, and I imagine the stench hits him immediately. The panic that must surge through him when he realizes there's a dead body. The sweet confusion over who it could be. This is beautiful.

I wonder if he's found Colton yet. Has he pieced together what's happening, or is he still reeling in shock? The thought of his confusion delights me. He must be unraveling right now, trying to figure out why everything keeps spiraling further out of his control.

By now, he should have picked up the note. He should be realizing just how deep in shit he is. Why hasn't he gotten out of there yet? I want to see him panic. The sirens in the distance are growing louder. Come on, Ray. Get out of there. It's far too soon for you to be caught just yet.

And then, there he is, my puppet, dancing. His movements are frantic, his face pale even from this distance. I can practically feel the fear pouring off him in waves. This is what I wanted. The look on his face, that utter shock. It's better than I imagined. He stumbles to his truck, tires screeching as he speeds off like Lewis Hamilton chasing his last checkered flag.

See you soon, Ray. We're not done yet.

Just for fun, I stay a while longer, watching as the police arrive. Several squad cars pull up, officers flooding into the bar. It's almost poetic, the way the pieces are falling into place. A nicely timed tip-off from a concerned citizen, about the stench, of course, was enough to send them scrambling. A little more pressure on Ray. Just enough to keep him on the edge.

The cops are swarming the place now, and it's getting a bit too crowded for my liking. Even from this distance, it's best not to tempt fate.

Time to slip away. Back to babysitting duty for me.... for now.

19

Chapter 19 – Vendetta

Detective Evelyn Kane arrives at Colton's crime scene. Her presence commands attention. The room quiets, heavy with her reputation. It was her case now. A murder with high stakes. The weapon was a police baton. The victim, Eddie Colton, was a notorious criminal. His name sent ripples across the department. If anyone could handle the complexity and heat of this case, it was Eve Kane.

At 5 feet 5 inches, she carries herself with an authority that makes her seem taller, almost imposing. Her red hair, tied back, sharpens her green eyes that sweep the room like a hawk. All the cops present, from seasoned detectives to the newest recruits, make way for her. Kane has earned her place. Nobody questions her, and nobody wants to get on her bad side.

She approaches the body, speaking briskly to Officer Brown, who stands just off to the side, scribbling notes.

"So, what do we have?" Kane's voice is crisp, businesslike.

Brown shifts on his feet. "Hey, Detective. The victim's male appears to be Eddie Colton, though the ID might have to wait until we get a formal confirmation from his family. Body's pretty beaten up, but the build, the location, it's him."

Eve narrows her eyes as she listens, her mind already spinning through the details. "Someone had a personal vendetta with him, I take it?"

"Yeah," Brown says, clearing his throat. "This wasn't just some bar fight. Whoever did this was out for blood and had the strength to back it up. I wouldn't want to take on Eddie alone."

Eve's lip curls slightly at Brown's admission of fear. A cop being afraid of a criminal, even someone like Eddie, is disappointing. She doesn't voice her criticism, though. Brown wasn't her concern right now. Colton was. "Thanks, Officer."

She kneels beside the body, studying the corpse's mangled form. Pathologist Simon Winter, standing nearby, continues his assessment. He's a meticulous man, good at his job, but Eve has seen more corpses than she'd care to remember, and this one would not shock her.

"Simon," she greets him, her tone still firm but with a little more familiarity than she showed Brown. "Cause of death?"

Simon glances at her, his brow furrowed as he considers the damage. "Hey, Evey. It looks like someone beat him to death, as obvious as that sounds. The police baton over there likely did most of the damage. But how many blows? That's a question for the lab."

"Eve. Or Detective Kane. Your pick, Simon." Her tone sharpens. Eve Kane allows no one to get too comfortable with her. Experience taught her that letting her guard down, even a little, led to others disregarding her authority, especially in a male-dominated job. She didn't tolerate disrespect in any form.

"Sorry, Eve," Simon mutters, looking away. "No other signs yet. It's tough to tell much more until we get him back to the

CHAPTER 19 - VENDETTA

lab."

"Who is Ray?" she asks.

"Huh?" Simon responds, but he catches Eve nodding toward the beer mat, with the message to Ray on the floor next to the body, "oh, no idea sorry. Another part of the puzzle, I suppose."

"Estimated time of death?" Eve presses.

Simon nods, glancing at the body. "Based on rigor mortis and the early stages of decomposition, I'd put it at about eighteen hours ago. Give or take."

Eve doesn't respond immediately. She straightens up, surveying the scene. The bar is a wreck, smashed glass, overturned tables, broken chairs, but oddly, none of the victim's blood splatters beyond where he lies. No blood trails, no signs of Colton being thrown across the room during the beating. Eve's eyes narrow in suspicion.

Something doesn't add up.

The destruction around the bar didn't match the body's placement. Someone might have trashed the place after Colton was already dead. An attempt to muddy the waters? To throw the cops off the trail? She wasn't sure yet, but she knew one thing: this would not be a straightforward case.

She turns, raising her voice to command the attention of the officers present. "Listen up." Immediately, everyone stands to attention, the energy in the room shifting under her authority. "This scene is already trashed, but we're going to comb through every inch. Fingerprints, DNA, hair, fibers, I want all of it. No detail is too small. Get everything bagged and tagged. I want updates from the lab as soon as possible. We're not missing a damn thing. Got it?"

A collective murmur of acknowledgment ripples through the

room as the officers disperse to follow her orders.

Eve Kane remains standing over the body for a moment longer, her mind processing the scene. This was brutal, personal, calculated. Whoever did this wanted Colton dead for a reason, and they wanted to send a message. The baton was key, but there was more to this than just a savage beating. She could feel it.

20

Chapter 20 – Shadows of doubt

Alison sat on the edge of her couch; her arms wrapped around herself as if she were offering herself comfort. The silence in the house had become suffocating. She had tried distracting herself in any way she could think of. She watched TV but had paid no attention. She had cleaned every inch of her house; it had never been so clean. She even cooked meals that nobody was going to eat. But nothing could drown out the gnawing anxiety. Where was Ray? Why hadn't she heard from him? Was he out there making enemies, making everything worse?

Her phone sat on the coffee table, taunting her. She kept thinking about calling Ray, just to hear something, anything. But she couldn't bring herself to dial. The idea of him screwing everything up wasn't out of the question. Ray was unpredictable. When he was in control, he was a force. She would trust him with anything. The problems came when he lost control. That was when things went sideways fast.

She took a long deep breath in and let it out slowly, trying her best to manage her anxiety, but it all felt too much. Her mind, always racing, started drifting back, back to the time when she saw the real Ray.

It had been a beautiful day, a rare moment of peace for their family. She, Ray, and Megan were out for a Sunday drive, heading to a lake just outside the city. Megan was in the backseat, humming to herself, tracing shapes in the fogged-up window. Alison remembered glancing over at Ray, seeing him relaxed for once, his grip on the wheel loose, a faint smile on his lips.

The calm didn't last long.

A car, a black SUV, had cut them off as they merged onto the highway. Ray had slammed on the brakes, only just avoiding a collision. The peaceful day shattered in an instant. The atmosphere in the car shifted. No more happy Ray. He was gone now.

"Stupid son of a bitch" Ray shouted, tightening his grip on the steering wheel.

"It's fine," Alison had said softly, hoping to defuse him. "We are both fine. Just let it go, Ray."

But Ray didn't let things go. Never. His face creased with anger. "No. People need to learn."

He floored it, speeding up to catch the SUV. Alison's heart had raced as she realized what was happening. "Ray," she said sharply. "Ray, don't. Please."

He didn't listen. He never listened when he was like this. He'd sped until they were right behind the SUV, so close that Alison had braced herself, thinking they were going to rear-end it. Megan had stopped humming, her eyes wide as she watched Ray from the backseat. The jovial mood was gone, replaced by an overwhelming tension.

Ray had finally swerved into the next lane, pulling alongside the SUV. He rolled down his window and gestured wildly for the other driver to pull over. The man, a middle-aged guy with glasses and a confused look on his face, did as he was told and pulled over to the shoulder.

Alison had felt a wave of nausea wash over her. "Ray, don't do this. Megan's in the car."

Ray had ignored her. He jumped out, his badge dangling from his belt, the weight of his authority turning him into something she didn't recognize. He stormed over to the SUV, slamming his fist on the driver's window. The man rolled it down cautiously, and Ray had leaned in close, barking at him.

She couldn't quite hear all of what Ray said, but she could see the man's face as it drained of all color. Ray was extremely intimidating and knew how to control people. The man had nodded frantically, apologizing nervously, his hands shaking on the wheel. Ray stood over him for a long time, letting his authority really sink in. Finally, he stepped back and waved him off dismissively, like the man was nothing but a waste of his time and energy.

When Ray returned to the car, he was still seething; the anger written all over his face. He said nothing. They drove the rest of the way to the lake in silence. Megan had been the first to break it, asking softly from the backseat, "Daddy, are you mad?"

Ray had sighed, then forced a smile. "No, baby. Just... people are stupid sometimes."

But Alison couldn't shake the unease that had settled over her. That wasn't just road rage, there was something darker in Ray's behavior that day. She had always been too afraid to mention it again, but the memory had stayed with her.

Just a few days later, she heard on the news that a driver of a black SUV, the same make and model as the one Ray had confronted, had been in a severe accident near to where they had pulled over. She hated she thought this, but there was a part of her that was convinced that Ray could have had something to do with it.

Alison blinked, forcing herself out of the memory. She hated thinking about that day. She hated the person Ray had become, or maybe the person he had always been, the one she didn't want to see.

Her eyes drifted back to the phone. Maybe she should call him. Maybe she shouldn't. What if she called him, and all she got was more lies? More anger?

There was a knock at the door, which startled her. She jumped up and walked slowly to answer it. She wasn't expecting anyone, and with everything that had been happening, she really wasn't ready to see anyone.

She opened the door slowly, looked around, but no one was there. She looked down and see an envelope lying on the porch. She bent down to pick it up, wondering why they didn't just post it.

She took the envelope inside, her curiosity peaking. Messy, scrawled handwriting addressed it to her. No return address. She opened it and pulled out a photograph.

Her breath caught in her throat. It was Megan.

Her sweet little girl, but something was wrong. Her hair was shorter. It looked like someone had hacked at it with scissors. Alison put her hand to her mouth. The sight of her daughter's hair hacked shorter shocked her to her core.

On the back of the photo, someone had written a message in the same messy handwriting:

Spoke with Ray yet?

Alison dropped the photo, her breath coming in shallow gasps. Panic surged through her veins. This wasn't just some

CHAPTER 20 – SHADOWS OF DOUBT

twisted game anymore. Megan was in danger, real, immediate danger.

And now, more than ever, she needed to know what Ray was doing.

21

Chapter 21 – Spiraling into shadows

How did I end up back here? Three double whiskeys deep, trying to numb the ache that comes from the crushing weight of failure. Not just failure, failure to protect my baby girl. There's no pain like it. I know the whiskey's a bad idea, but here I am anyway, knocking them back like water. At this point, I'd tell Jimmy to leave the whole damn bottle. Would make things easier for both of us.

The Broken Bottle is the same depressing, dark hole it's always been. Completely fitting for my mood, my life, everything right now.

I can't help but feel the pressure, as though I am being squeezed, all my breath being pushed from my body. I feel as though I am at the point of snapping, just one more squeeze and I will be gone.

That's when I hear it, Eddie Colton's name, floating through the haze of smoke and drunken murmurs around me. It cuts through the fog, pulls me back into the room, and I strain to listen.

"Is it true?" one drunk asks another.

CHAPTER 21 - SPIRALING INTO SHADOWS

"Dead as dead can be," the other slurs. "Up at his own bar. Rumor has it."

"Well, praise the lord," comes the reply, glasses clinking together in a grim toast.

I'm not surprised. Live by your reputation, die by it. That's how it goes. Eddie Colton's death? Nobody's shedding any tears. Not even his crew, I bet. Probably raising their glasses at the good news. But that these local idiots are talking about it means news is spreading fast, too fast. Whoever's trying to drag me into this mess has made sure the ball's rolling, and it won't be long before the cops come knocking.

Staying still is the worst thing I can do right now; I should be on the move. But right now, in this moment, I just cannot seem to find the strength to move.

The buzzing interrupts my thoughts. It takes a second to realize it's my phone; it takes all my energy to pull it out. What if this is just more bad news? When I see Alison's name on the screen, my stomach sinks.

She's probably calling to check on my progress, what I've found. Sorry, Al. I've got nothing. Scratch that. I've got worse than nothing. I'm just digging myself deeper, sliding closer to that inevitable six-foot hole waiting for me at the end of this nightmare.

I can't answer this call in here. I cannot let her know I am once again drowning in whiskey. She is counting on me right now. I stumble outside, the night air hitting me like a slap in the face.

"Hey, Al," I start, trying to sound casual. "I was just about to call...."

She cuts me off before I can finish my lie. Her voice is sharp, panicked. It sends a chill down my spine.

"Ray! What the fuck is happening? What haven't you told me?" Her voice is breathless, frantic.

I wasn't expecting this. Alison's not usually like this. Sure, she can get pissed, but she's always more controlled, cold, almost. That scary quiet some women can pull out when they really want to get their point across. But this? This is different. This is raw fear.

"What are you talking about? What's happened, Al?"

"I'm holding a picture. A picture of Megan," she says, her voice cracking, almost swallowed by sobs. "Ray, her hair... they've hacked off her hair. Oh my God, Ray, this cannot be happening to my baby!"

The ground feels like it's falling out from under me. I sink to the cold concrete, hardly able to stay upright as nausea washes over me. Megan. My little girl. I hadn't imagined what she looked like after someone dropped that parcel at my apartment. I didn't want to. Now Alison's seen the aftermath firsthand.

"Ray, are you still there?" she asks. I can hear her voice shaking, feel her panic through the phone.

"Yeah, I'm here. I... I'm so sorry, Alison."

"They wrote something on the back of the picture, Ray. It says, 'Spoke to Ray yet?' What the hell does that mean? What aren't you telling me?" She's crying harder now, her voice raw with confusion and fear.

"They sent me her hair," I mumble. "It was in an envelope, dropped at my place. No address. They were there, too. At my apartment. I... I'm so sorry, Al. This is all my fault. You were right. And I don't even know how to fix it."

For a moment, the line is silent, as we both consider how helpless we are, how I am not strong enough to get us through this. Then, her voice comes through, almost a whisper, "Go

CHAPTER 21 – SPIRALING INTO SHADOWS

to the police, Ray. Tell them what you've got. I'll do the same with this picture."

"I can't do that, Al. It's not possible now."

"Why the hell not?" Her frustration bleeds through the fear. "You can't do this alone. Megan needs more than just you running in circles."

"Because whoever's doing this, they killed someone, Al. A guy I arrested a long time ago. They're trying to pin it on me. They wanted me at the scene, but I ran. I didn't stick around to let them catch me there."

"How can this be happening, Ray?" she says, her voice faint, hopeless. "This is like some fucking twisted game. What do we do now?"

Her words hang in the air like a challenge. I don't have an answer. I can't even muster up a half-hearted reassurance. The truth is, I'm petrified. Everything feels like it's slipping out of control, and I'm too damn terrified to face what might come next.

But I must. For Alison. For Megan. Even if it feels like I'm running out of time, and I'm running blind.

Because I know one thing for sure, I can't afford to screw this up any worse than I already have.

22

Chapter 22 – In the dark

Megan deeply misses her parents. She's tried to be brave, like daddy would want her to be, but this strange place just feels so scary.

She sits on the little cot with her legs pulled up to her chest, her eyes covered by the thick blindfold the man makes her wear whenever he's around. She's tried to pull it down, to take a little peek, but he caught her, and he warned her not to do it again. He told her would be furious, so she doesn't try anymore. She knows he means it.

Earlier, he came in and told her to hold still while he cut her hair. She didn't understand why. She cried the whole time; she could feel the pieces of her hair falling. She loved her long hair; it made her feel like a princess. She worried her mum would be angry because her hair had been cut. She wanted to ask him to stop, but she could only sob. She was too afraid to stand up to him. The blindfold made everything scarier. It was like being in a room with a monster with the lights off. Sometimes she felt as if he was watching her, and that made her really uncomfortable.

CHAPTER 22 – IN THE DARK

The man never yells at her. He doesn't have to. His voice is soft when he talks, almost kind, like he's pretending to be nice. But there's something else in his tone, something cold underneath the softness. She knows not to push him, not to ask too many questions or make any sudden moves. She knows that sometimes the kindest voices can be the scariest, especially when you can't see the eyes that go with them.

But he hasn't hurt her. Not really. He's given her food: cold soup, stale bread, and a juice box. He brought her a blanket when she shivered, but it was only small, and it didn't make her feel warm. He speaks softly to her, like he cares. To Megan, this makes him even scarier. She tries not to think too much about it. She just wants mummy and daddy. She just wants to play outside again, to play with her toys and read her books.

She wishes she had some of her teddies here for company. Mr. Snuggles would know how to make her feel better, and Dolly. She's always been a chatty child, always talking to her teddies or to any adult who would listen. She feels like she hasn't spoken for so long now. She's not sure she even remembers how. Sometimes, she whispers little stories to herself, pretending her toys are here to listen. She tells them that mummy is looking for her. Daddy, too. She tells them it will be over soon. But she isn't sure she believes that.

The room is so quiet, the only sound she can hear is the drip-drip-drip of water somewhere behind the walls. She tries not to listen to it, but the more she tries, the more she hears it. So, she tries to imagine she's back in her own room, in her big comfortable bed and her beautiful nightlight. She closes her eyes beneath the blindfold and dreams of home.

She prays that the man will come back and say, "It's time to go home."

She hears his footsteps in the hallway. He's coming back. Her heart pounds so hard it feels like it might burst, every muscle in her tiny body locking up tight. She hates how scared she gets when he comes into the room. But more than anything, she doesn't want him to see it, doesn't want him to know just how much he terrifies her.

The door creaks open, and she hears the man's entering the room slowly, like he has all the time in the world. She feels his presence as he steps closer, hears his shoes on the cold concrete floor as each step brings him closer. She can't see him, but she can feel that he is looking at her.

"Hello, Megan," he says, in a kind soft voice, like he wants her to feel safe. But Megan cringes at the sound of his voice, and she squeezes her fingers into the blanket, gripping it like it's a lifeline.

She doesn't respond. She's too scared to speak.

"I brought you something," he says. She hears the rustle of something soft. "It's a little friend to keep you company."

He presses something small and fluffy into her hands. Megan feels it, soft fur, little plastic eyes, a tiny stuffed bear. She knows this isn't one of her teddy bears, but she is happy to have it, to have a friend, to have something to hold.

"Now say thank you," he says, his voice still soft but with an icy edge to it that makes her stomach drop.

"Thank you," she whispers, holding the bear close to her chest.

"Good girl," he says, sounding as though he is incredibly pleased with her. "You have been a very good girl, haven't you?"

She nods. She has tried to be good, as good as she can be. She holds the bear so tightly that its little arms dig into her ribs, wishing it were Mr. Snuggles, wishing it were anything from home.

"Alright, sweetheart," he says, as she hears his footsteps retreating toward the door. "You be good now. I'll be back later."

When the door closes, Megan squeezes the bear as tight as she can. It isn't from home, but she pretends it is. She pretends it brings all the smells of home with it, like mummy's perfume, and the clean laundry. She tries to hold on to that feeling, that smell. The pipe drips. The darkness behind her blindfold presses in on her. She wonders how long "later" will be.

23

Chapter 23 – New directions

I heard my phone ring from my pocket; the sound cutting through the fog of my thoughts. I had just put it back after the call with Alison, the weight of guilt still pressing down on me. Leaning against the cold brick wall outside the bar, I could feel the whiskey's burn doing little to dull the ache in my chest.

I took the phone out of my pocket and squinted at the screen: Joey.

I swiped to answer. "Joey. What is it?"

"Ray, we gotta talk," Joey said, his voice low and hurried, like he was trying not to be overheard. "I just got back from seeing Frank."

I straightened up, the fog in my head clearing a little. "What? You went to see Frank without me?"

Joey ignored the question. "Can you get to Angelo's?"

"Give me 15," I answered through gritted teeth, then hung up.

On the drive to Angelo's, I tried to calm myself. I knew Joey was trying to help, but the plan had been simple: Joey and I would confront Frank together. Frank would crack, maybe give

CHAPTER 23 – NEW DIRECTIONS

us something, anything, that could lead them to Megan. But Joey had gone rogue, deciding to see Frank on his own without me. Why?

When I got to Angelo's, Joey was already there, down the side alleyway, looking like a wagging dog who got the bone. So proud of himself. I could see the smirk on Joey's face before I could see Joey himself. That damn smirk.

The Chicago night was bitter, each breath I took forming a foggy plume in the air. As I walked toward Joey, his figure almost disappeared behind the mist of every exhale.

"What the hell, Joey?" I snapped, not waiting for pleasantries. "We were supposed to go see Frank together. Why'd you go without me?"

Joey shrugged, the smirk never leaving his face. "Had to move fast, Ray. Figured you'd just complicate things. You know how you are with Frank."

I stepped closer, my eyes narrowing. "Cut the crap. What did he say?"

Joey raised his hands in mock surrender. "Alright, alright. I talked to him. Told him you had caught me up about what had happened so far. That you were deeply sorry, blah blah. That you just want to find Megan, no matter what."

I stared hard at Joey, waiting for more. Joey wasn't usually a storyteller; he was quick and to the point, which was what I liked about him. "And?"

Joey sighed, rubbing his face as if frustrated. "He's still pissed, Ray. You should see his face. What the fuck did you hit him with, your truck?"

My patience wore thin; none of this meant anything. None of it was useful. "Spit it out, Joey. What did he have to say?"

"Frank knows you're desperate. He doesn't want you paying

him any more visits. Said he doesn't know where Megan is, said it doesn't matter where he got the CCTV image."

"Did he say anything fucking useful at all, Joe?" I said, exasperation bleeding through my voice. My patience and hope were waning fast.

Joey looked at me like he was enjoying my impatience. Like he wanted to drag this out longer and savor the fact that he was the one with the information. Was this just Joey getting back at me for not returning his calls? Pretty fucking petty, if you ask me.

Finally, Joey spoke. "He might have heard something, in the shitty circles he likes to run in. He mentioned a name, one we both know."

I stood up straight, a new sense of focus. "Who?"

"Tommy Russo. Remember him?"

I felt a chill run through me. Tommy Russo. That name was like a bad taste in my mouth. It must have been a decade or more since we had crossed paths. Tommy was a small-time hood with a big-time ego, someone who'd always wanted to prove he could run with the big dogs. A punk who'd held a grudge against me for busting up his operations, and his face, years back.

"Tommy's been out of the game for years," I muttered. "Why would Frank bring him up now?"

Joey's eyes were steady, his tone too calm. "Frank says Tommy's been asking around about you. Wants a piece of you for what you did to him. Maybe he's using Megan to draw you out, make you pay."

My stomach twisted. This didn't feel right. But Joey kept talking, his words flowing fast and confident, like he'd practiced them.

CHAPTER 23 – NEW DIRECTIONS

"I think it makes sense, Ray. Tommy knows how to hold a grudge. And Frank isn't the type to lie about something like that. Whatever sort of snake he is, he doesn't make shit up. It could be our best lead. We just gotta be careful how we play it."

I stared at Joey, my gut twisting tighter with every word. Was I just being led down another path? A path with nothing but misery and failure at the end of it? But this had come from Frank. This wasn't an anonymous source like the CCTV still or the parcel through my door. Joey had spoken with him directly.

I didn't have time to overthink. If Tommy Russo had Megan, if this were his way of getting back at me, I would burn Chicago to the ground to find him.

"Ray, what's going on in that head? You have said nothing," Joey said, snapping me out of my thoughts again.

"You heard about Eddie Colton?" I replied.

"Sure," Joey said, almost smiling about it; he hated Eddie as much as Ray did. "Scumbag got what he deserved, didn't he? It's been all over the news. What about it?"

"It was only hours ago I was standing over his dead body, Joe."

No emotion crossed Joey's face when I said this. He just looked me dead in the eye. Stared at me, a cold hard stare that felt like it lasted an eternity. Was he judging me? Jumping to the same conclusion everyone else would when they find out I was there? Is he picturing me beating the shit out of Eddie right now?

"Did you kill him, Ray?" Joey eventually asked.

"I wish I had the chance; he was dead when I got there," I replied.

"Okay... so what then? Why mention it?"

I explained the parcel, the hair, the drawing. Then I told him about the beer mat. "Don't you see? Someone sent me a clue that sent me right into the fire. Sent me exactly where they wanted me, so I would have to squirm my way out of it."

Joey's smirk seemed to get bigger every time I looked at him. But he didn't respond.

"What if this is just another lead that is sending me to another place where I am supposed to suffer further?" I continued.

Joey took a moment to respond, but what he said made sense. "If we ignore this lead, we have nothing else to go off. We follow this, we may get a step closer, hell, we may even bring her home."

"Alright," I said slowly, weighing his words. "But you should've told me before you went to see Frank. We need to be on the same page here, Joey."

Joey's smirk widened. "We are on the same page, Ray. Trust me."

I nodded, though my instincts screamed at me not to. How could I trust anyone right now? I couldn't afford to lose Joey now. He was the only friend I had in all of this. But Joey had changed the game by going to Frank without me. He was setting the tempo now, and I had no choice but to follow.

"We find Tommy. We sort this out. But from now on, no more surprises. We do this together," I demanded.

"Together," Joey agreed, but the word felt hollow. I turned, heading back out onto the street, my mind churning. Joey had always been a fast talker, but something about tonight felt off, like he was enjoying it. I knew Joey missed being a cop, missed the action, but my daughter was at stake; there was no time to enjoy being a cop.

We headed for the truck in silence, an icy dread creeping up

CHAPTER 23 – NEW DIRECTIONS

my spine. As I gripped the steering wheel, I couldn't shake the feeling that I was being led straight into another trap. But this time, there would be no room for mistakes.

24

Chapter 24 – Behind closed doors

Detective Evelyn Kane stepped through her apartment door. The warmth and familiarity of home relieved her after a long day. The details continue to swirl around in her head, continually pulling her mind back to the crime scene even as she tried to leave it behind.

She tossed her keys into the wooden bowl on the small table by the door. The keys joined some loose change, an old Metro Card, and a folded paper with a list of food items she meant to get from the store, but never did. The contents of the bowl are a dull reminder of how different her life is away from the job.

The apartment was small, but it was meticulously clean, extremely well organized. There were no signs of chaos that you might see in other homes. No piles of magazines or stray shoes by the door. Every item had its place, just as Eve liked it.

Her husband, David, was in the kitchen leaning against the counter scrolling through his phone, his face a picture of concentration. When he saw her, he smiled widely. The best part of his day was Eve coming home safe.

"Hey," he greeted her, setting the phone down. "Rough

CHAPTER 24 – BEHIND CLOSED DOORS

day?"

Eve nodded, slipped off her shoes and walked slowly, tiredly, across the hardwood floor. She leaned against the counter across from him and sighed. "You could say that."

David didn't push for details. He'd learned long ago that Eve would share when she was ready. Instead, he poured a glass of wine and handed it to her. Just one glass was one of the few indulgences she allowed herself after a tough day.

"Oh, thank you!" she said, taking the glass and sipping slowly. The warmth of the wine flowed through her, numbing just a small part of the tension in her shoulders. Yet her mind continued to race, the fragments of the puzzle she'd encountered at the crime scene stubbornly refusing to align.

"You want to talk about it?" David asked without pushing.

Eve sighed, setting the glass down. "It's this case. Eddie Colton's murder. Something about it feels... off. It was brutal, like most murders, but there's something deeper at play. There's a message hidden within, but I just can't grasp it."

David nodded, taking it all in. He wasn't a detective, but his steady aura had always provided Eve with comfort. He understood her job came with its pressures and the impact they had on her, even if he didn't always understand the details.

"What's bothering you about it?" he asked.

Eve's eyes narrowed as she focused on the floor, mulling it over. "I felt the scene was too pristine, almost staged. Colton was beaten to death, yet there wasn't nearly as much blood as you'd expect. The place was a mess, but not in a way that aligns with how violent the fight appears. I don't know, it just.... seems like someone is trying to push us in a certain direction."

Her way of thinking, which initially attracted David, fascinated him as he watched her. Eve Kane had an eye for detail, and her instincts were incredibly sharp. Yet, he understood that the job often demanded more from her than she was ready to acknowledge. "Maybe you're over thinking it" he proposed, aware it was a slim chance but feeling he wanted to help "It might just be what it seems. A brutal murder"

"Maybe," she said, but the uncertainty in her voice was clear. Eve trusted her instincts, and this case was bothering her in a way that others hadn't "But if it is, then why bother making it seem like something it's not?"

David shrugged. "That's your job to figure out, right? But maybe take a break for tonight. You've been at it all day, and it's not like you to bring work home."

Eve smiled faintly, appreciating the sentiment, but knowing she couldn't just turn it off. "It's never really off, you know that."

He nodded, knowing better than to argue. "I know. But still, you're home now. At least try to leave it at the door, even if it's just for a little while."

Eve considered his words, then nodded, more for his sake than hers. "You're right," she said, though she knew her mind would still sift through the details even as they sat down for dinner.

The evening passed quietly. David made a simple meal, pasta with a light sauce and a side of salad, something easy and familiar. They ate together at the small dining table, talking about anything but the case.

David shared his workday, recounting the dull aspects of office life. They contrasted sharply with Eve's reality. She listened with half an ear, chiming in occasionally, but her mind kept drifting back to the crime scene. The chilling image of Eddie Colton's vacant eyes and the message left behind.

CHAPTER 24 - BEHIND CLOSED DOORS

Later, as they sat on the couch watching a movie, Eve leaned against David, her head resting on his shoulder. It was a rare moment of vulnerability; one she allowed herself only in the safety of their home. David fully focused on the movie, but Eve's mind wandered. Her thoughts were still at the bar, still searching for the clue that would solve the mystery of Eddie Colton's murder.

David's arm wrapped around her, and he gently traced patterns on her shoulder and down her arm. It was a nice and comforting reminder that life held more than just her job. She closed her eyes, letting the warmth lull her. It gave her a moment of peace. But tomorrow she'd be back to the grind. She'd chase leads and try to solve an impossible puzzle. As she drifted off to sleep, her last conscious thought was of the baton, the blood, and the message that someone had gone to great lengths to convey.

Deep down, she understood that the case was only going to get more complicated from here.

25

Chapter 25 – Pieces of the puzzle

Kane woke up before dawn, her internal clock waking her from the light sleep she had found. The room was dark. David's steady breathing broke the calm of the early morning. He lay next to her, deep in peaceful dreams. Eve watched him for a moment, her thoughts already racing through the unresolved aspects of the case. For her, sleep was a rare luxury. The details of her most recent case always played on her mind through the night. The crack of dawn usually signaled a time for action.

Eve quietly got out of bed and headed for the bathroom, her footsteps not making a sound. When she turned on the bathroom light, she stood in front of the mirror, looking at her reflection. Her green eyes, tired, but sharp and ready for the day, were framed by the red hair she always kept tied back, a practical choice for someone in her line of work. The water from the shower was scalding, just the way she liked it, the steam quickly filling the small room. It was a ritual, this morning shower, the one place where she could collect her thoughts before diving back into the fray.

As the water poured over her, Eve's thoughts drifted to

CHAPTER 25 - PIECES OF THE PUZZLE

a message she had received late last night. It was a brief yet exciting update: Some preliminary results are in. It was the kind of message that sent a thrill through her veins; the adrenaline surging as soon as she read it. The shower felt too short, but she wanted to get in quickly, start putting the pieces of the puzzle together.

Back in the bedroom, Eve moved with purpose, dressing quickly in the semi-darkness. The case was tugging at her, demanding her attention, and she knew the lab would already be abuzz with activity. Before leaving, she bent down to kiss David on the forehead, a gentle gesture of affection that was as much for her as it was for him. He stirred slightly but didn't wake, and she was grateful. Not everyone has to be up as early as Eve. Let David rest.

The drive to the precinct was swift, the early hour ensuring that the streets were clear. The city was just beginning to stir, the first light of dawn creeping over the skyline. Eve's thoughts were already ahead of her, in the lab, with the results that could potentially break the case wide open.

As she walked into the lab, the familiar scent of chemicals and sterile air hit her, grounding her in the present. Doctor Nick Miller was already there, his small, fidgety frame hunched over a microscope. Nick was a nervous man, always seeming slightly startled, but Eve respected him. He was meticulous, a perfectionist in his work, and that was all that mattered to her.

"Morning, Nick," Eve greeted, her voice cutting through the quiet hum of the lab equipment.

Nick jumped slightly, but when he saw it was Eve, he relaxed, though only a little. "Eve," he responded, straightening up. His fingers twitched, as if they were continually on the brink of a nervous tic, yet his eyes remained sharp and focused. "I wasn't expecting you this early, but I suppose I should have anticipated it."

Eve allowed a small smile. "You know me. What have you got?"

Nick didn't waste time with pleasantries. He reached for a tablet on the counter, bringing up the preliminary report. "We ran the prints from the scene," he began, his voice steady now as he slipped into professional mode. "They came back faster than I expected, and they match someone from inside the departmental records."

Eve's eyebrows arched; interest piqued. "Who?"

"Ray Gordon," Nick said, watching her carefully for a reaction. "Former officer. His prints were on the bar, on a glass, and..." He paused for effect, "...on the baton."

Eve's mind raced, connecting dots even as new questions formed. Ray Gordon, the name from the note at the scene, simply Ray. It was a significant lead, but it didn't add up. Ray was a loose cannon, sure, but a cold-blooded killer? That didn't fit the man she knew.

"Ray," she muttered, more to herself than to Nick. "If he's the one who killed Colton, why leave a note addressed to himself? Why leave the murder weapon? He's a former cop; he'd know better than to leave anything that could trace back to him."

Nick shifted slightly, a hint of unease creeping back into his demeanor. "I'm just here to provide the facts, Eve. No conclusions, just the evidence."

Eve nodded, her mind already moving ahead. She needed to talk to Ray, to get a sense of where he was now, what had happened since he left the force. The evidence was damning, but something didn't sit right. Ray would know better than

CHAPTER 25 - PIECES OF THE PUZZLE

to make such obvious mistakes. Unless, of course, someone wanted it to look like he had.

"Thanks, Nick," she said, her tone curt but appreciative. "Keep digging. I'll handle Ray."

As she left the lab, Eve felt the familiar tug of the hunt. The initial findings were significant, yet they marked just the start of the investigation. The clues were aligning, but the overall image remained unclear. Ray Gordon was a key figure, but it was still uncertain whether he was the murderer or merely a player in someone else's scheme.

Eve Kane thrived on this, on the pursuit, the puzzle, the challenge. And as she headed to track down Ray, she knew one thing for sure: this case was far from over. If anything, it has just gotten more complicated.

26

Chapter 26 – Close quarters

As I drove, my fingers tapped the steering wheel in a nervous rhythm I couldn't control. Joey sat beside me, fiddling with his phone, his leg bouncing like a piston. I couldn't tell if he was anxious or excited; he chatted a lot, about nothing in particular. He was a little all over the map. Maybe the buzz of doing the police work was too much excitement for him. He had done nothing since his dismissal. Tough enough doing this with my own demons, never mind trying to figure out what was going through his head. I let him ramble as much as he wanted. I needed him now, more than ever.

The plan was simple: we were going to find Tommy Russo and get some proper answers. Joey's tip might have been thin, but it was the best lead I had. I felt like a puppet on a string. I was dancing to someone else's tune, and I hated that feeling.

As a cop, I always felt I had control. I had authority over the people, the badge, the uniform. It put me where I liked to be, in charge. I missed that feeling.

A familiar red-and-blue flash cut through the night, interrupting our drive. A police cruiser. Then another.

CHAPTER 26 – CLOSE QUARTERS

"Oh, shit..." I muttered, slowing down instinctively, thinking to myself I thought I had more time before they linked anything to me.

Joey glanced up, his face going pale. "Shit, Ray. Are they for us?"

As if on cue, the cruiser behind us hit its siren, a sharp wail that made me clench the wheel tighter. "Looks like it," I grumbled. "Hang on."

I pulled over, heart pounding. I wasn't ready for this, not yet. I knew it was inevitable at some stage, but they are usually slower than this. How can they already be on my tail? I thought. Then, I saw her. It was Detective Evelyn Kane. She was stepping out of the cruiser, with two officers flanking her like shadows. Kane is a brilliant detective. Well known, well respected, and brilliant at what she does. That's how they did this so quickly, damn it.

She was all business, her green eyes locked on me like a predator sighting prey. I rolled down the window before she even reached the door.

"Ray Gordon," she said, her voice cold and commanding. "Step out of the vehicle."

I glanced at Joey. "Stay calm," I whispered. His hand was twitching on his knee. He seemed more nervous than me.

"Sure thing, Detective," I replied, stepping out slowly with my hands visible. No point making this worse. "What's this about?"

She didn't waste time. "You know damn well what this is about. We found your fingerprints at the scene of Eddie Colton's murder. And your name... written all over the crime scene."

I kept my expression blank, but my insides twisted. Of course,

I knew this was coming, but hearing it said out loud made it feel even more real and dangerous. I was in deep.

Joey got out of the car, clearly on edge. "Detective, I was with Ray most of the night. Whatever you think happened, I can vouch for him."

Kane eyed him with suspicion. "You vouch for a man whose name was literally written in blood at a murder scene? A man whose fingerprints taint the scene? That's bold, Mr...?"

"Sanders, Joey Sanders," he replied, voice slightly shaky. "I'm his friend, former partner. And I'm just saying, Ray wouldn't kill anyone, not without cause."

Kane smirked. "Good to know Mr. Sanders. But let's get this straight. Both of you are coming with me. You can vouch for him all you like, but we're having a little chat down at the station."

Joey shot me a look, and I could tell he was debating staying out of it. Leaving me to deal with this alone. But I gave him a firm nod. "Come on, Joey. If you're so sure about me, this shouldn't be a problem, right?" I said, my voice challenging him to back me up.

He hesitated, then nodded reluctantly. "Right... right."

We climbed into the back of Kane's cruiser. Brushed shoulders as we sat locked in the back of what used to be our comfort zone. The station wasn't far, but the ride felt like hours. Joey's leg wouldn't stop bouncing. His hands were twitching. I could almost hear his pulse racing. The anxiety pouring off him was enough to help me forget my own concerns. Well, almost. I knew he was nervous, but I didn't get it. Why so jumpy? What was he afraid of?

When we reached the station, Kane led us into an interrogation room. It was typical.... cold, clinical, and unwelcoming.

CHAPTER 26 – CLOSE QUARTERS

The fluorescent lights buzzed overhead, flickering slightly. The room smelled like stale coffee and the faint scent of disinfectant. She told us to take a seat and then left us there; the door closing with a loud click that echoed in the small space.

The time ticked on, 10 minutes, then 20... the whole time Joey twitching about like a nervous wreck.

"They can't just leave us in here, waiting like this," Joey complained. I could tell he was getting frustrated now.

"You know the game Joe, we have played it ourselves, many times," I replied. "Just sit down, relax. We have nothing to hide."

He looked at me; it was almost as if he were pissed off at me for remaining so calm. I was the one being pulled in for questioning. I was the one who had left evidence at the scene. It was as if he were looking at me, telling me to wake up and react.

"You need to get your story straight, Ray," he said, "because if I were in her shoes, I wouldn't be letting you back out on that street tonight!"

"I have done nothing Joey, you know it, I know it. Whatever they have is circumstantial; that's why they haven't arrested me yet."

Again, he just looked at me, looking frustrated. With me? With the situation? I don't know, but he said nothing more.

Finally, after 45 minutes, Detective Kane returned. She pulled up a seat, sat across from us, her expression hard. I have heard enough about Kane; I know she is tough and knows how to push the buttons of suspects. How to break them. But they are guilty. I am not...not of what she is accusing me of, at least.

"Mr. Gordon," she began, "Let's get straight to it. Why were your fingerprints at the scene of Eddie Colton's murder?"

I kept my face straight. "I was looking for Megan. I got a clue that led me there. When I arrived, Eddie was already dead."

Kane leaned back in her chair, studying me. "Megan?" she asked.

"Someone took my daughter a couple of days ago. I have been trying to find her, but I think whoever has her is playing a game with me."

"I am sorry to hear that, Mr. Gordon," she replied, with what appeared to be genuine concern. "I sincerely hope your daughter is found safe."

"Thank you," was all I could muster in response. I sincerely hoped the same, with all my heart. But sitting here, going through this pointless exercise, wasn't helping.

After a moment, she leaned forward again. "Regardless of your personal circumstances, the fact remains that you were at my crime scene. Why?"

"Whoever has Megan, they sent me something. It pointed me to Colton's bar."

"What did they send you?"

I needed a moment to gather myself. The parcel and its contents shook me deeply. It was difficult to revisit the thoughts and discuss it. I couldn't let myself break down in front of others.

"Among other things, there was a part of a beer mat. A Colton's bar beer mat," I offered.

"So, from that, you headed straight there?"

"I did, yes," I answered as if there were no other answer, which to me was true. "It was a clue as to Megan's whereabouts. I headed straight there, hoping to bring her home."

Joey shifted in his seat. He was clearly uncomfortable with

CHAPTER 26 – CLOSE QUARTERS

this. He was my partner when Megan was born and for the first 6 years of her life. He knows as well as anyone how much she means to me.

"What happened when you arrived?" Kane continued her interrogation.

"I found Eddie on the floor, and I knew right away I had been played. I lost control, and I smashed the place up. It was only after that I saw the note, the tick tock note. Whoever it was had sent me there to be caught by you, but I didn't touch that son of a bitch."

"So, you hold some anger toward Eddie Colton, then?" Kane said, pleased with herself for catching me on my brief flicker of emotion.

"He was a scumbag. Every cop in the city had anger toward him. But I didn't kill him."

Kane sat back and studied me for a moment. It felt as though she were trying to read my mind. Attempting to physically see the words I may be thinking as they crossed my brain. She is good, but I am not guilty.

After what felt like an eternity of silence, Kane spoke again. "OK Ray, we don't have enough to hold you. Don't think that means you are in the clear. Rest assured that I will keep digging and I will be watching you. Stay out of trouble and do not leave the state, and you really should leave it to the police to find Megan."

"I believe Megan is close by," I responded. "I won't be going anywhere, not without her."

Kane stood up, motioning for the officers to escort us out. As we left, I looked over at Joey. He was still pale; he looked clammy. I felt let down by him. I couldn't shake it. He was supposed to be back up; he was supposed to be my support. It felt more like it was the other way around.

27

Chapter 27 – Fractured loyalties

We left the station and walked. The wind was icy and stung the skin on my face. Joey stuck close to me, nervous and twitchy. You could cut the tension between us with a knife. I just wanted to get as from the station as quickly as we could, then I could call a cab with no eyes on me.

We walked in silence, my thoughts racing as I replayed every moment of our interrogation in my mind. Joey had looked terrified; in a way I had never seen before. I could almost sense the relief pouring off him when Kane finally released us. I just couldn't understand it. He was acting like a guilty man. I kept looking his way as we walked, trying to figure out what was going on in his head, but he kept looking forward, giving nothing away.

The wind was strong, pushing against us, slowing our pace, delaying our escape from the station. The far-off noises of the city, the beeping horns, the sounds of sirens, seemed subdued beneath the weight of our situation. I felt an urge to shake Joey, to force him to share what was racing through his mind. Yet, I also recognized the need to tread lightly with my words. Joey was visibly on edge; that much was clear.

With enough distance from the station, I stopped, leaned against a streetlamp, and pulled out my phone. Joey waited beside me, his breath visible in the chilly air. I called for a cab, watching Joey out of the corner of my eye. He hadn't stopped fidgeting since we left the station, his hands constantly in motion, rubbing them together or tapping against his thigh. He looked rigid, as though he could snap at the slightest bend. I wondered again what was going on with him. My paranoia was getting worse by the minute.

The cab arrived within minutes, and we climbed into the back seat. I thanked the driver; Joey just stared out the window. The ride was short, but it felt like hours. Joey's leg bounced nervously, and he kept shifting in his seat. I could see his reflection in the window. He appeared anxious, clenching his jaw, and stared straight ahead to avoid looking at me.

My heart was pounding, the adrenaline still flowing, but I kept my focus on Joey for now. I wanted to know just what the hell made him act like that.

The cab pulled up near my truck. I paid the fare and thanked the driver again. I opened the cab door and instantly felt the cold air against my face again. I stood and watched Joey as he hurried toward the truck, eager to put this whole thing behind us. As much as I would have liked the same thing, I had some questions for Joey.

I climbed into the driver's side, put the keys in the ignition, but didn't start the engine. I just sat there for a moment, looking ahead, out at the empty road. I felt angry and impatient, more so now than at the station. After a few moments of quiet, I turned to Joey. "What the fuck, Joey? What happened back there?"

CHAPTER 27 – FRACTURED LOYALTIES

He didn't look at me. He kept his eyes on his lap, his fingers still twitching. "Just leave it, Ray. Drive," he muttered, his voice tight and defensive.

"No, fuck that, Joe. I'm not leaving it," I snapped, frustrated. "You were supposed to have my back in there. You looked like you were about to shit yourself the entire time. What's going on?"

He finally looked at me, his eyes filled with something I couldn't quite place. Fear, anger, guilt? I wasn't sure. "You don't understand, Ray," he mumbled. "You can't understand."

I softened my tone, trying to get through to him. "Then help me understand, Joey. Talk to me."

He turned fully to face me, his expression suddenly hard and cold. "It's the first time I've been back there since they kicked me off the force, Ray. Do you know what that felt like?"

I blinked. I was caught off guard. I hadn't thought about that, not once. "I get it, Joe. But...."

"No, you don't get it!" he cut me off, his voice rising almost to a full shout. "They kicked me out because of you, because I supported you after that mess with Leroy Jenkins. I lost everything because I stood by you. This is like Déjà vu, we are doing it all over again. What am I going to lose this time? What do I even have left?"

His words hit me hard. The guilt was instant. I realized I hadn't actually felt guilty about what happened to Joey before now. I had been so selfish. My pain and problems consumed me. I hadn't considered what Joey had gone through. "Joey... I'm sorry," I said, almost silent. "I didn't realize..."

He snorted, a bitter smile twisting his lips. "No, you didn't. You never do. But I don't blame you, Ray. I blame the assholes who let us go. Now, can we just drop this and get back to finding your daughter?"

I nodded, but I knew I would carry the burden of guilt from now on. "Yeah... sure. Let's get back to it." I started the engine and pulled away, but my mind was racing with everything just said. I still couldn't shake the thought that there was something Joey wasn't telling me.

The tension between remained it was palpable as I drove on. I kept my eyes on the road, kept the speed steady. My instincts were on high alert, telling me that something was off. I wanted to trust him; I needed to trust him. Yet, in that moment, that trust felt like a fading memory, drifting further away with each passing second.

28

Chapter 28 – The waiting game

The drive was tense, an awkward tension. Suddenly, I felt like I was driving with a stranger, not my old partner, not the man that was once one of my oldest friends. The tension gnawed at me, making it hard to focus on the job. We hadn't made a proper plan. We were doing this blind, and it was no good.

"Joe," I muttered. "We need a plan."

"No shit," he shot back. Then he turned and looked at me, and to my surprise, he laughed. It was an odd time for laughter, but it cracked through the tension like a knife, and I was grateful for that. "Let's just get there first. Stake the place out, then decide. Good?"

"Fine," I grumbled, though the thought of sitting around waiting made my skin itch. I wanted this done fast.

We went to Steel City Boxing, an old gym in Bridgeport. It was the type of place that held onto its grime and history. Tommy fit right in there. I parked a safe distance away. It was far enough to see the entrance without being seen. The rain smeared the windshield. The wipers gave brief moments of clarity.

Joey spoke first. "Settle in. This could be a while."

I didn't respond. My head was throbbing, my hands shaking. It felt as though my whole body was on. I tried to steady my hands on my knees, but they wouldn't stop. Alcohol withdrawal, creeping in again, even though it had only been a few hours since my last drink. What a goddamn mess I'd become.

I could feel Joey watching me, feel the weight of his concern ready to spill over into another lecture.

"You okay, Ray?"

"Fine, Joe."

"You look a mess," he said, sharper this time. "Are you fit to do this? We gotta have each other's backs, no matter what goes down."

"Jesus, Joey, not now," I snapped. "Let's just focus on that damn gym" I pointed at the building, dark and dull with grayed out windows, like a place that had no life in it.

Joey held his hands up in surrender, sitting back and staring out the window.

We waited. It felt like time stood still; minutes felt like hours. The rain was heavy, beating down on the roof. My eyes grew heavy; it was dark, and the truck was warm. The constant drum of the rain should have been enough to keep me awake. But I could feel my head drooping when suddenly.... bang, bang, bang.... on my window.

I jerked upright, my heart pounding. Joey looked as startled as I was. Then I saw him, a homeless man, face pressed close to the glass.

"Got any spare change?" he asked, his voice muffled.

My temper flared, and before I knew it, I rolled down the window. "Get the hell away from here, you dumb bastard!" I shouted, then rolled it back up, my chest heaving. The man muttered something under his breath as he shuffled away, but I didn't care. Let him hate me. Join the damn queue.

The homeless guy had gone, he had wandered off into the night. My adrenaline was pumping, and my nerves were on edge. I slowed my breathing, taking long deep breaths in and out, trying to calm myself. Joey said nothing. He seemed to have gotten over it already. He just kept his eyes on the gym, stayed concentrated on the task at hand. I could tell he was tense too, probably feeling the same undercurrent of dread that coursed through me.

"Keep it together, Ray," I muttered to myself. "Focus."

Minutes ticked by, feeling like hours. We watched the entrance of the gym like hawks, but nothing moved. The gym's dim outdoor light flickered intermittently, doing nothing to erase the dark at the entrance. I could see a few cars parked out front, but no signs of life. The place felt abandoned, yet I knew better. It was just sleeping, waiting to come alive.

"Maybe Tommy isn't here," Joey said after a while, his voice low, almost hopeful.

"He's here," I replied, my voice gruff. "I can feel it. We just need to be patient." Although being patient was exactly my special skill at the moment.

Joey nodded, but I could tell he wasn't so sure. Hell, neither was I. The longer we sat there, the more I felt like this was a dead end, a waste of time. My hands continued to shake, and my head felt like it was splitting open. The alcohol withdrawals were kicking harder with each passing minute, making it hard to concentrate. I breathed in through my nose, trying to steady myself.

I spotted some movement out of the corner of my eye. It was

a lanky, skinny man coming out from the side door of the gym. He took a quick look around before stepping out into the open. We knew him. It was one of Tommy's goons. He was the type who'd do anything for a quick buck or a pat on the back from Tommy.

"There," I whispered, nudging Joey. "One of Tommy's boys."

Joey squinted through the rain-soaked windshield. "I see him. Looks like he's checking the perimeter."

We watched as he paced, checking behind himself. He seemed nervous, as if someone might jump on him from behind. The cold was evident in his breath as it fogged in the air. Keeping one hand inside his jacket, as they usually do when holding a gun, ready to draw at a moment's notice. He was waiting for someone, that was obvious.

A few minutes later, another goon emerged from the front entrance. This one was shorter, stockier, wearing a hoodie pulled up tight against the rain. He had his head down, dashing across the street, and disappeared down an alley.

"What do you think?" Joey whispered.

"It looks like they're getting ready for something," I said, feeling the nerves tighten in my gut. "They're not just hanging out."

More figures appeared, one by one, from various parts of the gym. A couple of them milled around the entrance, smoking, checking their phones, trying to look casual but failing. My senses went into overdrive. I could feel the tension building, like this was all building up to something, something bad.

"That's too many people for a regular night," Joey muttered. "What the hell are they planning?"

"Doesn't matter," I replied, my voice sharp. "We wait."

CHAPTER 28 - THE WAITING GAME

We waited, watching. More of Tommy's boys trickled out, but there was still no sign of Tommy. My anxiety continued to climb; I could feel the sweat building on my brow. Something wasn't right.

"Where the hell is he?" I muttered impatiently.

Suddenly, a black sedan came roaring around the corner, screeching to a stop in front of the gym. The doors flew open, more men jumped out, they were shouting something, but it was impossible to hear over the commotion. There was a flurry of movement. Tommy's men scrambled, shouting orders at each other.

"What the fuck is going on?" Joey whispered urgently.

"Something's gone sideways," I said, my voice tight. "They all look shit scared" Joey smiled at that, a weird smile. Do I even know this guy anymore?

Out of nowhere, a gunshot rang out. The noise pierced through the air, stopping everything else for half a second, and then all hell broke loose. Tommy's guys rushed toward the sedan, some ducking for cover, others drawing weapons of their own. They were yelling, looking panicked.

"Where's Tommy?" Joey asked, eyes darting around the scene. "If his men are here, why isn't he?"

"I don't know," I replied. It made me feel uneasy. "But something's wrong. This isn't how he operates."

Another gunshot rang out, and we heard a scream of pain. One of Tommy's men went down, clutching his side. The others ran anywhere they could, jumping into the cars, running down the street, trying to get out of sight as quickly as they could.

"Ray, we need to follow them!" Joey urged, "They're leaving, and Tommy's not with them!"

I took off toward the sedan. "Maybe they'll lead us to him."

The sedan peeled out, tires screeching, and I jammed my foot on the gas, swerving into traffic behind them. Joey gripped the dashboard, his eyes fixed on the road ahead.

As we tore through the rain-slick streets, I kept glancing in the rear-view mirror. Tommy's men were all over the place, moving in different directions like they were running scared.

"They're spooked, Ray," Joey muttered. "Something's got them rattled."

"Yeah, but what?" I replied, my voice tense. "Where the hell is Tommy?"

We chased the sedan through the winding streets, headlights bouncing off wet pavement, the city a blur of shadows and rain. My mind raced, a hundred scenarios flashing through my head. If Tommy wasn't here, he was somewhere else, and whatever had gone down tonight, he hadn't planned on being a part of it. The sedan took a sudden turn off onto a side street, heading toward the industrial area near the river. I followed, keeping a tight hold on the wheel. I could feel the old buzz of the chase again.

"Keep close," Joey said. "If they lead us to Tommy, we'll get some answers."

I nodded, but my gut told me it wouldn't be so straightforward. The way his boys were acting, the desperation in their movements, it felt like they were running from something, like they had no direction. Why would this lead be any easier than the last? So far, everything has gone wrong. I was low on hope.

I had a sinking feeling that when we finally caught up with Tommy, we wouldn't be getting any answers.

29

Chapter 29 – Hanging by a thread

We kept our distance as the sedan came to a stop up ahead. The truck's rumble would spook them in this abandoned part of town. So, I parked a way back. We slipped out, moving low and using any cover we could find as we edged closer to the scene. Every creak of metal or the scuff of gravel echoed louder than it should. The silence down here wasn't right.

It wasn't just the sedan up there; two other cars were parked under a broken streetlight, casting jagged shadows. A dozen goons stood around, all stiff as statues, like they'd just seen something out of a nightmare. Not one of them looked easy, and each held a tension that I couldn't shake. I thought, What the hell are we walking into here?

We crouched behind a rusted pile of scrap metal dumped in the middle of nowhere. "What do you think is going on up there?" I whispered to Joey, feeling the weight of the unknown pressing in.

"Fuck knows," he muttered. "We need to get a look." He was right, but I was hesitant.

That's when I saw it. How I missed it before, I couldn't tell you. But beyond the huddle of henchmen, strung up high against the jagged outline of the metal beams, was Tommy Russo. His arms were stretched out like he was some twisted version of the savior himself, lifeless and abandoned. Dead.

My mind reeled; my stomach twisted. This couldn't be happening. Not again. I was bouncing from one murder scene to the next like some kind of sick joke. Someone was pulling the strings here, leading me by the nose to find bodies rather than clues. And every corpse I found just pushed me further from Megan.

Joey's voice cut into my thoughts. "Jesus Christ, Ray. That's Tommy. He's fucking dead!"

I opened my mouth, but no sound came out. My mind was spinning in circles. I couldn't believe they had led me to another dead man. How many dead ends could I keep chasing? I wasn't even sure what I was looking for anymore. I needed to get it together. Megan was out there somewhere, and this distraction was only wasting precious time.

"Ray," Joey hissed, jabbing his elbow into my side. "We better get out of here. Either his goons will find us, or the cops will. They're probably on their way."

But I stood rooted to the spot, staring at Tommy's lifeless body swaying slightly from the beams. Whoever was behind this was making a statement. They weren't just killing scum; they were taunting me. And with every fresh crime scene, the picture they were painting made me look less like a broken cop and more like a monster on a murderous rampage. My only hope now was to find this bastard before they buried me under a pile of corpses.

"Ray!" Joey's voice was sharp, pulling me out of the trance. "Snap out of it. We need to get back in the truck. Now."

CHAPTER 29 – HANGING BY A THREAD

I forced myself to my feet, feeling a dizziness grip me as I staggered forward. Fear was closing in fast, a cold, sharp terror that crept up my spine. Whoever did this wasn't just playing games, they had Megan. The thought hit me hard, the thought of Megan being held by this monster. I couldn't stand it; I doubled over and vomited on the ground.

"Shit, Ray! You're leaving evidence all over the damn place! Get in the truck!" Joey barked, hauling me up by my shoulder and practically shoving me into the back seat.

I flopped down, letting the shock wash over me as Joey slid into the driver's seat, his expression calm but eyes flickering with tension. He backed up slowly, like we were just another pair of bystanders minding our own business. But then he froze, staring out at something.

"Shit," he said under his breath.

I forced myself to sit up, my stomach still twisted in knots. "What is it?"

"They've seen us," he replied, his voice low, "and they're coming this way."

I tensed, fighting the urge to jump out and run. "Then drive, Joey! Get us the hell out of here!"

He smirked, glancing back at the goons with a casual nod, as if we were just passing through. He eased the truck into gear, his calmness a stark contrast to the thudding in my chest. Slowly, he pulled us away from the scene, all the while keeping an eye on the rear-view mirror.

"This whole thing's a shit show, Joey," I muttered as the tension finally spilled out. "Every lead we follow just drags us deeper. Every clue takes us further from Megan and straight to another crime scene."

Joey kept his eyes on the road, saying nothing, but his grip on the wheel tightened as he drove us back into the shadows.

30

Chapter 30 – In the shadow of the badge

Detective Kane leaned back; the stale office air thick around her as she reviewed notes from the Colton case. The last few days had thrown the city's underbelly into chaos, and her instincts told her this was only the beginning. Colton and Gordon, the violence, the evidence. It felt like the start of something dark. The kind of thing that meant no sleep for a cop until every piece was in place.

The call came through, short and clipped. Another one of Chicago's finest criminals had bitten the dust, and this time it was Tommy Russo. Kane's lips twitched. Another high-ranking thug hung out like yesterday's trash. And judging by the urgency in the voice on the radio, it would not be a typical scene. She grabbed her coat, threw it over her shoulder, and headed for the exit.

The drive over was faster than usual, the city streets giving way to more deserted, forgotten stretches of asphalt. By the time she arrived, the scene was crawling with uniforms and suits. The flashing red-and-blue lights cast eerie shadows on the cracked pavement and rusted metal in the lot. She took a breath, the weight of the city pressing down on her. This was no ordinary scene.

"Detective Kane," one uniform called as she approached, clipboard in hand, face tight with an anxious edge. "You're going to want to see this one."

"Let's hope it's worth the trip," she muttered, more to herself than to him. But as she reached the main cluster of officers, her gaze landed on the spectacle hanging high above, and her stomach twisted. Tommy, strung up for all to see, arms outstretched like some unholy saint. Her face remained impassive, but inside, she was firing on all cylinders. Another one, another bold display, another breadcrumb leading to... someone. And someone who had an agenda.

"Who was first on the scene?" she asked, pulling her gloves on as her eyes scanned the lot, instincts picking up every detail.

"Sullivan and Brooks," the officer replied, nodding toward two younger detectives huddled over a stack of evidence bags. She walked over, her boots crunching on the gravel, and the two of them straightened up as she approached, eyes wary.

"Sullivan," she said, glancing at the evidence laid out before them. "What are we looking at here?"

Sullivan ran a hand through his hair, glancing over his shoulder at Tommy's body swaying in the wintry morning breeze. "Found him just like this. No sign of struggle down here, no prints, no dropped weapons. Just Tommy, dead, and left for us to find. It's clean, Detective."

"Clean," she repeated, her voice dry, an edge creeping in. "So why do I feel like I'm walking into a set-up?"

Brooks cleared his throat. "There's more. We've got a group of Russo's goons hanging around the edge of the lot, watching.

CHAPTER 30 – IN THE SHADOW OF THE BADGE

Haven't budged since we got here, just watching us work like they're waiting for something."

Kane's gaze shifted, scanning the edges of the scene. Sure enough, shadows lingered by the chain-link fence, half a dozen of them, faces grim, eyes locked on every move she made. There was tension in the air, a kind of silent stand-off, but she knew better than to let them see her rattle. They were here for a reason; they wanted to see what the police would find. She could tell by their posture, their narrowed eyes, they wanted justice......their own brand of it.

"Alright, I want every inch of this place scoured. And have someone keep an eye on the muscle over there," she said, gesturing with her chin. "I don't want a single one of them wandering over or making a scene."

Turning back to the body, she took a long look, her mind racing. It wasn't just that Tommy had been strung up for them to find. There was something else, something that didn't sit right. An air of deliberation, a dark sense of purpose. Whoever did this wanted her, the cops, the city, all to take notice. She just didn't know why. But the pieces were falling too perfectly into place for her liking.

As she stepped back to survey the scene, something half-buried in the dirt caught her eye. The color stopped her cold. She crouched, brushing away the loose gravel. Her breath caught as she uncovered a torn, stained piece of fabric. It was a cop's blue uniform. She tugged it free, holding it up in the dull morning light. The fabric was rough, worn, and across its sleeve was a patch with numbers scrawled across it. Familiar numbers.

Her pulse quickened, an edge of adrenaline sharpening her focus. If this was what she thought it was, someone was playing games. And they wanted her to follow along.

"Bag this," she ordered, handing it to Sullivan. "Have it analyzed. Check out that number ASAP. I want answers yesterday."

Sullivan took the scrap, frowning. "This a badge number, Detective?"

"I think it is," she said, her voice tight, each word deliberate. "And I think someone's leading us around by the nose." Her eyes darkened. "And I don't like being led."

She cast one last look at Tommy's lifeless body, swaying high above, then turned on her heel. Whoever was behind this was getting bolder. More reckless. Somehow, Ray Gordon was involved. She'd bet her life savings that was Gordon's badge number she'd just uncovered. She didn't know if he was the pawn or the puppet master, but every instinct told her he was deep in this game. And if she didn't start unraveling it soon, she'd be playing catch-up with bodies piling up faster than she could keep track.

As she strode back to her car, she could still feel the eyes of Tommy's goons on her. Watching, waiting. She didn't care. Let them stare. She had a feeling that before long, they'd be seeing a lot more of her.

31

Chapter 31 – In the grip of doubt

We drove back to Joey's place in complete silence. My mind spun in endless loops, trying to get a grip on what was happening around me, but nothing made sense. It was surreal, like something out of a movie.... but it was happening to me, to my family, to my little girl. This wasn't supposed to happen. I was used to controlling the situation, not the other way around.

I hadn't even noticed Joey beside me, even though he was the one driving. When he finally spoke as he pulled up at his place, it was almost startling.

"Man, I am beat," he muttered, yawning and stretching his arms over his head.

I just nodded. A nod of agreement, of exhaustion, of... defeat. I didn't know how I was still standing, let alone thinking.

"Ray, you good?"

I looked at him with a deadpan expression. "How can I be good, Joe?"

He held his hands up in a surrender gesture, reading me like a book. "My bad, sorry! Stupid question. But listen, this isn't over. We'll figure it out, Ray. You know we will."

"Hmm," I replied, my voice sounding hollow even to me. "Whoever this is, they're smart. Crazy as hell, but smart. They won't make this easy."

Joey hopped out, clearing the way for me to slide into the driver's seat. "Look, we're no good to anybody if we can't think straight. Go home, get some rest. I'll do the same, and we'll catch up later, yeah?"

I gave him a weak nod, the best I could muster. It was all I had in me. I pulled away, heading home, supposedly to rest. But every time I considered closing my eyes, considered taking a break, a wave of guilt crushed the air out of my lungs. How could I even consider sleeping while Megan was out there, suffering God knows what?

The drive home blurred together. One of those mindless journeys where you make it all the way there without knowing how. I could've driven through red lights or hit every pothole on the road for all I knew. I barely remembered pulling into my driveway. I was parked, the truck in gear, and just... sitting there, panting. Every inch of me was in a daze.

It was too much. This feeling clawing at my insides. I couldn't handle this kind of helplessness. This kind of fear.

Just as I was about to get out, my phone buzzed in my pocket. I fished it out and glanced at the screen. For a second, I thought I'd read the name wrong, that my exhaustion was playing tricks. But there it was, clear as day: Frank.

I thought I'd seen the last of him after what I did, showing up at his place, tearing into him in front of his family. What did he want?

"What is it?" I answered, skipping any pretense of pleasantries.

"Ray, let's talk," he said. His voice was soft, stripped of

CHAPTER 31 – IN THE GRIP OF DOUBT

its usual arrogant edge. Just hearing him like that put me on guard.

"What do you want to talk about?" I said, my suspicion thickening.

"I have information. I think it's important that you hear it."

He had my interest, sure, but I didn't trust him an inch. "I'm not paying you money I don't have, Frank. Why the hell do you think..."

"I don't want money, Ray," he interrupted, and there was something almost earnest in his tone. "Meet me at the diner two hours, yeah?"

The doubt gnawed at me. Frank had already shown his true colors, the greedy, conniving bastard. I'd already shown him my limits, or lack thereof, with him. This didn't feel right. But he said he didn't want money, and that was so out of character it made my skin prickle. Maybe this was another setup, maybe I was walking into another trap. Maybe this was just my life now, waiting for the next trap to spring.

"See you there," I said and hung up.

More questions piling on top of each other, but I'd go. Whatever he had to say, I'd hear it out. I didn't bother going inside. Instead, I closed my eyes in the truck and let myself drift for a moment, letting the exhaustion settle into my bones.

It was a dangerous thing to let my guard down, but right now, the rest was all I had.

32

Chapter 32 – Threads of deception

Detective Kane sat at her desk, a coffee cup growing cold by her elbow as she sifted through the case notes. The scenes from the last few days ran like a film reel in her mind: Colton's body, now Russo's, violent, deliberate murders. And the same thread weaving them together: Ray Gordon. His name, his past, and now, his badge number, resurfacing like a ghost she couldn't shake.

It was too neat, too targeted. Whoever was doing this wanted her to think Ray was some renegade, that he'd fallen so far he was hunting down crime lords. But Kane was no fool. She could see the strings of a setup. The precision, the theatricality, it wasn't Ray's style. It felt calculated, almost... personal.

She pushed her chair back, rising with purpose. "Brown," she called over to the younger detective across the aisle. "Bring up the files on Ray Gordon. His cases, evaluations, suspension reports, anything that's got his name on it."

"Gordon?" Brown looked surprised. "I thought he was out of the game after that mess a few years back."

"He was. But now he's somehow tangled in the middle of

CHAPTER 32 - THREADS OF DECEPTION

this circus, and I want to know why. And I want to know who'd go to this length to pull him back in."

Brown gave a quick nod, logging into the precinct database and starting the search. Kane turned her attention back to her own notes, laying out the patterns, the gaps, and the questions that haunted her. Colton and Russo weren't just random victims; they were high-profile targets. They held power, connections. But their deaths, and Ray's connection to them, weren't sitting right. She needed more insight into who Ray was, who he'd been as a cop, and why he'd left the force in pieces.

A few minutes later, Brown handed her a slim file. "Not much here, Detective," he said, frowning. "Most of the records were sealed, but I pulled everything left unclassified."

Kane took the file, her curiosity sharpening. "Thanks, Brown. Can you grab me some more coffee while you're at it?"

She sat back down, flipping the folder open. The first page was Ray's personnel record, a dry list of dates, positions, commendations. But, as she read on, details emerged: recommendations from past captains, commendations for bravery, and high marks for leadership in the line of duty. Ray hadn't just been a cop; he'd been one of the best. That much was clear. But as she moved further into the file, the picture darkened. Notes of disciplinary action appeared, warnings, reprimands, each one painted a story of a man on the edge. A cop driven by instinct, sharp but volatile. And then came the suspension report.

It wasn't the full case file, just a few redacted lines, but it was enough to piece together. A case gone sideways, a suspect who'd been pushed too hard, dead…. a scandal. They forced

Ray out, and the department quietly covered up the case. But it had broken him. The once-celebrated detective left the force under a cloud, and by the looks of it, he'd never quite recovered.

Kane drummed her fingers on the desk, her mind racing. Whoever's doing this knows Ray's history. They're baiting him, taunting him, pulling him back to every crime scene with a cruel precision. They know his weaknesses, his connections, and they're using him as a pawn.

She reached the last few pages. Notes on his family, ex-wife, a daughter named Megan. Her heart tightened as she read the name. Megan had been listed as missing just days before this string of murders started. So that's it. They've got his daughter, and they're using her to twist the knife.

The thought made her blood run cold. She hadn't known Gordon personally, but she knew the type, good men who lost themselves in the job, who chased justice until it consumed them. She'd seen enough cops burn out, even a few she'd been close to. But Ray Gordon had the look of someone who was teetering right on the edge, and she could feel it. Someone was going to great lengths to push him over.

Kane closed the file, exhaling slowly. She needed to talk to Ray. That much was clear. But she couldn't walk into it blind. She needed an edge, something to get him talking, to break through his defenses. She could try questioning him directly, but if he were anything like his record suggested, he wouldn't crack easily.

"Brown," she called again, as he returned with her coffee. "I need more than files. Who's still around that worked with Gordon back in the day?"

Brown frowned, scratching his head. "Let's see... Joey Sanders, his old partner, still works odd jobs for a couple of

CHAPTER 32 - THREADS OF DECEPTION

the precinct guys. Got an address for him somewhere, if that helps."

Kane nodded. "I met him. Jumpy guy didn't enjoy being brought in with Gordon the other day," She paused, "I will catch up with him, see how he is on his own, away from this place. Reach out to any of Gordon's recent contacts on the force. Discreetly. I don't want this blowing back on him.... yet."

Brown nodded in response. But before he could go, Kane asked him one more question "Who is on the Gordon girl kidnapping?"

"I'll looking into it," Brown replied and headed off, leaving Kane alone with her thoughts and her coffee. She took a sip, eyes narrowing as she focused on the details. She'd dig deeper, find out everything she could about Gordon before she confronted him. The badge, the murders, the message, it all pointed to someone hell-bent on seeing Ray fall, or maybe just on making him suffer. Either way, they were counting on him walking right into their trap.

If she can get some information on the kidnapping, it may be a way to soften Ray up when she speaks with him. She needs him with his guard down; she needs him open, honest.

If she could uncover the truth before they pushed Ray over the edge, she might just save him. And, she thought grimly, maybe even his daughter.

33

Chapter 33 – Alison's solitude

Alison stood and watched the cashier scan her groceries one by one. Each beep felt distant, almost like a heartbeat in another room, faint, hollow, only just reaching her. Her thoughts drifted, tugging her back to the worry that had clawed at her for days. Her mind filled with Megan. Her face, her laugh, her warmth. Gone, pulled into some unseen darkness.

"Ma'am?" the cashier's voice snapped her back, an expectant look in his eyes.

"Oh, sorry." She forced a small, apologetic smile, taking her card out and paying for her shopping before putting it back into her purse. She mumbled a thank you and gathered her bags, her motions automatic, like someone else was controlling her limbs.

Outside, the sharp bite of the wind brought her back to herself. She loaded her bags into the trunk, feeling the weight of each one, the effort to care about such a menial task. As she closed the trunk, her reflection surprised her. She no longer recognized the drawn, distant face. Her eyes seemed too hollow, too old. She was exhausted. Days of hoping and

CHAPTER 33 - ALISON'S SOLITUDE

waiting had certainly taken their toll.

The drive home was quiet, a complete silence that was almost eerie. Every street blurred by a monotony of traffic lights and familiar turns, but the comfort of routine had worn thin.

Alison stepped out of the car, shut the door, and looked up at her house full of dread. She didn't feel the motivation to go inside. The thought of entering the silence inside broke her heart. But she forced herself to walk up the path with her grocery bags in hand.

As she reached her front door, the rumble of an approaching engine caught her attention. She turned, her brow furrowing as an unmarked sedan pulled up to the curb. The car door opened, and out stepped a man in a plain suit, mid-forties, with a worn but attentive face. He flashed a badge, his expression respectful but businesslike.

"Mrs. Gordon?" he asked, his voice soft but steady.

"Yes, well no, actually," she replied, her voice sounding uncertain. "Ms. Hayes, just call me Alison."

"Sorry, Alison, I'm Detective Marshall," he said, tucking his badge away. "I'm in charge of your daughter's case. I was hoping we could talk."

Her eyes narrowed slightly. Detective Marshall. Well, it is about damn time; she thought to herself. How can it have possibly taken this long to reach out to her? She wanted to lash out at him, but she held herself back. Megan needed her to stay focused.

"It's taken a while for you to get here," she said, her tone flat, masking the anger beneath it.

He nodded, acknowledging her frustration. "I am truly sorry. There have been some developments in other cases, our resources are stretched right now. But I'm here now, and I want to do everything I can to help bring Megan home."

She gave a small nod, her hand tight around her keys. "Let's go inside."

They stepped into the quiet house, and she led him to the living room. Detective Marshall took a seat, pulling out a notebook, as he gave the room a quick once-over. Pictures of Megan scattered across shelves, one of her old dance recital trophies, family photos that spoke to a life that had once been whole.

He cleared his throat softly. "I know you've probably been through this a dozen times already, but I'd like to get a sense of Megan, who she is, the people in her life, any recent changes. Anything that might help us understand who might have done this."

Alison felt a pang, a mixture of guilt and sorrow. Talking about Megan like this felt like tearing open a wound that had barely started to heal. But she forced herself to start.

"Megan... she's a bright girl. Fierce. She's got this way of seeing through people, you know? Like she knows exactly who you are, and she's not afraid to call you on it. Probably gets that from her father." Her voice wavered, and she had to pause to catch her breath. "She loves dancing, singing... always lighting up the house with her energy. I don't know anyone who would have a reason to hurt her."

Detective Marshall nodded, listening carefully, his pen moving steadily across the page. "Any friends or acquaintances who've recently come into her life? Someone you didn't know well?"

Alison thought back, "No... she had a close circle, mostly kids she's known for years. She wasn't one to trust easily." She hesitated, glancing at him. "But there's... there's Ray."

CHAPTER 33 – ALISON'S SOLITUDE

"Her father?" Marshall asked, jotting down the name, although he was already well aware of Ray and who he was.

"Yes. He and I... well, we're not together. He's... he's complicated. But he loves her. I know he'd do anything to find her." She looked away, ashamed of the uncertainty creeping into her voice.

Marshall's gaze softened, but his tone stayed professional. "I understand. I'll be speaking with him as well. It's my job to get a full picture of everyone close to her, no matter how complicated it might be."

She nodded, her fingers tracing the edge of a cushion as she steadied herself. "I just don't understand why anyone would target her. Or why now? She's just a kid."

Detective Marshall leaned forward; his voice was gentle but firm. "We're going to find out, Mrs. Gordon. And if there's anyone who has a reason, anyone who might have the slightest connection, we'll uncover it."

Alison thought for a second. She hesitated, then said, "There are things you should know." She bowed her head, almost ashamed she hadn't told the police.

Marshall studied her for a second. "Go on" he said.

"Her father, Ray, he is out there. He is looking for her. But we have both received things in the post...." She started to cry. The thought of what had happened. Her little girl's hair had been cut. She now felt stupid for not passing this on right away.

"What things Alison, what have you received?"

"Ray got a parcel with Megan's hair in it. I... I got a picture of Megan with her hair cut short." She was holding it together, but the tears flowed.

Detective Marshal sighed, a big, frustrated sigh. "This is crucial evidence, Alison. We should be reviewing it for clues before anyone touched it."

Alison just shook her head. She knew he was right; she had no words to offer.

He softened again toward her; he was good at his job. "Please bring me the picture and everything that came with it. I will bag and we will analyze. Hopefully, it will give us something."

"Of course, of course," was all she could offer in response.

They talked for a while longer, grasping at any possible thread, any lead that might bring Megan back. When he finally rose to leave, she felt a tiny sliver of hope.

"Thank you, Detective," she said, her voice nothing more than a hollow whisper.

He gave her a steady nod. "I'll be in touch. And if you think of anything else, no matter how small, call me. If you receive anything else, please don't touch it. Just call me."

She watched him walk to his car, the sinking feeling of isolation creeping back as soon as he drove away. But in the quiet that followed, a small spark lingered. Maybe this detective, along with Ray, could find Megan.

34

Chapter 34 – Worst fears

Megan couldn't believe it, she was outside. She could feel fresh air on her face. It felt cool and fresh against her skin after being stuck in that dark room. She thinks it has only been a few days, but it felt like weeks. Months, even. She almost didn't know what to do, frozen between fear and the overwhelming feeling of freedom.

Then she heard him.

"MEGAN!" The man's voice ripped through the quiet of the woods, sharp and furious. He was near. He sounded so angry, each syllable carrying a threat that made her heart skip. She had to get away. Now.

She picked a direction and ran for it. She ran with everything she had, pushing her little legs as hard as they could go. It was hard maintaining a grip on the floor, her feet slipping on dead leaves. The forest was unfamiliar; the trees looked the same in every direction, no clear path to safety. She didn't know where she was, only that she had to keep going.

"MEGAN, GET BACK HERE! NOW!" His voice cut through the air again, booming, closer this time.

Panic drove her forward. Daddy, she thought, a plea filling her mind. If Daddy were here, the man wouldn't shout at her like that. He'd protect her. She knew that she just had to keep running, no matter how tired she was.

Her heart pounded, her pulse raising further with every yard she ran. Her legs ached, cramp settling in as she ran harder than she ever thought she could. She pushed through bushes, squeezed between trees. Her breath was heavier with every step. Her lungs burned, her vision blurred, but she couldn't stop. She wouldn't stop. The man was getting closer, his voice closing in, wrapping around her like the shadows themselves.

"LAST CHANCE, MEGAN!" The words were terrifying to her. She could hear the fury in every word. It felt so close she could almost feel his breath on her neck.

She pushed herself harder, faster, so much faster than she ever realized she could run. She just had to keep running, just had to stay ahead of him. She could....

Then, BANG, a gunshot ripped through the stillness of the forest, echoing all around her, piercing the silence.

Megan stopped, frozen, her body locking in place. She felt the sharp, searing pain radiating from her back, spreading through her chest. She looked down, seeing the blood spreading across her shirt, a small hole in the center of her chest. She noticed she was no longer breathing heavily; she wasn't breathing at all. Her legs gave out, and she collapsed to the ground, landing on her front in the cold, dark mud. Then everything went black.

Ray jolted awake, my body drenched in sweat, my chest heaving, every nerve on fire.

"MEGAN! NO!" I shouted, the echo of her name tearing from my throat, filling the silent truck. I looked around, my eyes

CHAPTER 34 - WORST FEARS

wild, uncomprehending. It took me a moment to realize I was still in the truck, not in the woods, not watching Megan die. It was just me, in the stifling silence, trapped with the memory of that nightmare, the horror of it fresh in my mind.

I run my hands, shaking, over my face, trying to steady myself. My pulse racing, my breathing shallow, muscles tense. The dream had felt so real. Too real. It was everything I feared, everything I couldn't bear to face. I couldn't shake the image of Megan lying on the ground, her small body.... broken.... blood on her shirt.

It was just a dream. But I could still feel it, lingering like a shadow, refusing to let go.

I forced himself to take a deep breath, grounding myself in the present. I looked at the clock. I'd been asleep for longer than I planned, and Frank was waiting.

When I pulled up at the diner, I saw Frank sitting at the same booth as before. He didn't look so smug this time. Maybe having his life flash before his eyes stripped away that arrogance. I put the truck in park, wincing as I stepped out and made my way in. I was completely exhausted.

As I got closer, I saw the bruising on his face and neck. A pang of guilt, sharp and uninvited, ran through me. I nodded a silent greeting as I slid into the seat across from him, staying quiet. He'd invited me here, let him start the talking.

"No, sorry for being an asshole, Ray?" he sneered, the sarcasm thick enough to stir that flash of anger again.

"What have you got?" I asked, blunt, keeping my voice flat.

Frank shook his head, muttering, "You really are a prick, aren't you?"

"Just talk, Frank. I don't have time to nurse your wounds."

He leaned back, wincing, and took a deep breath. "After

you left my place, my wife, and kids... they were terrified. They cried for hours, Ray. I had to hold them, let them come to terms with what you did in our home. Their safe place." His eyes stayed on the table, the weight of his words hanging between us.

I could feel that knot of guilt tighten, a flash of remorse stirring under my skin. "I'm sorry, Frank." The words slipped out before I could stop them. His head jerked up, and from the look in his eyes, I knew he didn't expect an apology. Hell, neither did I. "I never meant for it to go down like that. I didn't want to scare your kids."

He nodded. "Well, it was when I was holding them, comforting them... I started thinking about you. About what you must be going through, not knowing where your little girl is. God knows what I would do in your position."

I stayed quiet, letting him talk, feeling the weight of what he was saying settle on me.

After a brief silence, he said, "You know, I used to be a cop, just like you. But I sold out. Started taking bribes, cutting deals. I didn't lose my family, but I lost myself along the way. Seeing you now, what's happening with you and Megan... it reminded me of what I've become."

I could feel my jaw clench. "A low-life money grabber?"

"Believe what you want," he replied, his tone clipped. "But I wasn't always the bad guy. And here's the thing about being a cop, Ray, we never lose our instincts. Even disgraced, those instincts stay sharp."

"What are your instincts telling you now, Frank?"

He leaned in, lowering his voice. "The image from the CCTV. Someone dropped it off at my place, but the way it happened... it's been gnawing at me."

CHAPTER 34 – WORST FEARS

I sat up, interest sparking. "How do you mean?"

"The whole thing was just too clean," he said, fidgeting, the discomfort clear in his eyes. "They dropped it off at my door, but no one saw a damn thing. The note was typed, precise. No fingerprints, no trace. They wanted me to get it to you, no question. It's screaming one thing, Ray."

"What?" I asked, the tension ratcheting up.

"Cop," he said flatly. "Whoever's doing this is one of us, or used to be. They knew I'd try to make a quick buck. They knew exactly how to get you involved."

"A cop?" The thought sent a chill down my spine. "You think a cop is behind all this? Why would they do this?"

"Maybe they're trying to frame you for something, or maybe you're a way out for them. I don't know, Ray. Did you piss off anyone while you were still on the force?"

I couldn't help but laugh at that. "The only people I didn't piss off are the ones I didn't meet. But I never thought about cops being on my enemies' list."

"Well, whoever it is, they know you. They know who you crossed and they damn sure want you involved."

I leaned back, running my hands over my face, taking in what he'd said. The more he talked, the more it made sense. Whoever this was had a deep-seated grudge, and they were dragging me right back into the past, one dead body at a time. But who could hate me enough to pull a stunt like this?

Frank reached into his coat pocket, pulling out a small envelope, and slid it across the table.

"There was a note with the image," he said, his voice low. "They wanted me to get it to you."

I opened the envelope carefully. There was a single sheet of paper inside. A bold, clinical font was used to type the words.

"You took what mattered. Now it's your turn to lose."

My hands tightened around the paper. The words were cold. They felt like a punch to the gut. More questions, no answers.

35

Chapter 35 – Beneath the silence

Back home, I dropped onto my bed, heavy and completely exhausted. My whole body ached, and I struggled to hold my eyes open, but sleep was the last thing on my mind right now. More than rest, more than escape. I wanted to talk to Alison. She was my only connection to Megan, the one other person feeling this same raw, relentless ache.

We might not share much anymore, but right now, she was the only person who'd understand this hell I was living.

Without giving myself a chance to second-guess it, I grabbed my phone, scrolling until I saw her name. It felt strange. Her number still saved a thread of the past I hadn't let go. I hit dial, each ring stretching out painfully until her voice finally broke through.

"Ray?" Her voice was tentative, guarded.

"Hey Al," I replied, feeling awkward. "I... I just wanted to check in."

There was a pause, a complete silence that strangely broke the awkward feeling. We both knew I didn't have any good news to share. There wasn't much I could say to ease her worry.

But that wasn't what this was about.

"How are you holding up?" I asked, knowing full well how absurd the question sounded.

"How do you think?" she replied, her tone edged with bitterness, the tiredness cutting through. "My daughter's missing, Ray. Every day that passes..." Her voice trailed off, and I heard her take a deep, shaky breath. "I'm barely holding it together."

Her words were like a mirror, reflecting the same raw pain gnawing at me. It wasn't fair what she was going through. The anger, the helplessness, the fear.... I knew it all too well.

"I wish I could say something that mattered," I whispered, more to myself than to her. "But the truth is... I don't have a damn thing to say. Nothing that makes this any better."

Another silence settled between us, heavy with unspoken regrets and the things we'd lost. I thought of all the moments we'd missed, of the life that could have been if things hadn't spiraled the way they did. But Megan was all that mattered now. Finding her was the only thing left.

Alison broke the silence. "You're out there looking, though, aren't you? Doing... something?"

"Every minute I'm awake," I replied, my voice rough. "I'm following every lead, talking to people I never thought I'd speak to again. But it's like... it's like someone's playing games with me. Pulling me into something I can't see my way out of. And Megan's at the center."

After yet another brief silence, Alison told me, "A detective came to see me today, said he is working on Megan's case. Said he would do all he could to bring her home safe."

"Well, he took his sweet time to begin this all he can do," a perfect mix of anger and sarcasm in my reply.

CHAPTER 35 – BENEATH THE SILENCE

"I made my feelings clear on that, but it's good to know they are looking too. He wants to talk with you, too."

"I will look forward to that."

"I never wanted this," she said softly, her voice a low whisper. "For any of us."

"Neither did I." The admission hung in the air, and I felt a crack open between us, something raw and real. Maybe, despite everything, that was enough. For tonight, at least.

Before we ended the call, she whispered, "Find her, Ray. Please... just bring her back."

"I will," I promised, the weight of it sinking into my bones. "Whatever it takes, Alison. I'll bring her back."

I hung up, feeling the silence of the room settle around me once again, but it didn't feel as heavy. For the first time in days, I wasn't completely alone.

I lay down and I closed my eyes. I needed to rest.

36

Chapter 36 – The call

I was waking up slowly, sluggishly, to the sound of my phone buzzing on the pillow beside me. I found it difficult to open my eyes as my sleep had been short but heavy. The light from the screen hurt my eyes, made it difficult to focus on the caller id. When my vision cleared, there was no name. It was unknown. My gut instincts kicked in instantly. I just knew it was whoever had Megan. I didn't want to answer, but I knew I had to.

I answered wearily, "who is this?"

A pause. I could hear someone breathing, a faint hint of a laugh escaping through the line. "Oh, Ray," the voice purred, distorted by some fancy voice changer. "I think you know who this is, don't you?"

I bolted upright, feeling every nerve in my body lock tight. I didn't know who exactly, but I knew it was him. The one who had Megan. Anger surged up, sharp and unfiltered, spilling over before I could hold it back.

"You son of a bitch! If you've hurt her, I swear to God, I'll...."

"Now, now, Ray." His voice was so calm he could've been lounging on a beach somewhere, a cocktail in hand. But then,

CHAPTER 36 - THE CALL

a twisted darkness seeped into his tone, chilling and cutting. "Remember who's in charge here."

I clenched my jaw, forcing myself to breathe, to slow down. I wouldn't give this sick bastard the satisfaction of my anger. He'd get a kick out of it, feel my fear like a prize. "What do you want?" I asked, as steady as I could manage.

"What do I want?" He let out a soft laugh, cruel and detached. "I want to take back the years you stole from me. But most of all, Ray, I want you to suffer. I want you to die. But not before we play our game."

His voice cut through me, so calm and controlled, so filled with anger, yet without a trace of humanity. I swallowed back a flash of nausea.

"Who are you?" I asked quietly, the desperation creeping into my voice. "What did I ever do to you? Why drag Megan into this? Why not just come after me?"

"Where's the fun in that?" he sneered, sounding amused. "Sure, I could have killed you at any time, but I am not letting you off that easily. Where's the satisfaction in that? You're understanding what I'm capable of, aren't you? Just ask Eddie... or Tommy. Oh, wait..." And then he laughed, a low, mocking sound that made my skin crawl.

I fought the urge to scream back. "You know, the cops don't think I had anything to do with these murders. So, what's the point?"

"There's always a point, Ray," he snapped, the arrogance in his voice unwavering. "You're just too fucking stupid to see it. What a fall from grace... our hero in blue. Look at the state of you now."

He was baiting me, pushing me, testing my patience. But I wouldn't give him the reaction he wanted. I took a slow breath, forcing myself to stay calm, to think. Focus, Ray. There had to be something on this call, something that would give him away.

"What did I do to you?" I asked, more pleading on my part, hoping he'd give something up. "What could I have done to make you want this?"

"You fucked everything up, Ray," he spat, his tone colder, more bitter. "You always fucked everything up."

I dropped the phone onto the bed, my hands gripping my face, fingers digging into my skin as the anger pulsed through me. I'd never felt this helpless, this caged. Reasoning with a psychopath was a waste of breath. There was no getting him to be decent, no pulling humanity out of this monster. I would have to take him down.

I lifted the phone back to my ear, not saying a word.

"You still there, Ray?" His voice carried that mocking amusement, like he'd known I'd come back.

"I'm here," I replied, my voice flat. "But I still don't know what the fuck you want from me."

"I already told you," He replied, a hint of twisted joy in his tone. "I'm going to make you suffer. And this is just the beginning. Bye-bye for now..." And with that, the line went dead.

I stayed there, staring at the phone, my body rigid, every nerve on edge. I'd heard the monster speak. Calm, calculated evil. And he had my daughter. This was a nightmare I would never recover from. But if he thought he could scare me into breaking, he didn't know me well enough. He'd just lit a fire.

I could feel it, something I hadn't felt in a long time, my old instincts kicking back in, pulling me up off the bed, driving me forward.

CHAPTER 36 – THE CALL

No more fuckups.
No more drinking myself numb.
Now was the time to show my worth to Megan.

37

Chapter 37 – Unmasking the past

Joey lived out west. Not the friendliest part of Chicago, but then again, a former cop forced off the force has no pension to fall back on. This was to be expected.

As Detective Kane drove to Joey's, her mind churned over every detail of the case. She could see the steady decline in living standards as she drove further west. She hoped this wouldn't be a wasted trip, but surely his former partner could fill in the gaps about Ray's past.

As she entered Humboldt Park, she spotted Joey right away. He was just stepping out of his door, double locking it with practiced caution. Cops, former cops, we all like the extra layer of security. She watched as he double checked it was secure, leaning his weight against the door and trying the handle. He seemed satisfied it was locked and turned to walk away.

She drove up and parked at the curb right outside. He spotted her car and stared at her. His gaze was steady, and his posture calm. It was nothing like the jumpy, evasive man she'd questioned back at the station. As she got out of the car, he smiled at her, a casual, friendly gesture, as if his friend he

CHAPTER 37 – UNMASKING THE PAST

was expecting had just arrived.

"Mr. Sanders," Kane said casually as she strolled toward him.

"Please, call me Joey," he replied with a big smile on his face. "What can I do for you, Detective?"

Kane, not easily surprised by much, was taken aback by the complete change in this man. He could just as well be a completely different person. She studied him for a second, but he didn't crack. He remained calm, composed, a smile of complete bliss on his face. "I was hoping you could help fill in some gaps. About Ray? About his time on the force?"

Joey sighed and leaned back against the wall of his home, then he let out a small laugh. "Gaps about Ray Gordon.... how long do you have Detective? The man was a bulldozer. He went through everything and everyone so he could enjoy his power trip."

"So, would you say he was difficult to work with?"

"I very much enjoyed working with Ray when he was smart," Joey's reply was very polite, but there was menace there. He gave the impression he liked a bit of what Ray got up to when he was breaking the rules. "It was when he acted with no thought that was when he was hard to control."

"You sound like you admired his way of working?" she probed. "I have been looking into his time on the force. He had a lot of complaints about him."

"Like I say, he wasn't always too smart," Joey grinned. "Had he used his brain more, he might still be out there doing some good around here. The force needs people who will work hard. Even if it means cracking a few heads."

Kane nodded. She took mental notes. She now understood, not Ray, his files told her all she needed to know about him as a cop, but Joey and the kind of cop he was.

"What about you, Joey? What kind of cop were you? Did you like to crack heads on the side too?"

Joey stood up, gave a wink, and responded coldly, "I used my brain, Detective."

Kane got a chill up her spine. She had to stop herself from showing a physical shiver. She never allowed herself to show any vulnerability, and now wasn't the time to begin. But she could imagine this man. He was big, very imposing, and in a uniform. He was also extremely cunning. What he could have gotten away with didn't bear thinking about.

"Will that be all, Detective Kane? I got stuff to be doing."

"Just one more question," she said. "Can you think of anyone who would want to hurt Ray? Anyone who comes to mind that might be top of the list?"

Joey laughed. Then he turned and walked before answering. As he walked, he replied, "He has a list as long as your arm, Detective. I hear two of them are already dead. Guess that makes your job a little easier," and he just kept walking.

"I will be in touch," Kane shouted as she watched him walk away. She wished she could get inside Joey's head and read exactly what he was thinking. She was certain he had information that would help.

38

Chapter 38 - The Bridge Between

Detective Kane stood at the precinct, waiting in a small conference room. A disordered pile of crime scene photos and documents lay splayed before her.

The clock ticked, echoing through the quiet room as she scanned her notes once again. She knew she was onto something, but every time she thought she'd pinned down a lead, it unraveled in her hands.

The door opened and Detective Marshall stepped in. He looked weary but focused, a hint of impatience in his eyes as he took a seat across from her.

"Kane," he greeted, nodding slightly.

"Marshall. Thanks for coming on short notice." Kane's voice was all business as she gestured to the scattered files on the table. "We've both been circling the same case from different angles. I thought it was time we shared some notes."

Marshall's eyes flicked over the documents, his brow furrowing. "I've been looking into Megan's disappearance; I have made no connection to these murders. Where's the link?"

Kane leaned forward, pointing to Ray's name on a printed

report. "Ray Gordon. He's the thread between these crimes. Ray is connected to both murders, and his daughter's disappearance aligns with the timeline of these murders. It feels personal, like someone's making a point, using Ray as a scapegoat, a pawn, or just to punish him. But to what end?" She paused, gauging Marshall's reaction.

He nodded, considering her words. "I spoke to Alison, Megan's mother. She mentioned that she and Ray have received disturbing packages, clippings of Megan's hair, a photograph with her hair cut shorter." His jaw tightened. "Whoever's behind these wants them in a constant state of fear. They're taunting them. Megan is the pawn here."

Kane nodded, crossing her arms, her expression darkening. "The murders, the way they've been staged. Colton and Russo. Both high-ranking crime figures, men Ray would've crossed paths with when he was on the force. Both left in a way that leads straight back to Ray. It's deliberate, calculated. But it is too obvious, so they aren't trying to frame Ray."

Marshall exhaled, leaning back in his chair. "I've seen people play games, Kane, but this... this is sadistic. They know how desperate the family will be to get her back; they know Ray's character. If we don't get ahead of this, he's likely to fall right into their trap."

"That's exactly what they're counting on," Kane replied, her voice hard. "We need to get to them before Ray does. Whoever's doing this wants to break him completely, and we will not let that happen. We'll work together on this. Share everything."

Marshall gave a nod, his face set with determination. "Agreed. I'll need to go over every detail from your side, and I'll share all we have from the kidnapping case."

CHAPTER 38 - THE BRIDGE BETWEEN

"Appreciated Marshall," Kane replied. "I met his former partner earlier, Joey Sanders. He has information. He knows Ray's past better than anyone. But he is tough to crack. He is pissed about being let go and there is something off about him. If we get anything that links back to Joey, we pick him up right away, got it?"

"Got it," Marshall replied, accepting orders from Kane as if he was happy for her to take the lead on this. Murder trumps kidnap, he thought to himself.

Kane leaned forward, her eyes focused and determination pouring out of her. "Let's get this job done and get that girl home safe as quick as we can."

Marshall gave a firm nod, his voice steady. "Agreed. We're not letting anything slip through the cracks."

They shared a look, a silent agreement between them, both knowing what was at stake. With one last glance at the case files spread across the desk, they set to work, each bringing years of experience and grit to bear.

39

Chapter 39 – Silent doubts

I sat in my truck waiting on Joey, the man who used to have impeccable time keeping, suddenly loves to make me wait. I let my mind wander as I waited as I thought about Alison and what she must be feeling right now. I was out here doing all I could, and I felt helpless. It must be eating her alive, sitting and waiting for the phone to ring.

It is a strange thing to want to do all you can for someone who left you, took your child away from you. But right now, I just wanted to find Megan and then place her in her mother's arms. I wanted to watch the pain drain away as they embraced each other and watch the safety to return to each of them. To feel the pain lift from me.

Just as I allowed myself a moment to feel the joy of this feeling, my passenger door flung open, and Joey hopped in. He nodded at me "Ray."

"Like to make me wait around, don't you, Joe?"

"You going to lecture me about my time keeping now, Ray? Going to put me in the book for being late?" he said with a smile on his face.

CHAPTER 39 – SILENT DOUBTS

I wasn't amused. Lately, not much amused me.

"If you must know, I am late because I had a little visit from Detective Kane. She had some questions for me about you. Wanted to know just how naughty you were back in the day," he said as if he were passing on any accusations as a message from Kane that she was out to get me.

"Oh yeah, and what did you tell them?" I asked. I knew just how much he knew and with how jumpy he was at the precinct, I was nervous he would say anything to get rid of her.

"Don't worry Ray, your secrets have always been safe with me. I am not about to go telling Detective Kane any of your stories. She is just like the rest. She'll chase her tail until she tires and then give up." He clearly had no respect for her. "We are on our own here, as always."

I looked at him. He was so self-assured and didn't seem at all ruffled by the visit from Kane. After what I saw the other day, I half expected to look down and see piss stains down his trousers. But he was as calm as I remember ever seeing him. "I am not so sure; she seems to know what she is doing. I think she has good instincts; she may surprise us."

Joey laughed, a low hearty chuckle as if he enjoyed my 'joke,' "oh Ray" he said, "so trusting of them still."

I fought back the urge to respond. He was annoying me, talking to me as if he were better than me. As if I were stupid to think there could be a detective better equipped than us to do this job. I took a breath and composed myself before I spoke to him again.

"I got a call from Frank," I told him. "I went to see him."

Joey sat up straight, all his bravado seemed to drain away in that one moment "what the fuck Ray, I thought we agreed to leave Frank to me?" he said with clear anger in his voice "you are just going fuck another lead."

"He called me Joe. What the fuck you want me to do? Ignore any lead? Run it by you first before I look for MY daughter?" I snapped back at him. He really had my back up today.

He sunk back into his seat a little, the weight of understanding of my situation making him take a moment. "What did he have to say?"

"He thinks a cop is behind all of this."

He looked at me as if I were crazy for believing this, but he was uneasy with the suggestion. That was clear. "Cops are too dumb to get away with something like this, Ray, you know that."

"They haven't gotten away with it, not yet. I am relying on dumb. Dumb make mistakes."

He smirked at that. He always had a thing for seeing others as dumb. He always felt he was superior, especially where intellect was involved. I thought back to a time when I really saw Joey, the real Joey.

Joey and I had been tracking Nicky Stone for hours. The guy was smart, slippery, always just a few steps ahead. We had split up to cover more ground in the crumbling industrial district by the river. It was a wasteland of abandoned warehouses and boarded-up buildings, long deserted.

I rounded a corner. My flashlight cut through the foggy dark. Then, it caught my eye. A faint light glowed through the boards of a broken-down building just ahead. I slowed, instinctively quieting my steps. Inside, I could make out two figures in the dim light.

As I crept closer, I could see it was Joey, his bulky frame looming over a smaller man slumped against a wall. My stomach twisted when I recognized Nicky. His wrists were

CHAPTER 39 - SILENT DOUBTS

bound, his head hung low, and a fresh cut on his cheek glistened under the dim light.

My hand moved to my gun, ready to step in, when Joey's voice drifted out, smooth and unsettling.

"Don't bother begging, Nicky. You did this to yourself," Joey murmured, his tone almost gentle, like he was explaining something simple. "You crossed too many lines, ran your mouth too many times."

Nicky looked up, a glimmer of hope flashing in his eyes as he spotted movement by the window. I froze, pressing my back against the wall, caught between instinct and horror as I watched.

Joey leaned in, his voice dropping to a whisper, but I heard every word. "You think anyone cares about what happens to a rat like you? No one's looking, Nicky. No one's coming for you."

Nicky's face drops as he realized what was happening. He tried to pull away, scrambling against the wall, but Joey was faster. He moved with practiced ease, his hand reaching out, pressing down hard on Nicky's throat. He showed no emotion, there was no remorse for what he was doing.

I felt as though I was in shock, watching Joey go about this as if it were nothing. Joey held Nicky's gaze as the man struggled, his legs kicking weakly against the wall, his fingers clawing uselessly at Joey's arm. Joey maintained his calm throughout, his grip steady, unrelenting.

Finally, Nicky's body fell limp in Joey's hand. Joey took a step back, letting Nicky's body fall to the ground. He straightened his collar and glancing down at Nicky's lifeless form with mild disinterest, as though he'd just taken out the trash. He turned, casually wiping his hands on a rag he found on the ground, leaving no trace of the violence that had just occurred.

I moved away from the window, my was heart pounding, I still wasn't sure I believed what I had just witnessed. I forced myself to breathe quietly as I heard Joey's footsteps approach.

Joey reappeared on the street, calm and casual. He spotted me and raised a hand in greeting, as if nothing unusual had happened.

"Find anything?" he asked, his tone light, almost cheerful.

I shook my head, struggling to keep my face neutral. "No. Nothing here," I replied, looking him in the eyes. He didn't show any sign of anything that had just unfolded down there, not a trace of remorse. Just the same easy going smile I had known for years.

People have always known me for crossing the line, but nothing like this, not cold-blooded murder. And the thing that got me kicked off the force, this thing with Leroy…… that had driven me to drink. At least I knew I had a soul, but Joey, I wasn't so sure. I suddenly questioned whether I could trust Joey to help find Megan. Or was he more of a loose cannon than I ever was?

Joey was clever, not as clever as he thought, but clever enough to never get caught.

Back in the present, Joey brought me back to reality. "Ray? Did you hear me?"

I shook my head, as if I were waking from a nightmare. "What? What did you say?" I asked.

"Fuck me Ray, it was a simple question. What else did he say?"

At that moment, I decided I didn't trust this man to find my daughter. He could kill the kidnapper, not have a second thought, and I would never see her again. Not only that, but I

CHAPTER 39 - SILENT DOUBTS

felt as though I didn't really know him anymore. "Not much Joe, I think he was just wanting to make amends, maybe keep me from kicking his ass again."

He didn't look too convinced, but said, "I can believe that he doesn't want that again."

I made my excuses for getting back home, told him I need to rest and refresh. I would catch up with him later, but I didn't want him near this, not anymore.

40

Chapter 40 – Crossroads

I drove home thinking about Joey, convinced I'd done the right thing. I have always known who I was, a loose cannon, reckless. But this was different. I was focused now. With Megan at stake, I didn't plan on making any more mistakes. I knew Joey would cloud my judgment, make me second guess my every thought. I'd rather work with Kane than Joey on this one.

Still, there was a pang of guilt that gnawed at me. Joey was the last real ally I had. Even after all we'd been through, he was, or had been, my friend. But that didn't matter now. I had to focus on Megan, and I couldn't afford the distraction or doubt. To get her back, I needed clarity, not old loyalties.

As I turned onto my street, I noticed an SUV parked outside my house. The plates were civilian, but everything about it screamed cop car. As I got closer, I recognized Kane in the passenger seat. Funny, I thought. A few hours ago, I hadn't wanted to see her ever again. But right now, I was glad she was here. Her presence gave me something I hadn't felt in a while: hope.

I pulled up and climbed out of my truck. Both doors of the

CHAPTER 40 – CROSSROADS

SUV opened, and Kane stepped out, followed by a man I didn't recognize. He looked serious but soft, the kind of guy who wouldn't intimidate anyone. Maybe that's why he was paired with Kane, I thought, hiding a smirk.

Kane spoke first. "Ray, you look like shit. No, worse, like shit that's been chewed up and spat back out."

"Always a pleasure, Kane." I gave a dry laugh. "I was just hoping someone would stop by to tell me how great I look."

"I'm serious. When's the last time you actually slept? I don't want to show up here for information only to find a body." Her voice had a note of actual concern, more for me than just the case.

I hesitated, then gave in to the blunt truth. "It's not rest I need; it's a drink. Try drinking yourself into oblivion for two years straight, then stopping cold. Hits you like a freight train." I looked away, half embarrassed by my admission.

She nodded, and I caught a hint of compassion in her expression. She'd probably seen her share of cops who'd fallen from grace. I wasn't handling it well, but I was sure there were others who'd fallen even harder. She gestured to the man next to her. "This is Detective Marshall. He's assigned to Megan's case."

"Pleased to meet you, Mr. Gordon." He extended a hand. "Wish it were under better circumstances."

"Call me Ray." His handshake was firm but nonthreatening, and as I sized him up, I felt my instincts returning. He wasn't here to play games; I could trust him. For the first time, I felt like I was back in the game.

"What can I do for you, detectives?" I asked, surprising even myself at how willing I was to talk.

Kane took the lead. "Marshall and I are working the cases

together. The murders and the kidnapping they go hand in hand."

"It's good to know you two are on it," I said, genuinely encouraged.

"These murders," Marshall spoke up, "they have your fingerprints all over them, Ray. A lot of evidence pointing back to you."

I took a deep breath, waiting for the other shoe to drop.

Kane stepped in, her tone firm. "Yeah, your name is all over it. Everything's way too neat, way too obvious. So, we're confident you're not involved."

I let out a breath, a strange sense of relief settling over me. "Glad to know you're not wasting time looking into me."

"Actually," she countered, "looking into you might be exactly what we need. Whoever's behind this knows you. Knows your past, knows your cases." She paused, studying my reaction. "We think you're being punished, Ray. They're using your past to pull you in and make you feel every blow."

I leaned back against my truck, absorbing her words. Of course, it made sense. Whoever was doing this had a deep understanding of my life, my history. They weren't just setting me up; they were sending a message. I was willing to hear more, so I kept quiet, letting them talk.

Kane's eyes flicked to Marshall, then back to me. "What's your connection to Colton and Russo?"

"Not much to tell." I shrugged. "They were lowlifes. Guys I'd dealt with when I was on the force. I wasn't the type to back down, and they found that out the hard way."

Kane raised an eyebrow. "The hard way?"

"I got physical with them," I said, not bothering to hide it. "Didn't make a show of it, but I didn't back off when they

CHAPTER 40 – CROSSROADS

pushed. Guys like them, they get embarrassed, angry. But they never got even. Not with me."

Kane took a step closer, her gaze steady. "Was this standard practice for you?"

"Oh, come on. Thought you just said I was off the hook."

"I'm not pointing the finger at you, Ray. I'm trying to understand how many others might have a grudge." She kept her tone calm, clearly wanting me to open up.

I thought it over. "Look, I have a contact, the one who sent me the car image from the time of the kidnapping. He thinks it's a cop doing this."

Marshall's eyes widened slightly, and he looked at Kane, who seemed equally intrigued. "Why would a cop be behind all this?" she asked.

"Frank thinks the drop-off was too smooth. Whoever it was moved quickly and knew what to do without leaving a trace."

"Frank?" Marshall interjected. "Frank who?"

"Frank Mulligan. Not someone I'd normally trust, but... he's onto something this time. And I think he's right. This person's too careful." I was about to outline my next steps when Kane cut in.

"No, Ray. There are no 'next steps' for you," she said, her voice hard. "You need to step back and stay out of this. Leave it to us. We'll get your girl home safely."

A part of me knew she was right, but I couldn't just sit back. "Sorry, Detective. I can't do that. I can't sit here waiting while someone else does my job for me. I'm not letting up until I bring her home."

Kane took a step closer, almost pleading. "Ray, hear me when I say this, if you interfere, we'll have to bring you in for obstruction. Don't make us do that."

I stayed silent, unwilling to make a promise I couldn't keep. I watched them, trying to gauge whether they will put it all on the line for Megan.

Marshall opened the car door, and Kane glanced back at me. "We'll do everything we can, Ray. Leave your phone on, don't go far. We'll need to speak with you again." She paused, giving me a hard look. "And for the love of God, don't get in the way. You'll only make it harder."

Without another word, she climbed into the SUV, and they drove off, leaving me alone on the street, wrestling with a truth I couldn't accept.... could I really step back and leave them to it?

41

Chapter 41 – Raising the Stakes

I know he feels it now. That creeping doubt, the helplessness slipping under his skin. Ray thinks he's still got something left to prove, something left to save. Well, he can't, this is nothing but another failing in the waiting for him. He does not know what I have in store for him. This whole time, he's been running in circles, chasing ghosts I've laid out for him, thinking he's moving closer to her. Every step he takes, every call he makes, it's all by my design.

And still, he's just as clueless as I knew he'd be.

But this? This is where it starts to hurt, Ray. This is where I show you how deep I can make the knife go.

I picture him now, stumbling and scratching at my scraps. He thinks he's onto something, that he's making headway.

Pathetic.

The man's grasping at straws, each one slipping through his fingers like sand, and he thinks that'll be enough. But I know better. I've always known better.

There's an art to this kind of suffering, you know. Ray wouldn't understand, but I do. I've been crafting this plan for years, rehearsing it, replaying it in my head until every piece fit perfectly. And it does. The whole thing fell into place as if it were waiting for me, just begging to be put into motion.

He'll come close, sure. I'll let him. I'll let him get so close he thinks he can feel her breath on his shoulder, hear her voice just around the corner. And then I'll yank it all away, and he'll realize it was nothing more than smoke, a trick of the mind. I want him to feel that sting, that gut-wrenching despair. The kind that tears at you, that eats you alive.

This is how he's going to pay. Step by agonizing step.

I walk over to the door that leads to the basement, listening for any sounds below. Just the faintest rustling, the quiet breaths of a girl too afraid to cry out, too afraid to hope. Good. I want her scared. I want her feeling what I felt, what he made me feel. She's my pawn, the perfect piece on this board, and I'll play her however I want.

The satisfaction sits heavy in my chest, a dark, steady pulse. This is my game. My rules. Ray's going to break down; he's going to lose everything that matters. And when he finally realizes that, I'll be there, watching every flicker of pain cross his face, savoring every second.

And the best part? He'll never see it coming. He'll never understand the depth of what he did, the reason behind every step of my plan. But he will feel it. That's the only thing that matters now.

Even with all the control I feel right now, I can't help but let the anger boil over inside me. I hate that man, how I have stood face to face with him, 'chatted' with him, 'sympathized' with him.... it all made me sick to my stomach. I don't even realize I have tipped the table over until it is laying on the ground, cups and papers scattered all over the floor. It's a blind fury

CHAPTER 41 – RAISING THE STAKES

he makes me feel inside, this man who thinks consequences don't exist. But I will use this, and he will feel it. He will feel every last bit of it!

42

Chapter 42 – Megan's Fear

Megan presses her back against the icy wall, as if somehow it could wrap around her, hold her safe the way her daddy would if he were here. She can hear the man upstairs. He sounds so angry, so out of control. She trembles, trying to make herself small, wishing she could feel her mummy's or daddy's arms around her, pulling her close and safe.

She tries to block him out. If she can't hear him, maybe he isn't real. She hums a lullaby to herself, the one mummy used to sing every night, and lets her mind drift. She imagines her bedroom, the way her big comfy bed would feel, her soft pillows and warm blanket wrapping her up like a hug. In her mind, she can see all her favorite books stacked on the bedside table, the adventures of Supertato waiting to make her laugh. Her teddies would be lined up, all there to keep her company, and her nightlight would cast a gentle glow, making her room feel safe and warm.

The smell of her mum's perfume floats into her memory, like it always did when mummy would tuck her in. Her imagination is so strong that she almost believes she's back home, back in

CHAPTER 42 - MEGAN'S FEAR

her cozy room, wrapped in her parents' love. But then a loud crash from above breaks her focus, a heavy, angry sound that jars her back to this dark, cold place. To reality.

Her heart thuds painfully, and she curls tighter into herself, feeling the emptiness and fear closing in. Her brave front crumbles, and the tears come, unstoppable and heavy. Her cries echo in the empty room. She sobs, shaking with fear. Each tear reminds her how far she is from home, from safety, from everything that once made her happy.

43

Chapter 43 – Shotguns and silencers

Detective Kane sat in the passenger seat, staring out the window, replaying her conversation with Ray. She could see the fire, the anger, and the unbreakable determination in his eyes. She knew he wasn't about to back down. The question that gnawed at her was whether he'd be an asset in this, or just a disaster waiting to happen.

"What did you make of Ray?" she asked, turning to Marshall.

He adjusted his grip on the steering wheel, his knuckles whitening slightly as he kept his gaze fixed on the road ahead. "He looks like a desperate man. And given the circumstances, he's near broken."

She nodded, her gaze shifting back to the road. "Yeah. And desperate can be dangerous. You think he'll back off?"

Marshall's response was blunt. "Would you?"

She leaned back, letting that sink in. She didn't answer because she knew he was right. If it were her daughter, no threat from any detective would keep her away. She'd do whatever it took. Warnings be damned.

"How do we control him, then?" Marshall asked. "If we

CHAPTER 43 – SHOTGUNS AND SILENCERS

can't stop him, maybe we can keep him in check. Manage the damage?"

Kane frowned. "Not sure it'll be that simple..." Just then, her phone buzzed. She raised a finger to Marshall to pause their conversation and answered, "Kane here. What've you got?"

Officer Brown's voice came through, "Detective Kane, I've been asking around about Joey Sanders, talking with the guys at the precinct. There's some... interesting stuff."

"Let's hear it," Kane said, her tone shifting to business.

"They all said the same thing, almost like a script. Joey and Ray were thick as thieves on the force. Both rough around the edges, didn't take any crap. Power went to their heads a little. 'Power-mad' was the term that came up."

Kane nodded as she listened. So far, nothing was surprising.

Brown continued, "But here's the difference. They all said Joey was the smart one. Rough, like Ray, pushed limits too. But Joey was more... tactical. Fewer complaints. Ray was like a shotgun; Joey, a silencer."

"Interesting," Kane murmured, remembering Joey's confidence during their earlier conversation. "He told me something similar. Said he used his brain more than Ray."

"One other thing," Brown added, as if bracing her for something unexpected. "They said he was a bit... strange. Cold, calm, calculated. Not the type you'd want to mess with. Ray was pretty much his only friend; the rest kept their distance."

"Good work, Officer," Kane said, ending the call. She turned back to Marshall, "Let's monitor Joey Sanders. There's more to him than we're seeing right now."

Marshall nodded, his eyes never leaving the road. He was completely focused on the kidnapping, and if watching Joey helped them get closer to Megan, he was ready to pursue that lead for as long as it took.

44

Chapter 44 – Game of Nerves

I lay in bed, staring up at the ceiling. Sleeping was a joke at this point. My mind wouldn't shut off, wouldn't let me drift off while my daughter was out there with this monster. The thought of closing my eyes and finding rest felt almost like betrayal.

But I knew I couldn't go on much longer without sleep. Without rest, I'd be no good to her when it mattered most. So, I turned on my side, closed my eyes, and tried, really tried, to switch off my mind, to force my body into some kind of rest. If only to be sharper tomorrow. Just sharp enough to find Megan and bring her home. The thought of holding her, of promising I'd never let her go again, let me breathe easier for a moment. It was actually working. My mind was finally drifting, my muscles easing, a lightness beginning to settle over me.

And then my phone rang. Of course it did.

I reached for it and checked the screen: Unknown. Him. Again. I gripped the phone, a surge of anger pushing down my exhaustion as I answered. I didn't say a word.

"Rayyyyy," came his taunting voice, a whisper that crawled over my skin.

I kept my silence, jaw tight. Let him do the talking. Let him crack.

"Ray, I'm already annoyed with you. It will do you no favors to ignore me."

His voice had changed, gone from cool to aggravated, his words tight and clipped. Maybe he'd slip up, let something fall. I stayed silent, willing him to make a mistake.

I forced myself to breathe evenly, feeling the chills creeping up my spine, my pulse thumping in my temples. I was pushing him, and I knew it. I could almost feel his anger seething through the line. He had Megan. She was his only leverage. He wouldn't hurt her, not yet. He needed her.

"Enough of this shit, Ray. Speak. Now!" His fury spiked, hot and raw. I could feel it vibrating through the phone, but I held firm. I would not let him make me his puppet.

"Big fucking mistake, Ray!" he barked, the sharpness in his voice jolting through me. This man was beyond reason, someone who'd already shown how far he'd go. But if I came face-to-face with him, I'd make sure he paid. His voice dropped, laced with venom. "I already didn't like how much time you've been spending with those detectives. But this insolence of yours..."

I hung up. Satisfaction mixed with a sick twist of doubt. Had I made things worse? Had I just pushed him too far? My mind raced with a thousand what-ifs, each one threatening to tear me apart. I had to believe he wouldn't risk losing his leverage. He was angry now, and if I was right, he'd slip up. Eventually, he'd make a mistake.

I sat back, feeling a wave of nausea twist in my gut. Not the

CHAPTER 44 – GAME OF NERVES

usual tremor from lack of a drink; this was something deeper. This was fear, the kind that chokes you when the stakes are life or death. But fear or not, I'd held my ground, and for now, that had to be enough.

45

Chapter 45 – Echoes of the Past

Detective Kane wanted to dig deeper, wanted to know more about Ray, Joey, and their time on the force. What she'd learned so far had been interesting, but expected. The stories about Ray all lined up with his files: complaints, violence, a man pushing every limit. But Joey? That was the enigma. His name scarcely appeared in Ray's reports, despite their partnership and closeness.

Why didn't he register? Why didn't his name pop up in all the chaos surrounding Ray?

Kane pulled Joey's file, hoping to find some dirt. There was nothing but minor complaints and routine accusations officers deal with daily. Yet people talked about him differently. Words like "cold" and "calculated" kept coming up, and his behavior during their last meeting had unsettled her. It was too smooth, too calm. Her instincts screamed not to trust him. She needed more, and she wanted it directly from someone who'd seen Joey in action.

At the precinct, she spotted Officer Jeffords, one of the old-timers. Over 20 years on the force, he'd already been helpful

CHAPTER 45 – ECHOES OF THE PAST

to Brown, and Kane figured he might have even more to share.

"Jeffords," she called, catching him on his way back to his desk. "With me."

Jeffords hesitated, looking around like he was hoping she'd meant someone else, but then sighed and followed her into a meeting room. He looked like he'd just come off a long, rough shift, but Kane wasn't about to let him clock out just yet.

"Detective Kane," he said, showing enough respect to not irritate her but not going overboard.

"Take a seat," she said, cutting straight to business. "I understand you spoke with Officer Brown recently about Gordon and Sanders."

Jeffords sat slowly, adjusting himself in the chair like he was settling in for an interrogation. "I did, yeah. Told him everything I know."

"I appreciate that," Kane replied, sitting opposite him. "From what I hear, everyone's been helpful. But I wanted to hear it from you directly. No middleman." She let her words hang in the air, giving him room to speak.

Jeffords shifted again, unsure of where this was going. "Alright... but I'm not sure I've got much else to add."

Kane leaned back slightly, keeping her tone calm but firm. "Just tell me what you told Brown. Same thing. I'm not here to catch you out."

Jeffords nodded, exhaling slowly. "Like I said, those two were close. Worked well together, no partner squabbling like you get with some. But honestly, they didn't talk much, not to anyone else. It was like they didn't need to."

Kane nodded, letting him keep going.

"Ray..." Jeffords paused, a slight grin tugging at his mouth. "That man's a mean son of a bitch. Pardon my language,

Detective."

Kane shrugged. "I've heard worse. Go on."

"Word around the precinct was that Ray didn't back down from anyone. You crossed him, you paid for it. The bosses loved him for it, didn't care how he got results, just that he got them. There's no shortage of stories about him grabbing guys by the throat, throwing them around like rag dolls. It's why the brass kept him around so long."

"Checks out," Kane said. "Everything I've heard matches that. What about Joey?"

Jeffords straightened in his seat, crossing his arms. He took a moment, as if weighing his words. "Joey was... different. Quiet. Tactical. Didn't make waves, but he got things done. He left little for people to notice. Hell, I'd bet even Ray didn't know half the stuff Joey got up to."

Kane frowned, her instincts kicking in. "What kind of stuff are we talking about?"

Jeffords shifted again, his voice lowering slightly. "He was cold, Detective. Dead in the eyes, like nothing rattled him. He'd come back from a beat, hardly say a word, but there was always this... energy about him. Like he'd been somewhere dark and come out just fine. It put people off. They kept their distance, everyone but Ray."

Kane felt a chill creep up her spine, her mind racing with possibilities. Joey was calculated, clever, and arrogant. The kind of man who could hide his skeletons well. Too well.

"Thank you, Jeffords," she said, standing to let him go. "If anything else comes to mind, you know where to find me."

Jeffords nodded, straightening his uniform before heading out.

Kane stayed behind, her mind working through everything

CHAPTER 45 – ECHOES OF THE PAST

Jeffords had said. Joey Sanders was becoming more than just an enigma. He was a puzzle she was determined to solve.

46

Chapter 46 - No Safe Place

As I pull into the gas station, the only thing I can feel is complete and utter exhaustion. Hours of driving around the city, blindly looking for anything, anyone, who might give me a crumb to follow. Informants, old contacts, anyone who'd once been willing to talk. Problem is, I've never been the guy to build lasting friendships. Now, with no badge or uniform to back me up, most of them wouldn't even look me in the eye.

If I'm going to find Megan, it won't be because someone handed me the answer. I'd have to fight for every inch. Unless Kane... No. I shake the thought away. She doesn't want me involved, and she's probably right. Maybe I should just go home, sit by the phone, and wait. Maybe I should call her and tell her about the mistake I made yesterday when I hung up on him. It was still eating away at me. Why hadn't he called back?

I step out of the truck, stretching my arms high above my head, feeling all the aches and pains from sitting in the truck all day. I fill the gas all the way up again.

Inside, I wander the aisles and end up in the candy section again. Sugar highs and crashes, better than living on whiskey,

CHAPTER 46 - NO SAFE PLACE

I guess. I grab two king-sized bars and head to the counter.

The cashier barely glances at me. He's young, with long, unwashed hair, and the distinct smell of weed hangs on him like cologne. How do these kids keep a job when they're high all the time?

I hand over the candy bars and give him my pump number. As he rings me up, my phone buzzes in my pocket. Not a call this time, a text message.

I pull it out, not recognizing the number. No words, just an image. I squint at the screen; the picture taking a moment to register. A front door. Just a random....

No!

I can almost feel the blood draining from face, my heart rate jumping in an instant. It's not random. That's Alison's front door.

"Fuck!" I shout, the word echoing through the small store. Heads turn, startled.

The cashier blinks at me. "Uh, sir? Your candy?"

But I have already left sprinting across the forecourt for the truck.

I jump in, slamming the door and peeling out of the lot without a second thought. The stress and anxiety have my heart hammering in my chest, sweat beginning to form down my back as I speed toward Alison's house.

What was he doing there? What has he done?

I try to tell myself it's a warning, just a sick way of reminding me he's in control. But my gut says otherwise. Images flash through my mind: Alison hurt, Alison... worse. This is my punishment. This is what I get for that call yesterday. Stupid. Reckless. Never poke the psycho. Say what he wants to hear. Be where he wants you to be. Keep him happy.

Just keep him onside.

I fly up the driveway, skidding to a stop, and leap out before I fully park the truck. The front door is unlocked, and I throw it open so hard it slams against the wall.

"ALISON!" I shout, my voice cracking with panic. "ALISON, WHERE ARE YOU?"

I tear through the house, room by room, until I reach the back. And there she is.

My Alison.

Bloodied and tied to a chair.

The sight of her stops me dead in place. I feel as though my legs are going to collapse underneath me. I slowly force myself forward toward her. It is breaking my heart to see her head slumped forward, blood trickling down her face.

I put my hands up to her face, slowly pushing her hair aside, terrified I may break her further. My hands are trembling with the shock. She flinches at my touch, and makes a small, weak sound. "Alison, it's me. Ray. You're safe now."

I pull her close, holding her against me as tears sting my eyes. "I've got you," I murmur. "It's okay now. I've got you."

She tries to speak, her lips moving weakly. "Evan..."

"What?" I pull back to look at her. "Evan? Where is he?"

Her voice is barely a whisper. "Upstairs."

My heart sinks. I ease her back into the chair. "Stay here. Don't move. I'll get you help, but I need to check on Evan."

My training kicks in as I move toward the stairs. Every instinct is on high alert. He could still be here. I move cautiously, my back to the wall, each step creaking under my weight.

I reach the top and head toward the master bedroom. The door is ajar. I approach it slowly and inch my way in, wary of

CHAPTER 46 - NO SAFE PLACE

anything that I may be about to see, or that could jump out at me.

When I am in the room, I see him. Evan is lying on the floor.

His throat has been slit, the blood pooling around him. His hands are frozen mid-reach, as if he'd tried to stop it, to save himself.

I slump onto the bed, staring at the scene in front of me. Evan, an innocent man who had no part in my past, no connection to my mistakes. He's dead because of me. Because of the monster I brought into our lives.

What the hell could I have done to deserve this?

I pull my phone from my pocket, ready to call 911, but a new message pops up. Another picture.

It's Alison's front door again. Only this time, it's open, the way I left it. And there's a message:

I CAN GET TO YOU ANY TIME, RAY. DO NOT TEST ME AGAIN.

My body goes cold. I sprint back down the stairs, back to Alison. She's still there, tied and trembling.

I glance out the front door, scanning the street, but there's no one. How the hell does he keep doing this?

I dial 911, my voice shaking as I tell them to send Detective Kane. "It's all connected," I say, then hang up before they can ask questions.

I kneel beside Alison, taking her hand in mine. "Help is coming," I whisper. But even as I say it, I feel the dread settle deeper. What else will he do?

47

Chapter 47 - Focused Fury

I pace the hospital corridor, the floor squeaking under my boots with every step. Sitting feels impossible. Waiting feels worse. Alison is in there, behind a guarded door, being treated by the doctors. My mind is continually running with thoughts of all the mistakes I have made, from my past right up to my very latest, which has led to Alison being hurt. I am hurting everyone who has ever cared about me.

Where the hell is Kane? She should've been here by now. She needs to see this for what it is, a message. A declaration. This bastard isn't just coming after me; he's tearing apart the people I care about to send his twisted message.

The anger simmers inside me, hot and potent, but there's a difference now. I'm not spiraling. I'm not grasping at every fleeting lead or drowning myself in whiskey to dull the pain. I feel sharper, more focused. The rage that has always clouded me has become a tonic; it is what is now fueling me to push on.

I stop pacing and lean against the wall, letting the coldness seep through my shirt. My mind is running through every angle. Every step of this game, he's playing with me. It is

CHAPTER 47 - FOCUSED FURY

impossible to know the rules. He is making them up as we go along, but I have to beat him. There is too much at stake here.

The door to Alison's room opens, and the doctor steps out, clipboard in hand. His expression is calm, professional, the look that tells me Alison's still breathing.

"Mr. Gordon," he says, his tone measured. "Good news. Alison is going to be fine. She has clearly been through a lot. Blunt force trauma to the head has resulted in a concussion, but nothing life-threatening. She's also suffering from shock, which is to be expected. With plenty of rest, she should recover in a few days."

I nod, swallowing the lump in my throat. "Thank you, Doctor." It's all I have.

He offers a simple nod, maintaining his complete professionalism. "She's sleeping now. Let her rest for a while."

As he walks away, I sink into one of the plastic chairs in the waiting room. The hard edges dig into my back, but I hardly notice. My mind is already moving again, piecing together everything I know.

This isn't just about hurting me. It's about control. He is pulling me about, making me run from lead to lead, from scene to scene. Stabbing at the most vulnerable parts of my life. But he doesn't know that he is fueling his worst nightmare, he doesn't understand what I am capable of.

He doesn't know it yet, but I'm coming for him.

I pull out my notebook, the same one I used to carry on the force, and start jotting down everything I can think of. Connections. Patterns. What I know about his methods, his timing, his targets.

He's careful. Meticulous. He planned everything to the last detail. But he's human, and humans make mistakes.

Somewhere in all of this, he's left a crack. A weakness I can exploit.

My pen hovers over the page as I think back to the last message he sent, the photo of Alison's door, the one I'd left open in my panic.

I CAN GET TO YOU ANY TIME, RAY. DO NOT TEST ME AGAIN.

It wasn't just a threat. It was proof. Proof that he was watching, that he was in control. Proof he was always one step ahead of me. But how? Was it because he knows me? Because he knows how I think?

My thoughts are interrupted by the sound of boots approaching. I glance up to see Kane striding toward me; her face set like stone. Marshall is trailing behind her, looking uncomfortable in the sterile hospital environment.

"About time," I mutter, standing to meet her.

"Don't start, Ray," Kane snaps, her voice low but firm. "What's the situation?"

I motion toward Alison's room. "She will be okay. Concussion, shock. She is sleeping now."

Kane nods, glancing toward the door. "And Evan?"

I hesitate, the image of his body flashing in my mind. His throat slit, his blood soaking the carpet. A man who had nothing to do with this, gone because of me.

"He didn't make it," I mumble.

Kane's jaw tightens, but she doesn't press. She knows what this means.

"This guy isn't just sending a message," I say, my voice hardening. "He is making a point. He wants me to know he is in control. He wants me scared, distracted and dancing to his tune."

"And are you?" Kane asks, her eyes boring into mine.

CHAPTER 47 - FOCUSED FURY

"No," I reply without hesitation. "Not anymore."

She studies me for a moment, then nods. "Good. Because we need you sharp. This guy's escalating, and we are running out of time."

I glance down at my notebook; the pages filled with half-formed thoughts and scribbled connections. "I am going to figure him out, Kane. He thinks he is untouchable, but everyone slips up eventually. Everyone."

"And when he does?"

I meet her gaze, my expression as hard as hers. "When he does, I'll be ready to do whatever it takes."

Kane takes a deep breath, her tone steady but laced with frustration. "I know you won't stop, Ray. And I don't blame you. If I were in your shoes, I would probably do the same thing. But you must keep me informed. Marshall and I are your best shot at solving this. Understood?"

I nod slowly, knowing she is right. "He called me again."

Her eyes narrow, a flicker of annoyance crossing her face. She is not happy I've kept this from her. Before she can speak, Marshall steps in, leaning forward with intent. "What did he want? What did he say?"

"It's more about what I said, or didn't say," I admit, my voice quieter now as guilt settles in.

Kane crosses her arms, her patience visibly thinning. "What exactly does that mean?"

I hesitate, dragging a hand through my hair. "He called to taunt me, to mess with my head. I would not let him have that satisfaction. He mentioned being unhappy with how much I have been talking to you two, warned me not to piss him off anymore." I pause, looking away, knowing the next part is going to hit hard. "He told me to speak, but I hung up on him."

Kane's jaw tightens, her expression hard. "And now Evan is dead," she says flatly, her disappointment cutting through the air like a blade. "Ray, you cannot play games with this man. He is dangerous, capable of anything. You know that."

I slump back in my chair, her words weighing heavily on me. "I know. I thought... I thought if I didn't give him what he wanted, he would slip up, make a mistake. But it backfired." My voice falters as the remorse crashes over me. "Evan didn't deserve this. And Alison... I am just grateful she's still alive."

There is a brief silence, thick with unspoken tension, before I recount everything: the photos, the messages, the way he's always one step ahead. Kane listens intently, her sharp gaze never leaving me.

When I finish, she nods curtly, her expression unreadable. "We will take your phone, have our techs go over everything. Maybe we will get lucky and pull something from the messages or images."

Marshall adds, his voice firm but less cutting, "In the meantime, do nothing reckless. You need to be smart about this, Ray."

Kane stands, leveling me with a final look. "We'll keep you updated. But if you get another call, you tell us immediately. No more solo decisions. Understood?"

I nod again, and they turn to leave, the weight of their warning lingering in the air.

Left alone, I exhale deeply, the guilt still clawing at me. Kane's right. I cannot afford to screw this up again. If I am going to beat this bastard, I need to stay sharp. No more mistakes. From now on, I'll play this game his way, but I will do it on my terms.

48

Chapter 48 – Bound by grief

I had been pacing the sterile halls of the hospital for hours, unable to sit still for a minute, but Alison is finally awake and is asking for me. That familiar dread at the thought of facing her kicks in. I pushed him too far, and he punished me by doing this to her, by taking Evan from her.

I take a moment before pushing the door open. The sight of her stops me cold. Alison, my Alison, she had been beaten. This monster had put his hands on her. He had made a mess of her face, leaving it broken and swollen, almost beyond recognition. The monster had crushed even the last faint glimmers of hope from her eyes. The guilt is too much to bear. I almost break down crying right there, but I cannot do that. I am here for her. She needs me to be strong.

I take her hand in mine, fighting all the emotion I am feeling. I speak softly, "I am so sorry this happened to you. I will find this bastard, and I will put him down. I promise you."

She doesn't look at me, her gaze fixed downward. But she grips my hand tightly, as if she is holding on to the only familiar face she has left. Then, in a trembling voice, she asks the question I have been dreading.

"Evan? Is he... is he really gone?"

My throat tightens, and I squeeze her hand gently, though it feels like my heart is in a vice. "Yeah, Al. He's gone. I am so sorry. He didn't deserve this."

At that, her grip slackens. Her hands rise to cover her face, and she breaks sobbing, huge tears rolling down her cheeks. She is inconsolable, and I'm utterly useless, standing there like a goddamn statue.

"Do you need anything?" I finally ask, desperate to do something, anything, to help.

She doesn't answer my question, she just wipes away her tears and asks, "What am I supposed to do now, Ray?" sounding completely defeated.

I don't know if she wants an answer, so I stay silent, letting her get it all out.

"Ray," she continues, her voice cracking, "I have lost everything. Evan is dead. And Megan... I may never see her again."

"Don't," I cut in, my tone sharp. "Don't you dare say that, Alison! Don't even think it!"

She turns to me, her eyes glassy with tears. "I have to accept reality, Ray. If I don't, it'll break me. I don't have Evan anymore. And you..." Her voice falters, but she pushes through "You are not the Ray I once knew, not anymore."

The tears come again, rolling down her bruised cheeks, and she whispers, "I feel so alone. I have lost everything."

I sit down beside her on the bed, pulling her into a firm hug. Her weight rests heavily against me, her pain palpable. "You'll never be alone," I say, my voice steady despite the storm raging inside me. "I will always look out for you, Al. And I will never

CHAPTER 48 – BOUND BY GRIEF

stop looking for Megan. I swear to you, I will bring her home. You will hold her again. I promise."

She leans into me fully now, her body trembling as she lets herself fall apart in my arms. I hold her tighter, feeling the weight of my promise settling in. "Alison," I begin hesitantly, the guilt clawing at me, "this is all my fa...."

She cuts me off, pulling back slightly to meet my eyes. There's fire in her voice now, burning through the pain. "Don't. Don't do that, Ray. Just... get this son of a bitch. Do what you do best. Make him pay. And bring Megan home."

I nod, unable to speak. The determination in her eyes leaves no room for argument. I will do what she asks. I will make the bastard pay.

We fall into silence, holding each other in a moment of shared devastation.

49

Chapter 49 - The Whistling Shadow

Joey hadn't heard from Ray, and their last conversation left him irritated. Ray wasn't exactly sharing details, which gnawed at Joey. Why bring him into this mess if he didn't want the help? The whole thing reeked of mistrust, and Joey wasn't one to sit idle while someone kept him in the dark.

So, he walked. Wandering the streets of Chicago, a habit he had fallen into in recent years. It reminded him of his days on the force, pounding the pavement, chasing bad guys. Even it wasn't the real thing anymore, it gave him a purpose. He still felt he could take on bad guys. He didn't need a badge for that.

Tonight, Garfield Park called to him. The West Side, dangerous even for cops, felt alive in a way nowhere else did. It was desolate, broken. Streetlights flickered weakly, their dim glow casting long, jagged shadows. Figures lingered in alleys, smoke from something.... cigarettes, trash fires, God knows what, hung in the air. Joey lived for the danger, for putting himself in dangerous places and finding his own unique way out.

As he rounded a corner, Joey spotted someone he hadn't seen

CHAPTER 49 - THE WHISTLING SHADOW

in years. Darius "Slim" Carter. A former informant, though Joey never called him that to his face. To Joey, Darius was just another street rat, one of many he had used and discarded during his time on the force.

"Joey Sanders," Darius said, his wiry frame shifting as he took a step closer. His voice carried a mix of bravado and irritation. "What the fuck you doing around here? You know you ain't welcome. No badge, no shield, no nothing now."

Joey smirked, letting the insult roll off him. Darius had always been all talk, a scrawny guy with no bite to back up his bark. Still, his cockiness amused Joey. "Slim," Joey said, his tone light but edged with mockery, "still out here playing king of the rats, huh? Figured you would have scurried into a hole by now."

Darius stiffened, anger flashing in his eyes. "The fuck you call me? You think you're still big shit, huh? You ain't got a badge now. You're nothing."

Joey chuckled, low and menacing. "And yet, here you are, still running your mouth. You're lucky I have a soft spot for old acquaintances."

Darius took a step back, his bravado faltering. "What you want, man? You come out here looking for trouble?"

"Not trouble, Slim," Joey said, stepping closer. "Just some... closure."

"What the fuck does that mean?" Darius asked, his voice wavering.

Joey didn't answer. He moved fast, the knife in his hand before Darius could react. He pushed the blade hard and fast into Darius's gut. His eyes widened, shock and pain taking over as he staggered back, clutching at the wound.

"Why..." Darius gasped, blood spilling over his fingers.

Joey tilted his head, his expression calm, almost serene. "Why not?"

Darius didn't have any chance to fight back, his strength and his legs slipping away along with the blood as it left his body. Joey sat cross-legged beside him, watching with a detached curiosity as the life drained from the man's eyes. "You know, Slim," Joey said conversationally, "I used to think the badge meant something. That it gave me power. But now I see it was just a leash." He leaned closer in a menacing whisper. "I don't have a leash anymore."

Darius tried to speak, but no words, just blood coming from his mouth. Joey sat comfortably, watching him struggle. There was no emotion on his face, no regret, no hesitation. Just a cold, calculated stillness.

When it was over, Joey stood and wiped the knife clean on a rag he pulled from his pocket. He looked down at Darius's lifeless body, then at the dumpster a few feet away. "Fitting," he muttered to himself.

He picked up Darius like he weighed nothing, dumping him unceremoniously into the dumpster. The rag followed. Joey straightened his jacket, tucked the knife away, and started walking. He whistled a cheerful tune as he disappeared into the shadows of Garfield Park; the sound echoing faintly behind him.

50

Chapter 50 – Reaching out

I close the door to Alison's room gently, careful not to disturb her. She is finally asleep. The sheer exhaustion and emotional toll of it all sent her into an uneasy, much-needed rest. Her mental condition was as delicate as her physical right now. I need to leave her to rest and recover.

As I step back into the corridor, the weight of the situation presses down on me. I have lost my phone to Kane, who wants to comb through it for evidence. It's the right call, but now I'm completely cut off. No way for the psycho to contact me, and that leaves me uneasy. If he can't get to me, what's stopping him from lashing out again, this time at Megan?

The payphone catches my eye, an almost forgotten relic of another time. No one uses them anymore, but it is there, bolted to the wall, waiting. Before I fully realize what I'm doing, I'm dialing Frank's number from memory. The card he handed me earlier in all this was still in my pocket, but I didn't need it.

The phone rings. Once. Twice. By the seventh ring, I am about to hang up when his voice comes through the line. "Frank Mulligan." His tone is brisk, professional.

"It's Ray," I say.

There's a pause. "Ray? What number are you calling from?"

"I'm at the hospital," I reply, glancing around the quiet waiting area. "Kane has my phone. She's doing some tech work on it. I got another call from him."

Frank doesn't answer immediately, and I imagine him piecing together what I just said. Finally, he asks, "Why did he call?"

I take a breath, bracing myself for the admission. "To mess with me, I think. To remind me he is in control. I didn't let him. I didn't say a word. Just listened and hung up."

"Why the hell would you do that?" Frank's voice sharpens, cutting through the static of the old line.

"I was tired of him thinking he owns me," I snap, my voice low but filled with frustration. "I wanted him to know I am not some puppet on his strings. I thought he'd call back, but... instead, he went after Alison."

Frank lets out a breath. "What did he do, Ray?"

"He beat her. Badly. The lousy, cowardly son of a bitch. And Evan's dead." The words come out raw, jagged. Saying them makes them feel real all over again.

"Jesus Christ." Frank's voice is flat, and I can't tell if it's shock or just that cop detachment he always had. "You need to play this smarter, Ray. If he calls, do not push him again. You hear me?"

"I hear you," I mutter, even though the words sting. He is right and I hate it. "I've been thinking about what you said. That this could be a cop. I think you're onto something. He is too good at this. Too clean."

The silence stretches again, and I can almost see Frank on the other end, nodding in agreement.

CHAPTER 50 - REACHING OUT

"I'm going to reach out to some old contacts," I continue. "My old chief, maybe. He wasn't exactly a friend, but he respected the results I got. He might help, given the circumstances."

"Good plan," Frank says, his voice measured. "What do you need from me?"

The truth hits me as I stand there gripping the phone. I need nothing from Frank. I called him because I didn't know who else to talk to. Joey's out of the picture for now, and Frank is the only one who really offered anything in all of this. "Nothing. Not right now," I admit. "But thanks for picking up."

There's a brief pause before he speaks. "Keep me in the loop, Ray." And then the line clicks dead.

I hang up the phone and stare at it for a moment, the quiet hum of the hospital filling the space around me. I don't know if calling Frank was the right move, but at least I don't feel as alone in this fight.

I head back to the waiting room and take a seat, my mind already racing. If this bastard is a cop, then this is going to be tough. He may always be two steps ahead of me. None of us knows who we can trust.

51

Chapter 51 – Lines of deception

Joey leans back on the park bench, his mind settling into a rare moment of calm. After the night he's had, he feels some balance returning. The frustration of Ray's cold shoulder is eased by the small release he granted himself earlier. There's nothing as satisfying as draining the life from someone who has no right to share his air. Therapeutic, really.

He pulls his phone from his pocket, scrolling through his contacts until he lands on Ray. Maybe it's time to show him just how useful he can still be if Ray can get past his stubborn pride. Joey taps the call button and listens to the ring, his free hand tapping absently on his thigh.

After several rings, the call connects, but the voice that answers stops him cold.

"Mr. Sanders, how can I help you?"

Joey frowns and pulls the phone away from his ear, glancing at the screen. Ray Gordon. He hasn't mis-dialed. Confused, he presses the phone back to his ear. "Who is this?"

"This is Detective Kane, Joey," she says smoothly, her tone professional but edged with curiosity.

CHAPTER 51 - LINES OF DECEPTION

Joey pauses slightly but maintains his cool. "What are you doing with Ray's phone? Where is he?"

Kane's voice remains steady, measured. "Mr. Gordon has been receiving some very interesting calls and images on this phone. It's with our tech team now, and we're confident we'll get to the bottom of it."

There is a deliberate pause on her end, and Joey knows exactly what she's doing. Fishing. Probing. She doesn't trust him, and that amuses him more than it unnerves him.

"That's fantastic news," he replies, his tone light and sincere. "I'm sure you'll get exactly what you need."

The silence that follows lingers longer than most would be comfortable with, but Joey lets it hang, enjoying the weight of her scrutiny. He can practically hear her thinking, trying to gauge his reaction, trying to pick apart his words.

Before Kane can respond, Joey speaks again, his voice calm, almost pleasant. "I'll catch Ray later. Goodbye, Detective."

He ends the call without waiting for a reply, slipping the phone back into his pocket. It annoys him that Ray has shown a mistrust in him, but with Kane, he doesn't care.

52

Chapter 52 - Old Faces, Dead Ends

I felt a twinge of guilt about leaving Alison alone in the hospital, given everything she'd endured. But she needed rest, and I needed answers.

Driving to the precinct felt surreal. The building that used to feel like a second home now felt as though I was driving straight into enemy territory. I parked across the street and watched the buzz of cops coming and going. Uniforms everywhere, notepads in hand, suspects in cuffs. All of them living the life I had once dominated, wielding the power of the badge like it was my birthright.

Now, I was an outsider. Worse, a cautionary tale whispered among rookies. I had fought too hard and crossed too many lines to hold on to what they took from me. Watching them, oblivious to the opportunities they had, made me hate them for squandering what I had lost.

I couldn't afford to waste time thinking about that. I had to stay focused. There were people in that building who would love nothing more than to watch me fail, and I couldn't give them the satisfaction.

CHAPTER 52 - OLD FACES, DEAD ENDS

Walking into the precinct felt like stepping onto foreign soil. The air was tense, the hum of voices and clacking keyboards muted by my apprehension. I paused just inside the door, caught between nostalgia and dread. For a moment, I froze, stuck in the doorway like a man without a country.

Then I saw her, Officer Mia Parker. One of the few who didn't treat me like a pariah during my time here. Tall, confident, with braided hair and a stunning face that could charm the most hardened criminal. Her smile lit up as I approached the desk.

"Well, if it isn't Ray Gordon," she said, her voice warm, laced with that signature sass. "What brings you here, sugar?"

I chuckled despite myself. Mia always had a way of softening my rough edges, even when I didn't want her to. "Hey, Mia. Good to see you."

She tilted her head, studying me with a mixture of amusement and concern. "No offense, Ray, but you look like shit. When was the last time you got any sleep?"

I sighed. "Sleep hasn't exactly been easy to come by lately. You know how it is."

Her expression softened, sympathy replacing the teasing. "I heard about your little girl, Ray. I am so sorry. If you need anything, you know where I am."

"Thanks, Mia," I said, lowering my gaze. "Actually, there is something. I need to see the Chief. Think you can help me out?"

She smiled at that. "You know he's not gonna be happy to see you, right?"

"Probably not," I admitted.

With a mock sigh, she set down the file she had been holding. "Come on, sugar. Let's go ruin his day."

I followed her through the precinct, past familiar faces, most of them pretending they didn't see me. Others whispered to each other as I passed. I felt like a naughty school kid being led to the Principal's office. It didn't matter. Nothing mattered except finding Megan.

Mia stopped in front of the Chief's door and knocked before pushing it open. "Chief, a little blast from the past for you," she said with a grin before turning to me. "Good luck, honey."

I nodded, steeling myself before stepping inside.

Chief Doug Hayes hadn't changed much. Still the same hulking man, sweat clinging to his graying hair as he sat wedged into a chair that looked like it might give out beneath him at any moment. His scowl deepened the moment he saw me.

"Fuck me, Gordon. What are you doing here? Aren't you tangled up in some active investigation?"

"Good to see you too, Chief," I said dryly.

"Cut the crap, Gordon," he growled. "We kicked your ass out of here. You're not supposed to keep coming back."

"I haven't exactly made a habit of it," I replied, trying to keep my tone steady. "But you're the ears of this place, right? I figured you'd know that already."

He leaned back in his chair, which creaked under his weight. "Damn right I hear things. I also heard they pulled you in for questioning. You're making a mess, Gordon."

I ignored the jab, leaning forward. "I need your help, Chief. I believe the person who took Megan is a cop."

His expression darkened. "Get the fuck out of here, Ray. None of my men would stoop to this. None of them."

"You sure about that?" I pressed. "Because whoever did this knows me. They know my history, my habits, my family. This

CHAPTER 52 - OLD FACES, DEAD ENDS

is not random."

He sat forward, his chair groaning again. "Listen, people talk, Ray. They tell stories about you to the new guys; make you sound like some kind of bogeyman. But that's it, just stories. Nobody here would target you or your family. You've lost your damn mind."

I rubbed my face, frustration bubbling over. "This cannot be another dead end, Chief. Someone out there knows something, and I need you to help me find it."

He sighed heavily, his tone softening. "Ray, I am sorry about what's happened to you. Truly. But you need to back off and let the detectives do their job. You will only get in the way."

I stood, feeling the weight of his words pressing down on me. "You know I cannot do that, Chief. Thanks for your time."

As I turned to leave, his voice followed me. "Don't get in the way, Gordon. For your girl's sake, don't do it."

53

Chapter 53 – Riverside reckoning

As I leave the Chief's office, I pause just outside the door, letting the weight of yet another dead end settle in. My gut twists with frustration. I think of Megan, wondering if she knows I'm doing everything I can to bring her home. God, I hope she does.

Taking a deep breath, I square my shoulders and start moving again, weaving through the precinct's familiar halls. Whispers follow me like shadows, the same low murmur of voices as on the way in with Mia. I keep my head down, resisting the temptation to grab some rookie by the collar and demand answers. It wouldn't help. Cops don't talk about cops, not to someone like me.

"Ray!" Kane's voice cuts through the noise. I look around and see her hand in the air waving me over.

I make my way over, hoping beyond hope she has something for me to chase.

"Tell me you haven't been caught doing something stupid?" she asks, half serious.

I manage a dry chuckle. "Not yet. Had to see the Chief, see if

CHAPTER 53 – RIVERSIDE RECKONING

he could give me anything useful."

"And?"

"Another dead end," I admit, the words tasting bitter in my mouth.

She hands me my phone, her expression unreadable. "The tech team has done what they can. They will keep working in the background, but here, it's back in your hands."

I take it cautiously, like it might bite me. "Please tell me they found something."

"Nothing unexpected," she says, shaking her head. "The calls came from a burner phone. GPS tracked the photos to Alison's doorstep. No surprise there. He is bold, I'll give him that. We canvassed the area, but nobody saw anything or anyone suspicious."

"What about the burner? Any leads there?"

She shrugs. "We're combing the area where it was likely dumped. If we find it, we might trace where it was bought, but that's a long shot."

"Better than no shot at all," I mutter, not much hope there, but hope all the same.

She places a hand on my shoulder. "We're on it, Ray. I promise."

Just then, my phone buzzes in my hand. Unknown Caller.

"It's him," I say, my voice quiet, as if I don't want him to hear me speaking to Kane.

"Speakerphone," Kane orders, pulling me into a nearby office and shutting the door behind us.

I press the speaker button but stay silent, waiting.

"Come on now, Ray," the voice drones through the phone, low and menacing. "Let's not go down that road again."

"What the fuck do you want now?" I snap, my anger

simmering.

The kidnapper's tone shifts, sharp. "I hope we've learned our lesson here, Ray. Poor Alison didn't need to be caught up in all of this, did she? But you, you just couldn't fucking listen, could you? You have no idea what I am capable of, do you?"

I force myself to stay calm. This bastard wants to push me over the edge. Not this time. "I get it. You're in charge. Just tell me what you want. Tell me how to get Megan back."

He chuckles darkly. "Where's the fun in that, Ray? Because of you, I'll never see..." He cuts himself off abruptly, like he's said too much.

"Never see who?" I press. "What did I do to you?"

His tone cools again, chilling me to the bone. "Never mind that, Ray. I have something for you, something more urgent. I warned you to stay away from the cops, didn't I?"

Kane and I exchange a glance, her jaw tightening.

"Feel free to take your little detective friend along for this one," he sneers. "I've got the other one... well, marshaled, you might say." His laugh is a low, cruel growl.

My stomach drops. "What the hell does that mean?"

"Of course you wouldn't understand," he says, his smugness dripping through the phone. "But Kane will. She's much smarter than you. Riverside Parking Garage. Hop to it."

The phone goes dead.

I look at Kane, her face pale, her hands clenched into fists.

"It's Marshall," she whispers, her voice thick with dread. "He's done something to him. I haven't heard from him all day. Shit, Ray. Who the fuck is this guy?"

"We know nothing yet," I say, though I'm not sure if I believe it. "This could just be another mind game."

Her head snaps toward me, her eyes blazing. "Mind game or

CHAPTER 53 - RIVERSIDE RECKONING

not, I am not waiting to find out. My car. Now."

She storms out of the office, grabbing a nearby officer as she goes. "Get units to Riverside Parking Garage immediately. Tell them to wait for me."

I follow her through the precinct, my pulse pounding as the urgency of the moment takes hold. As we sprint to her car, I realize she's forgotten, or doesn't care, that I'm a civilian. I'm not about to remind her.

She fires up the engine; the lights flashing as we peel out of the lot, tires screeching on the tarmac.

54

Chapter 54 – Marshall's fate

Kane weaves through traffic like it's an obstacle course, dodging cars with such precision it feels like we're in a chase scene from a movie. Each swerve and whistle past the other vehicles pushes the anxiety up further through my chest.

I imagine the possibilities ahead. Every scenario ends the same: Marshall, lifeless, another casualty in this nightmare. The thought churns my gut, and I feel the weight of it pressing down on me.

Every step of this lunatic's plan feels personal, like a punishment. I keep hearing his words over and over: 'Because of you, I'll never see...' Never see who? What did I do to him? The questions circle like vultures, picking away at my focus.

As if reading my thoughts, Kane speaks up, her tone firm but not unkind. "This is not on you, Ray. Do not go missing on me now. Stay focused."

I nod, staring straight ahead at the road. I don't respond. I can't. The words wouldn't come even if I tried.

"When we get there, you stay in the car," Kane says, her voice sharp with authority.

CHAPTER 54 – MARSHALL'S FATE

"What the fuck? You can't just leave me in the car," I snap back, my frustration bubbling over.

"This is going to be an active crime scene," she replies, her tone hardening. "I can't have you trampling it. You're not allowed to be there."

"What if he's still there? What if the bastard's right in front of us? I can't just sit back and wait. You know that."

Kane grips the wheel tighter, clenches her jaw as if she is holding back. She doesn't say anything right away. She is clearly considering how best to manage me, a potential loose cannon, at the scene. The wail of sirens grows louder as we get closer to the scene, the red and blue lights reflecting off nearby buildings like a warning beacon.

Finally, Kane pulls the car up just past a cluster of patrol vehicles, their lights flashing in the dim evening light. She slams the brakes, the car screeching to a halt.

She turns to me, her expression deadly serious. "Fine. But you stay with me at all times. No running off, no playing hero. You're a civilian now, Ray. You listen to me. Got it?"

Her composure under pressure is impressive, a rock in the middle of this storm. For a moment, I almost feel like thanking her.

"I got it," I say, my voice low but steady. "Thanks, Kane."

She gives me a curt nod, already half out of the car. I follow, the tension in my chest tightening with every step.

Kane heads off and speaks with the first officer on the scene she can find. After a tense minute or two, she returns.

"We've got cops all over this parking lot. If he's still here, he isn't getting away."

I nod, but my response is grim. "It's not him we're here to find, though, is it? He's long gone by now."

"Marshall," she mutters, almost to herself. Her voice is low, heavy with the weight of what's waiting for us.

Kane calls over to the nearest officer, giving a description of Marshall, but it feels pointless. She may as well be saying let me know when you find a dead man. The officer nods and gets on his radio, relaying the details to the others.

"What car does Marshall drive?" I ask, the thought striking me.

Kane's expression sharpens, realization dawning. She turns back to the officer and describes the vehicle. He immediately radios the description, his voice tense as he orders everyone to report back upon finding it.

"Let's go," Kane orders, and we head straight into the parking lot, starting at the bottom and working our way up one level at a time.

The air feels thick with dread, every echo of our footsteps bouncing off the concrete walls, heightening the tension. Then we hear it: noise from frantic officers from somewhere above us.

"We've got something!"

Kane and I stop dead in our tracks. This is it. We look at one another, and she takes off at a speed that surprises me. I chase behind, staying as close as I can, my heart pounding in my chest.

We reach the level to find officers clustered near a car that matches Marshall's description. Kane doesn't hesitate. "Step back! Everyone secure the area and keep it locked down. Nobody enters or exits this lot without my clearance."

She glances at me, her tone unwavering. "Stay here, Ray."

I freeze, torn between obeying her command and charging forward. But something in her voice anchors me. She doesn't

CHAPTER 54 - MARSHALL'S FATE

need me getting in her way right now.

Kane approaches the vehicle, her flashlight in hand, and begins a slow, deliberate inspection. Her eyes dart across the car, taking in every detail. When she reaches the rear of the vehicle, she stops dead.

"Blood," she says quietly, almost to herself.

She steps back; her face tight, her composure slipping for just a moment. Then she straightens, nodding to one officer. "Pop the trunk."

An officer steps forward with a crowbar. With a sharp crack, the trunk pops open. Kane hesitates, taking a breath before reaching to lift it fully.

The moment she sees inside, her expression hardens, but there's no hiding the anguish in her eyes.

Marshall is there. And he's gone.

The sight of Kane's face is enough to make my knees buckle. I knew this was coming, but the reality hits harder than I imagined.

Kane takes a step back, regaining her composure with visible effort. "Call it in," she orders, her voice hollow. "Get the Medical Examiner here."

She walks back toward me, the weight of what she's seen etched across her face.

"I'm sorry," I begin, my voice cracking under the guilt pressing down on me.

Kane shakes her head, cutting me off. "This isn't on you, Ray. You're not making him do this. He's making his own decisions. Don't take his sins on your shoulders."

I nod, swallowing hard. "How?"

She bows her head for a moment before responding. "Stabbed. Over and over. It wasn't quick." Her voice falters for the first time. "Marshall was a good man. He deserved better."

Before I can respond, my phone buzzes in my pocket. My stomach tightens as I glance at the screen.

"Answer it," Kane says sharply, fire flashing in her eyes.

I exhale and pick up. "Hello?"

It's not him. Relief washes over me as I listen to the voice on the other end. I nod, murmuring a soft "Thank you" before hanging up.

"Hospital," I tell Kane. "Alison's ready to be discharged. I need to go pick her up."

Kane nods briskly. "Go. Keep your phone on. I'll keep you informed."

"I need to get back for my truck," I add.

Kane gestures to a nearby officer. "Take him back to the precinct."

Before I leave, I turn back to Kane, my chest heavy with the weight of it all. "I'm sorry. Truly."

She doesn't respond. She's already heading back to the scene, her focus shifting back to the task at hand.

55

Chapter 55 – Boundless evil

I carefully help Alison into the truck, handling her as delicately as I would a newborn child. She is so fragile right now, physically, and emotionally, and I am terrified of breaking her. I fasten her seat belt across her, being careful not to press on any of her bruises.

Her silence is deafening.

It is only when I am seated in the driver's seat that I realize she cannot go home. It is a crime scene. Hell, I am not sure she even wants to go back there again.

I glance at her. "Al, where do you want me to take you?"

She doesn't respond, just stares out the windshield, her expression hollow. I imagine, in some cruel way, she'd rather go anywhere but here, leave the city, leave the memories. But we both know that's not possible.

"I'll take you to my place. You can rest," I say, starting the engine. "And we can figure out where we go from there."

"Thanks," she whispers, her voice barely noticeable.

I drive in complete silence. The world outside of the truck feels like a blur. I think about Marshall. When he met Alison, he was the one who gave her hope, the one who reassured her they were going to work hard to find Megan. She deserves to know the truth, even if it shatters her again.

"Al," I say quietly. She can probably sense the dread in my voice. "There's something I need to tell you."

Her head turns slightly, the look on her face already breaking my heart. "I cannot take any more bad news. Please Ray, don't tell me any more sad news."

"I know," I say, staring out of the window at the road ahead, "but you need to hear this."

She breathes out sharply, like she's preparing herself for the bad news. "OK," she says, closing her eyes. "Tell me."

"It's Detective Marshall," I say after a pause. "He's...he's dead."

She turns to face me, shock etched all over her face. She can't find any words, just sits and stares at me for a long moment. But then the tears start. She sobs uncontrollably, struggling to catch her breath.

"He was supposed to find Megan," she chokes out between sobs. "He told me...he told me they'd find her. He gave me hope, Ray. How did this happen?"

"It was him," I say, my voice low. "The bastard who took Megan. He did this. He killed Marshall for helping me."

Alison gasps sharply, like she's been struck. "If he can kill the detectives, what chance do we have, Ray? What chance does Megan have?" Her voice rises, teetering on the edge of panic.

I cannot even comfort her; I have had the same thought, and it terrified me. Instead, I say the only thing I believe. "He's doing this to get to me, Al. He won't hurt Megan. She's his leverage, his way of making me suffer. As long as she's with

CHAPTER 55 - BOUNDLESS EVIL

him, I still have time to figure this out."

She stares at me, her tear-streaked face etched with despair. "Then you have to figure this out, Ray. Because you're right, this is about your past. You're the only one who knows it all. The only one who can stop this."

Her words, although completely true and expected, hit me hard. Anyone who gets close ends up dead. Marshall, Evan... God, what if Kane's next?

The rest of the drive is silent. Alison retreats into her grief, and I let her, consumed by my own thoughts.

When I pull up outside my place, I hesitate. "He knows where I live," I say. "He's been here. I'll call Kane, get some protection outside. You'll be safe."

She doesn't respond, just shrugs. I can see it in her eyes. She doesn't believe in safety anymore.

I help her out of the truck and into the house, moving as carefully as I did before. Once inside, I sit her on the couch, grab a blanket, and drape it over her shoulders. She's trembling, though whether from the cold or the shock, I can't tell.

"You need rest," I whisper.

Alison doesn't look at me, just leans back into the couch, her eyes fixed on something far away. "Just find her, Ray," she whispers. "Find Megan."

"I will, I promise."

56

Chapter 56 – Burden of truth

Alison has been asleep for a couple of hours now. I have sat and watched every breath, in then out, in then out. It is as though I am hypnotized by her breathing. For the first time in days, she looks at peace. Sleeping lets her escape, if only for a little while.

As I watch her, I think back to when we were together, how she always had questions, how I always avoided answering them. It always left her questioning me and the man that I was. She always felt I was hiding something. And this was true. I never let her in, never let her see who I was when I was out on streets wielding my badge like a weapon. I was afraid she would hate me for it.

The guilt is a raw wound that never closes. I kept her at arm's length, forcing her to live with a stranger instead of a partner. And now, after everything, she deserves the truth.

My chest aches at the thought of opening up, but I make my decision in that moment to tell her the truth. She deserves to know it all, even if it pushes her further away from me.

Some more time passes. I have no idea how long as I have

CHAPTER 56 – BURDEN OF TRUTH

been lost in my thoughts. Alison stirs, slowly opening her eyes, a moment of confusion as she takes in her surroundings. She isn't at home. For Alison, nightmares only begin when she opens her eyes.

She rises to a seated position and looks at me. She can see it all over my face that there is something I want to say. "Ray? What is it?"

Right now, I am as emotional as I can recall ever being. I can feel anxiety in my chest. It is a like a force trying to push its way through my sternum. It aches.

"Al," I say softly, wanting to make this painless. "I was never fully honest with you. I know you know that. But I think it's important to be honest now. More than ever, you deserve to know who I was."

She sits further forward, moving to the edge of the seat, looking as though she cannot believe I am finally opening up to her. "OK, go on."

"I was a dangerous man, a nasty police officer. I took what I wanted, and I didn't care who I hurt." I hang my head in shame. "Sure, most were bad, but I never saw a line. I bulldozed my way through anyone and everyone. There were no consequences, not for me. I felt like a god in that uniform. It was addictive, and it drove me further and further into my ego."

I look up and see Alison staring at me. There is no surprise there. She knew this already that was clear to see. She didn't speak; she let me continue.

"I hurt people Alison, I hurt terrible people. And now.... Now Megan....." I break down into tears. I know how many lives I affected with my past, but Megan was so small, so innocent. I couldn't bear the thought of her in the company of this monster any longer and the fact that this was down to me.... It broke me more every time I thought about it.

"I crossed a lot of lines. I was physical with some of the nastiest this city offers, and do you know what, I enjoyed it. I loved taking their power away. It was as if I was untouchable. People heard that Officer Gordon was nearby, and they would take notice."

Alison has tears in her eyes. I notice her swiping them away as she listens intently to every word I say. But she never speaks, never interrupts. She has been waiting for this for a long time.

"The night it all caught up with me, the night I finally took it too far, the night I....." I hesitate, once I admit this, I can never take it back "The night I killed a man in cold blood" and I hang my head in shame again. As I tell the full story of the night, I killed Leroy Jenkins.

Two years ago.

Olivia Rodriguez, a four-year-old girl, had been missing for three weeks now. Someone took the poor little thing from her own front yard while her parents prepared her lunch just meters away. They say they didn't hear a sound, no signs of screaming or struggle. Whoever had taken her was quick and quiet. They knew what they were doing.

I had made sure I was aware of everything happening on the case, being a father to a little girl myself. This one struck a chord with me, a violent, painful chord.

There had been chatter now for a few days. People suspected Leroy Jenkins of taking little Olivia. We—the force, Joey, and I—knew him well from past run-ins. He was a nasty piece of work, a really intimidating man even to me, so only God knows how terrified this little girl must have been.

When the call came out over the radio that Leroy had been spotted nearby, there was no way I was missing the opportunity to track this son of a bitch down. Joey answered the radio call to confirm we were responding. I hit the accelerator and headed straight for the address. No sirens. I wasn't about to give this bastard a chance to run.

"We are catching this evil bastard, Joey," I said, voice full of determination. "We are bringing him in, and we are going to make him pay."

"Agreed," Joey nodded as he said it. "We got to be smart about this, Ray. This is one nasty piece of work we are working with here. Let's do this the right way."

I nod and squeeze my eyelids as if it helps me focus, to drive faster. We will do this one right. We will get our man, and hopefully we will save this little girl.

As we get nearer the scene, I slow the car down, turn off the headlights and creep as close to the property as we can without being detected. We jump out into the pouring rain, the crack house up ahead our target. I swear I could already smell the place from here. I didn't want to spend any longer inside than necessary.

"You head up and around back, I got the front," barking my orders over the noise of the falling rain. And off he goes.

I walk up to the front door slowly; it is locked, but everything about the door and frame looks weak. I barge the door open, and I am inside. I have my service weapon drawn and torch in hand to allow me to see anything in the shadows of this awful place. It is no surprise to me that someone like Leroy would choose to spend his time here.

I start with the front room, planning to make my way around the house, but there he is, in the very first room. He is just standing there looking at me with this huge grin on his face. Is he high? Is he really that arrogant to think he is getting out of this?

I point my gun and torch at him. "Jenkins, on the ground now," I order.

He just laughs, he is enjoying this "Come make me bitch" he says smiling.

I am not scared of anyone, but getting into a physical confrontation with this monster wasn't a wise move. I kept my distance, and I ask him "Where is she?"

What he does next makes my skin crawl. He rubs his hands and licks his lips. "Ooh, that little one tasted so sweet."

I have to stop myself from throwing up right there and then.

He continues, "You got a little girl, don't you, pig?"

I don't even realize I am doing it; it is like the anger took full control of my senses and did what I likely would have been too afraid to do. I have squeezed my finger on the trigger three times. Three bullets into the sick son of a bitch's head and he hits the ground, the thud of him landing as loud as the gunshots that just rung out.

I have no regret that he is dead, only that now we won't know where Olivia is. But the sense of relief that he will never get near Megan, well, that helps a little.

Joey comes bursting into the room, gun drawn. He sees Leroy on the ground. "What happened Ray?"

I don't respond. I am too disgusted by what I just heard. I am too angry at what he has done to that little girl, and I am too disappointed that we won't find her.

Joey continues to talk. "Ray, we can't cover this up. Others are on their way right now. We weren't the only ones to respond to that call."

I honestly don't give a shit at that moment. I turn and I head outside. I can't be in that rotting place any longer. I cannot

CHAPTER 56 - BURDEN OF TRUTH

be near that scum's body for another second. Once outside, I leave the property and head for the curb and take a seat. I know what this means for my future, but I could not allow him to roam the streets any longer.

Back in the present

When I finish talking, Alison reaches out her hand. I take it lightly in mine. "Oh Ray, he was a monster. The world is a better, safer place for him being gone." She is genuinely sympathetic. But then she continues, "All the other stuff, I don't agree with it. You should have been better. But this, they should have given you a damn medal."

I just sit back, relieved to have unburdened myself.

57

Chapter 57 – Brother in doubt

I had left Alison under the protection of two officers, but I still couldn't shake the fear that anything could happen while I was gone. This psycho wanted me scared; well, he can tick that one off his to do list. I am petrified every minute of the day for those closest to me. But I have to move forward.

Kane had sent the officers with a message; she wants to see me down at the precinct. I wasn't about to sit around waiting to be asked again. I wanted to know what she had, so I had hopped straight into my truck and drove straight over there.

Kane had set us up in a boardroom of sorts, with files spread out all over the desk. I knew those files weren't for me, but Kane had stopped caring. She had a new, steely look of determination in her eyes. I could see it; she would do whatever it takes. He had gone too far, made an enemy of her, and she isn't the kind of enemy you want.

"What's the official word on Marshall?" I asked, knowing it was a sensitive question.

She looked up at me. I had broken her concentration. It was as if she hadn't even known I was in the room until I spoke

CHAPTER 57 – BROTHER IN DOUBT

"Stabbed 57 times. It was a frenzied attack."

"Jesus Christ" I wasn't expecting that, not from a man who has shown so much control.

As if reading my mind, Kane continued, "Very different from the other killings." She returned to studying the files on the desk. "He has a new state of mind. He is no longer planning; he is acting in rage. This feels the most dangerous yet."

I step closer to Kane, wanting her to feel the urgency in my voice. "We have to find him. If he is in a rage, he may act out and hurt Megan before he is done with me."

"That's the plan Ray, that is what we are trying to do here," she appeared to be lacking patience at this point.

I took a seat at the desk and put my head in my hands. Reviewing all the information in front of me was only going to remind me what we were dealing with here.

"I want to know more about your old partner, Joey Sanders," she says, looking me directly in the eye.

I look back at her, half in disbelief, half expecting the attention to turn Joey's way at some point. "You don't really think.... Surely Joey wouldn't do this to me?" I asked.

"I am just gathering as much information as I can here, but I will give it to you straight. That man creeps the bejesus out of me. I think he has a dark side to him, and I think he believes he is too smart to be caught doing whatever it is he does."

I sit there and I think back to the times I had seen the dark side of Joey. But he had done everything quietly, under the radar. Joey rarely faced repercussions for his actions, unlike me, and when he did, he easily dismissed them with simple explanations.

Kane, interrupting my thoughts, asks, "Is there anything from your time together that suggests there may be more to him?"

I want to protect Joey. He was my partner for a long time, my friend. But lying won't get me closer to the truth of what is happening here. "There were times, times he worked it alone. He preferred for me to go do something else and let him do what he needed to do, his words."

"What the fuck does that even mean, Ray?" she snaps. I can't help but think that Marshall's killing has hit her harder than she would care to admit.

"I don't actually know," I admitted. "there were times when he creeped even me out. When he was like that and he wanted to be alone, I had no problem with it. He would always come back in a much better mood."

"Do you think he is capable of murder?" she asks, taking a seat next to me.

I turn and look her dead in the eye. "I know he is."

I take some time to tell her about the Nicky Stone case, how that had unraveled, what I had witnessed, and how Joey acted in the moments after it. It was the same way he acted after each time he had worked it alone. He was content. He was at ease.

"I'm sorry, Ray. I know he was your friend. But he is my number one suspect," she says. She stands and heads for the door. "We need to speak with him. We need to find out where he was when they butchered Marshall." She grabs her coat and holds the door open, ready for me to follow.

I can't believe this could all be Joey. I knew he had secrets, and that people didn't like him. I had seen some dark stuff when he thought he was alone. But we were always good. Even after he was kicked off the force for my actions, he held nothing against me. Not that I was aware of.

CHAPTER 57 – BROTHER IN DOUBT

I follow Kane out the door reluctantly. If this were to be true, I didn't know how I would handle it.

58

Chapter 58 – Broken bonds

Kane drives, her hands tight on the wheel, her eyes fixed on the road, while I replay the worst-case scenarios in my head. Joey Sanders, my former partner, my closest friend on the force. Could he really be the monster behind all of this? No matter how many questionable memories resurface, the idea that Joey would harm Megan or Alison seems impossible.

But Kane is a sharp detective, her instincts better than most. I have to trust her, even if it means confronting the possibility that I've been blind to something right in front of me.

"I'll do the talking, Ray," she says, her voice firm. "You're here to observe and maybe provoke a reaction. If he sees you with me, it might trigger something."

It makes sense, but I still feel uneasy. "Got it," I mutter, gripping the armrest as she weaves through traffic.

"Understand this," she glances at me briefly. "You cannot lose it in there. No laying hands on him. Got it?"

"I hear you," I say, raising my hand like a scout's honor. "Best behavior"

As we head west, the neighborhoods grow more run-down.

CHAPTER 58 - BROKEN BONDS

The streets reflect the decline Joey must have experienced since being kicked off the force. By the time we park outside his place, a sinking feeling settles in my gut.

"You ready?" Kane asks, her hand on the door handle.

No. "Let's do it," I say, stepping out of the car.

Kane knocks hard on the door. No answer. She knocks again, louder this time. Finally, Joey opens it just a crack, enough for us to see his unshaven face and tired eyes.

"Why the fuck are you banging on my door?" he asks, his gaze shifting from Kane to me.

"Let's just talk, Joey," I say, trying to keep things calm. "Let Kane ask her questions, and we'll leave you alone."

He hesitates, running a hand through his messy hair before opening the door wider. Without another word, he turns and walks inside.

Kane and I follow. The place is dimly lit but spotless, every surface wiped clean, everything in its place. That's Joey, chaos on the inside, order on the outside.

"You just keep showing up, don't you, Kane? And you," he says, nodding at me. "What is this? You two partners now?"

"I brought Ray because he knows you better than anyone," Kane replies coolly. "He might notice if you're lying."

Joey's eyes narrow. "Lying about what?"

Kane steps forward, her tone sharp. "Where were you around midnight, the night before last?"

"At midnight?" Joey repeats, scratching his head. "Same as any other night, passed out in there." He jerks a thumb toward the bedroom.

"You got anyone to corroborate that?"

"Corroborate?" He sneers, then turns to me. "Ray, what is this?"

I glance at Kane for permission. She nods, and I take a step closer to Joey. "They murdered Kane's partner, Marshall, the other night. It was a message for helping me."

Joey's face falls. He stares at me; the color draining from his face before sinking into the armchair. For a moment, he's silent, rubbing his face as if trying to wake from a bad dream.

Finally, he looks up. "Ray, you're here because you think I did this? You think I took Megan?"

Just hearing him say it aloud crushes me. I can't even look him in the eye. "I don't know what to think, Joey. Just answer Kane's questions."

"I can't fucking believe this," he mutters, shaking his head. "No, I don't have anyone who can vouch for me. I sleep alone."

Kane presses on. "What about three days ago? Early afternoon?"

Joey's eyes dart around the room, as if searching for an escape. Finally, he sighs and leans back in his chair. "I walk a lot. Clears my head. That's all I do these days" He fixes his gaze on me. "Or help an old friend when I'm asked."

"Not much of an answer, Joey," Kane snaps.

Joey's frustration boils over. "I told you, I'm alone. I like it that way."

I step closer, lowering my voice. "Joey, someone attacked Alison. Left her in the hospital. They killed Evan. This is fucking serious."

"Holy shit, Ray," He gets to his feet, his voice trembling with emotion. "You think I'd hurt Alison? Megan? You can't believe that."

His words hit me hard, and I turn to Kane, shaking my head. "It's not him."

Joey's face twists with anger. "Not him? You're damn right

CHAPTER 58 – BROKEN BONDS

it's not. What the hell, Ray? You show up with her, accuse me of this, and now you're done?"

"I'm chasing my tail here, Joey," I say, my voice breaking. "You have no idea."

Kane steps in. "Mr. Sanders, this is my line of questioning, not Ray's."

"Get the hell out. Both of you" Joey points to the door, his voice cold.

Without a word, Kane and I leave. Outside, I lean against the car, trying to catch my breath. Joey's reaction had been genuine, I was sure of it. But that left me no closer to finding Megan, and no closer to knowing who this monster really was.

59

Chapter 59 – On the hook

After Kane dropped me back at the precinct, I trudged to my truck like I was walking through quicksand. Each step felt heavy and deliberate, as though moving forward at all was too much effort.

I'd just betrayed my only friend, the one person who had willingly stepped into this nightmare with me, offering to help find Megan. I dropped him without proof, without hesitation, at the mere suggestion that he could be involved. Deep down, I knew Joey had his demons, even after leaving the force. But putting Megan or Alison in harm's way? That wasn't one of them. I was sure of it. Well, as sure as I could be, I wasn't exactly getting much right these days.

I climbed into my truck; I hesitated and then started the engine, but I didn't move. I just sat there, drained. I pressed my head back against the headrest, took a deep breath, and closed my eyes. Thoughts of Megan ran through my mind. I thought about how long it had been since I'd seen her, held her, told her just how much daddy loved her. It was enough to make me ache for her.

CHAPTER 59 – ON THE HOOK

A tapping on the window forced me to come back to the now. I opened one eye, and when I saw who it was, I blinked hard to make sure I wasn't imagining things. Mickey Finch.

I buzzed the window down. "Mickey. Long time. What's going on?"

"You know me, Mr. G. Plodding on" He gave me the same simple grin he always had, even back when he was my most reliable CI. Mickey was a guy who'd had a rough hand dealt to him but never played the victim. Polite, and always honest with me. He was one of the few people I genuinely liked in this world.

"I think I've got something you might be interested in," he said.

I smiled at that, just for a second, like we were back in the old days. But reality set in fast, and I shook my head "Mickey, I'm not on the force anymore. I can't do anything with it."

He frowned. "Can I hop in?"

"Sure, get in."

Mickey slid into the passenger seat, giving a little shiver like he was shaking off the cold. Then he turned to face me, all serious now. "I think I know who killed that detective"?

My heartbeat jumped up instantly, and my whole body was shaking. Mickey was never one to bullshit. If he said he knew something, he knew something. I felt hope for the first time. "Tell me."

"I was in the car park where they found him," Mickey started, "Just trying to escape the cold. Now, I didn't know it was a detective in that trunk at the time. Swear to God. But I saw this guy... kept stabbing at him, even though it was obvious he was already dead."

I wanted to grab Mickey and shake the name out of him, but

I kept still. "Go on."

"He was in a state, man. Like... rage. Crazy. I just stayed low, didn't want to end up next. Anyway, after he finished messing with the body, he leaned back and stretched. That's when I saw it."

My back straightened as if I were sitting up to pay attention. "Saw what?"

"That scar. Left side of his neck, nasty-looking, shaped like a hook" Mickey traced the air with his finger to show the shape, but I wasn't looking.

Everything started spinning. I gasped for breath, and my stomach lurched as if someone had punched me. "Frank" I whispered.

Mickey leaned back. "Yeah, that's the dude. He always gave me bad vibes, but I remember that scar clear as day."

It couldn't be. Frank, calm and collected Frank, who'd stood there and let me choke him out without so much as a fight. He'd fooled me completely. I thought back through every interaction we'd had, everything he had said, how he had been so friendly after he reached out the second time. "Fuck, fuck, fuck!" I was grabbing at my hair as I held my head in my hands.

"Mr. G, I'm real sorry about your girl. I hope this helps," Mickey said earnestly.

I turned to him, my voice shaking. "Mickey, thank you. Really. You might've just saved Megan's life."

He nodded, gave me a small smile, jumped out of the truck, and off he went.

I just sat there, not know where to move. It all made sense now, Frank's calm demeanor, his calculated moves, his willingness to help me. It wasn't help. It was control.

But why? What had I done to him? I couldn't think of

CHAPTER 59 – ON THE HOOK

anything I had ever done to him. I'd avoided Frank for most of my career. He wasn't trustworthy to a working cop. So why was he doing this to me?

I grabbed the steering wheel while I wrestled with my next decision. Kane had been good to me, brought me closer than anyone else had to finding Megan. But if I brought her in, I wouldn't get Frank alone. I wouldn't get my chance to make him pay.

No. This was personal. I was going to get Megan back. And then I was going to break his neck.

60

Chapter 60 – Let's be Frank

I drove to Frank's place, my mind racing with questions and suspicions. I knew Frank, sure, but not on a personal level, not really until Megan went missing, and he stepped in to help. Why would he do this? I'd never crossed paths with him in a way that could have hurt him, not directly. He'd been on the sidelines of my world, just another guy trying to keep himself out of trouble.

But now, none of it made any sense. I felt like I was missing something critical, some connection I hadn't pieced together. If I need to squeeze his neck with my bare hands to get it, then that's what I'll do.

I thought back to the first time I stormed his house, tearing through every room like a madman. Megan wasn't there. She couldn't have been. He had his kids and wife in that house. There were too many risks. He wouldn't keep her there.

Would he?

The more I thought about it, the more I considered how close I had come. My head spun. If he wasn't hiding Megan there, then where? And why the hell would he do this to me at all?

CHAPTER 60 – LET'S BE FRANK

As I pull up to Frank's place, I feel that gut wrenching nervousness in my stomach again. I had no idea how this was going to play out. I had no idea how much control I had over myself right now. When I just suspected he had her, I lost control. But now that I know he has her, there was no telling how I would react to seeing his smug bastard face.

I knock on the door as if I am just a visitor, here to see a friend, no urgency in it. I don't want to give anything away. I can feel my senses revving up to react the moment the door opens. But it isn't Frank, it's his wife. A wave of disappointment hits me. I was hoping we could be alone for this part.

When she sees me, the realization sets in, and she panics. "No, don't you dare. I will call the police."

I hold my hands up in a surrender motion, I keep my voice as calm as I can manage "I am sorry for what happened last time, truly I am. Frank has been helping me since I was last here, I was just hoping to speak with him."

She seems to be a little surprised by how calm I am. In truth, I think I am too. She relaxed a little, but kept her guard up. "Frank isn't here."

I grit my teeth. Damn it, I was really hoping to catch him off guard. But I do my best to hide my frustration. "Do you know where I can find him?"

She hesitates before answering. "I don't know anymore," she said, somewhat depressed. "He hasn't been himself the last few days. He's hardly ever here."

He has been escalating, seems to be losing some control, makes sense that he would stay away from his family. I probed a little, "what do you mean? Not been himself?"

She sighs and bows her head. "He.... He has been a little distant, like he is lost in his own little world. If I try to snap him out of it, he gets annoyed, easily. It is not like him." She looks back up at me, concern on her face. "Do you know what is going on with him?"

"I just hoped to talk about some details of Megan's case with him," I lie. It's an easy lie, given what's at stake. "He has been helping me piece some stuff together."

"I am sorry about your little girl," she says, genuinely sympathetic. "I don't know what I would do if...." She trails off and doesn't finish that thought. I don't blame her; it is too much to bear.

"Thank you," I say, though my mind is already racing. I need to keep the conversation going, to get inside the house. Maybe there's something here, something I can find. "What do you think has Frank acting out?"

She shakes her head, a look of helplessness. "I honestly do not know. It's not like him at all."

"Do you mind if I come in? Maybe we can talk? Maybe Frank will come home" Another moment of hesitation, but sympathy for Megan seems to tip the scale. She opens the door and gestures for me to come inside. As I step in, I look around the room. I am not sure what I'm expecting to find. He's hardly going to leave a map with a pin in it for all to see. Still, I know I need to be here. I just don't know why yet.

"Can I get you anything? A drink?" she asks. She is courteous. She's as blind to what Frank is capable of as I was. I think of telling her to bring a bottle of whiskey and leave it on the table, but I ask for water. She nods and heads to the kitchen. Alone, I stand there, taking in the home of the man who's turned my world into a nightmare.

My phone buzzes in my pocket, breaking my thoughts. Without thinking, I pull it out and answer. "Hey Ray, did you

CHAPTER 60 - LET'S BE FRANK

like what I did with Detective Marshall?" His voice is cold and sinister, and even though I know who it is now, it chills me to the bone. I take a deep breath, surprised. How do I handle this? What do I say to Frank now that his mask is off? He still thinks he's in control. I need to shake that, plant some doubt.

"Not a smart move taking out a detective," I say, forcing calm. "You've got more than just me to worry about now."

He chuckles, a low, grating sound. "You think that concerns me? Those idiots will make themselves dizzy chasing their tails trying to figure it out." His arrogance pours through the phone. Now that I can put a face to it, it infuriates me even more.

Frank's wife comes back with my water. I gesture to her I'm on the phone and step into another room to continue. "You really think you're smarter than everyone else, don't you?" I say, my voice sharp.

"I don't think it, Ray. I know it. I'm smarter than all of you. We'll play this for as long as I choose."

It's like he's snapped the last thread of my composure. My patience is gone, and I can't hold back. "Listen, Frank, you're not clever. You're just another dumb fuck who thinks he can get away with murder. Now I have got you Frank, it's only a matter of time before I wrap my hands around your neck."

The other end of the phone goes silent. The smugness, the arrogance, it all vanishes. For a moment, I feel the smallest flicker of satisfaction. "I'm at your home right now, Frank," I say, my tone low and deliberate. "With your wife." But the line goes dead.

Shit. What have I done? I had him talking. I could've set a trap, got him to meet me somewhere, but now he's gone, and I have to find this sick bastard before he can hurt anyone else.

I step back into the living room, thank Frank's wife, and head for the door. As I hop into my truck and pull away, my mind is already racing.

61

Chapter 61 – Game changer

Frank drops the phone onto the table in front of him, Ray's words echoing in his head: "Listen, Frank, you're not clever. I am at your home, with your wife."

Shit! How does he know it's me? I must have made a mistake. But how? Where?

His anger builds rapidly, and he completely loses control. Before he even realizes it, the phone is flying through the air, smashing against the wall. The table follows, flipped over with a crash that fills the room. A roar tears from his throat, raw and primal, so loud and full of rage it feels like it could shake the walls.

Frank is breathing hard now, his chest heaving. Slowly, he glances down at his hands, the skin on his knuckles scraped raw, blood dripping where he's punched the walls without realizing. Pain finally registers, but it's dulled by the frustration eating away at him.

He slumps back against the wall, his mind racing. This wasn't supposed to happen. Everything had been going so well. Ray was supposed to dance to his tune, follow the breadcrumbs, but now, now the bastard knows. And it changes everything.

For the first time, a shadow of doubt creeps into Frank's mind. He has been so careful, so meticulous. But had he slipped? Missed something? The thought claws at him, each unanswered question gnawing away at his composure.

Then his doubt turns into anger, cold and consuming. He has to re-calibrate. Ray, knowing the truth, doesn't mean the game is over. It means the rules are different now. He leans forward, running a bloodied hand through his hair. If Ray thought this was bad, Frank would make sure the next moves crushed him.

Maybe it was time to send Megan back to him. Not whole, but in pieces.

Megan heard everything from her room. She pressed her hands tightly over her ears. She never liked loud noises, but these when they were scary like this.... it was all too much. Her small body trembles, tears streaming down her face as she tries to stifle her sobs.

The sounds terrify her, like thunder crashing right outside her window. She presses herself into the corner of the room, gripping her blanket as if it can shield her from the bad man.

"Daddy will come. He'll find me," she whispers to herself. She says it again, and again, trying to make it true.

She pictures Daddy lifting her up, holding her tight, telling her everything will be okay. She misses him so much, misses the way his hugs made her feel safe, like nothing could hurt her. But now, the cold, dark room feels like it's swallowing her whole.

The blanket she clutches is too thin to keep her warm, but she hugs it anyway. It reminds her of home, of the big comfy bed she used to curl up in when she felt scared. She closes her

CHAPTER 61 – GAME CHANGER

eyes, imagining she's there again, with Daddy's strong arms wrapped around her.

But the noises from the other room snap her back to the present. She flinches at the sound of another loud thud, and her heart races, the fear freezing her in place.

She can only hope the man stays out of her room.

62

Chapter 62 – Mending bridges

As I drive aimlessly through the streets, the realization hits me like a gut punch. I have just screwed up my best chance of finding Frank. Just an hour ago, he thought he had all my trust. Hell, there's no thought about it. He had my trust. I was blind to his deception. What an idiot I had been.

The thought keeps circling my mind, taunting me. I could have called him, played along, let him come to me. Then I could have pushed my thumb into his eye until he told me where he was keeping her. Torn him apart piece by piece. But my anger, my goddamn need to show him I was onto him, has left me in a deeper pit of desperation than ever.

All this time, I've been trying to keep it above board, to think clearly and do this the right way. But that's gone now. If I want to beat Frank, I need to think like Frank. I need someone who knows how to work with a twisted mind like his. There's only one person who can help me with that. I just hope he's still willing to take my call.

I pull over, grab my phone, and scroll to Joey's number. Before I hit dial, I take a deep breath. I'm going to have to

CHAPTER 62 – MENDING BRIDGES

wade through his anger and disappointment first. He has every right to it, but I don't have time to dwell on that. I press the call button, and the phone rings. And rings.

In my head, I see Joey staring at my name, debating whether to let it go to voicemail or tell me to go to hell. I hope he thinks about Megan.

Finally, the call connects.

"What the fuck do you want?" His voice is sharp, cutting straight to the bone.

"Joey, listen, I know you're angry...."

He doesn't let me finish. "Angry? I'm way past that, Ray. That you even considered I could do this to you. To Megan. To that little girl of yours...." His voice cracks slightly before he cuts himself off.

"I know," I say quickly, desperate to keep him from hanging up. "I never genuinely believed it, Joey. I was just following Kane's lead. I should have trusted you. I'm more sorry than you'll ever know, but right now, I need you."

He laughs, bitter and humorless. "After all that, you want me to help you? Fuck that, Ray. You're on your own."

The panic rises in me, and I shout before he can end the call, "Think of Megan, Joey! Not me. I know who has her!"

Silence. The kind that feels like it's stretching on forever. I imagine Joey, on the other end of the line, weighing his hatred for me against his care for my daughter. Finally, his voice comes through, quieter.

"Who?"

I steady myself, relieved he's willing to listen but still choking on the name. "It's Frank. It's been that bastard all along." My voice shakes as I say it, the anger burning through every inch of me.

"Fuck!" It's all he manages, the shock settling in. "I talked to him, Ray. Looked him in the eye. I didn't pick up on a goddamn thing. Are you sure?"

"I'm positive," I reply, knowing I'm about to admit to yet another colossal Ray Gordon fuck-up. "And I fucked it again, Joey. I confronted him. Now he knows I know."

I can feel Joey's frustration radiating through the phone. He doesn't say it, but I can imagine the thought running through his head: Why the hell doesn't Ray ever think before he acts?

Finally, he exhales heavily. "Where are you now?"

"I'm on my way to you," I say, bracing myself. "Sorry."

"No, that's fine. That's good. Get here, and we'll talk more," he says, his voice softening slightly.

It feels like a slight weight lifts off me, having Joey back in my corner. I say nothing else. I just hang up and head straight for his place.

63

Chapter 63 – False hope

Detective Kane has sat in the same room, staring at the same evidence for hours. But she is no further along. She has no new information. There were photos, witness statements, and reports. But nothing fit together. She cannot tie anything to Joey, and it was infuriating to her.

The killing of Marshall had made this personal for her. He was a colleague, and he deserved better. Kane felt a weight of responsibility for what happened to Marshall. She was the senior detective on this. She should have been able to protect him.

This wasn't just about solving the case anymore, this was no longer about justice, this was about revenge.

All the evidence was just blurring together. There was no meaning to it. It was just random pieces of information that led nowhere. She was desperate for something to jump out at her, something with Joey's name on it. She wanted that bastard behind bars.

She leaned back in her chair, pushing the palms of her hands over her eyes. She needed a break; she needed time to clear her head, but just then an officer popped his head through the door.

"Detective Kane?"

Kane didn't bother to move her hands from her face. She spoke right through them. "What?"

He hesitated before stepping into the room. "Got something for you."

"Yeah? What is it?"

"Another murder, out west, Garfield Park," he said, all business but slightly nervous.

She removed her hands and stood up. "Do we know who it is?"

"Yeah, some small-time thug," He referred to his notepad, "Darius Carter. Single stab wound, from what I have been told."

Kane circled the room, thinking this through. Small-time criminal doesn't fit the profile, this may have nothing to do with the case. It may just be another random act of violence in a violent part of the city. But the timing, the timing, made it interesting.

While she was thinking, the officer continued, "witness says they saw Joey Sanders in the area."

She stopped dead. "Say that again."

"Sanders, Joey Sanders," he repeated.

She was conscious not to go diving in here, but this was too much of a coincidence. "Did they give a description of Joey? Did they actually witness him doing anything?"

"They gave his name. They know him well; he's a former cop, and not very popular. People tend to remember him. Witness just says he was walking around that area, at that time. He was just whistling, but she didn't witness any crime. But she said he gave her the creeps."

CHAPTER 63 – FALSE HOPE

It was a week witness statement, but it was something to bring him in for. She could feel the frustration shifting. It didn't matter how circumstantial this was, a witness statement was more than enough to get him here. "Good work," she said as she grabbed her coat. "Get me that witness, get them here, and don't let them leave until I have spoken with them."

"Yes, ma'am," he said as he turned to leave.

"And get an APB out on Joey Sanders. I want him in custody yesterday," she ordered.

She grabbed her keys and headed out of the meeting room, and addressed the entire office. "Right, listen up. Our old friend, Joey Sanders, has been linked to a murder out in Garfield Park. I want a full team with me. Sanders has been playing us long enough. It's time we put an end to it."

Kane strode on through the precinct while officers scrambled to their feet, grabbing their gear, falling in line behind her. She stopped and followed up with, "This bastard is dangerous, but this is for Marshall. Let's make it count."

She headed for her car and tore away from the car park with sirens blazing. A trail of blue and red lights in her rear-view mirror.

64

Chapter 64 – Frank's trap

When I arrived, he was waiting outside. He moved toward the truck with some urgency, jumping into the passenger side. When he got in, I felt the urge to apologize to him. I felt I had let him down. "Listen, Joe...."

But he cut me off. "We don't have time for that Ray, let's figure this out. Let's bring Megan home."

I nod my head in agreement. I agree, that's the only thing we need to focus on right now. "I don't know where to go next. Trying to do the right thing has got me nowhere," I admit. "I think it's time to mix it up, go old school, like we did back in the day." I look at him, hoping he agrees.

He looks at me with a fierce intensity. "We have to use our brains Ray, we don't barrel into this, he has already shown he is too smart for that."

It felt good to have him in my corner, to be trusting him again. I felt I had the backup I needed to get this done. "What are you thinking?" I ask him.

He sat back and puffed out his cheeks, his brain working away at possible answers to that question. "How long has he

CHAPTER 64 – FRANK'S TRAP

known that you know?"

"An hour, maybe a little more."

He nods and stares off into the distance. "OK, that's good. It is conceivable that you haven't spoken with me yet."

I just sit in silence, looking at him. I don't know where he is going with this. I wait for him to continue.

"I can call him, ask him to meet me, tell him I need his help."

"You think that will work?" I ask, unsure if this was the right move. "He always seems to be a step ahead. Do you not think he will find it too risky?"

He nods again. "Possibly, probably even. But we won't know unless I try him" He doesn't wait for me to agree, he already has his phone out and is calling Frank. I feel my whole-body tense at the thought of hearing his voice on the phone again. Joey put the phone on speaker so I could hear the conversation.

To my surprise, he answers quickly, "Joey, what's up?" I cannot quite believe how casual he is when he answers. Maybe that is a good thing. Maybe he thinks Joey is out of the picture.

"Frank, I need to talk. You got some time?" Joey says, putting on an acting masterclass.

"Sure Joe, what you need?"

"Can we meet? I don't want to discuss over the phone."

There is a period of silence on the phone. It is eerie. He hasn't responded and my anxiety kicks in harder. The only reason he wouldn't agree is that he is onto us. Joey is the one to break the silence. "Frank? You there?"

A heavy sigh comes through the phone and then Frank's voice, but he isn't as relaxed this time. His voice has an angry bitterness, a sinister sound. It makes Joey and me exchange a nervous look. "Yeah, of course, Joe. Where should I meet you? Shall we just jump straight to it and meeting Ray's fucking living room?" His voice is raising the longer he speaks, he is clearly angry. "How fucking stupid do you think I am, Joe? And you Ray? You are listening, aren't you? How do you still not get this? I said do not piss me off Ray!"

Joey and I sit quietly, not sure what to do or say next. We hadn't planned on his response being like this, so much for using our fucking brains.

I try something different. "Frank, just give Megan back. You can have me, but let her go back to her mother."

He just laughs down the phone. It is a dark, horrifying sound. "It will not be that easy, Ray. I want you to come alone. Hear that, Joe? Stay the fuck away or I will chop her up and send her to you both in pieces. Got it?"

I cannot bear the sound of this bastard threatening my daughter. It enrages me. I am almost out of my seat; the anger pushing me closer to the phone. But Joey lays his palm on my chest and gives me a look. He points to his temple and says, "Think."

I take a moment to compose myself and then I respond, "Where and when?"

"That's a good little boy Ray, now Joe, tell me you understand?" his voice sounds smarmier the more he speaks.

"I hear you Frank, I understand."

"Good, good. Now give the phone to Ray and fuck off," he orders Joey out of the way.

Joey hands me the phone. He opens the truck door, waits a second and then shuts it hard. But he remains in the truck.

"OK Frank, we are alone. What the fuck do you want?" I ask him.

He laughs again. I am sick to my stomach at the sound of his laugh. I want to ram my fist down his throat. "You already

CHAPTER 64 – FRANK'S TRAP

know this, Ray; I want you to suffer. But right now, I want you to get to Langley's Industrial Depot, down by the old freight yard. Alone Ray! You think you can do that?"

"I know it. I can get there."

I was in no way prepared for what came next. "Daddy, please do what the bad man says. I am scared Daddy. Please come get me" Megan's voice came down through the phone. The sound of her voice it broke me.

I hadn't heard her speak for so long. I just wanted to keep her talking. But when I tried to speak, I broke down completely. "Megan, sweetheart, Daddy is coming for you. I promise baby" I don't know if she could understand me. I was speaking through tears. I looked at Joey and he was shaking.

Then Frank's voice comes back through "Fucking pathetic Ray. You have one hour. And no tricks. I know you have your little friends helping you. If I see them. She is dead. Get going," with that the phone went dead.

I needed time to compose myself. Hearing Megan has sent my senses spinning. He knew exactly what he was doing. He was trying to keep me off balance, to keep me from thinking straight. I was his little puppet, and he was making sure I was still dancing to his tune.

Joey leaned forward and placed a hand on my shoulder. "I don't care what Frank says, Ray. You're not walking into that deathtrap alone. Not happening."

"You know Langley's?" I asked him.

"Langley's?" Joey repeated, his face darkening. "That place is a maze. Old warehouses, rusted catwalks, half the walls falling apart. If Frank wanted a stage to screw with your head, he picked the right one."

I closed my eyes for a second, trying to steady myself,

imagining Megan trapped in some corner of that labyrinth.

"You hear that, Ray?" Joey said suddenly, his head snapping toward the back window.

I heard it too. Sirens growing louder, closing in. My heart dropped as blue lights flashed all around us. Tires screeched to a halt and doors slammed shut. Joey cursed under his breath.

There were cops everywhere, and Kane was leading them. She was heading straight for my truck; she looked angry and strode with purpose.

65

Chapter 65 – In the cross-hairs

Kane yanks the passenger side door open, her hand already gripping her gun, ready to draw it at any moment. "Joey Sanders, step out of the car. You're under arrest on suspicion of murder," she barks at a stunned Joey in the seat beside me.

I couldn't believe this was happening. Just a few moments ago I felt I had the support of an old friend in my attempts to find Megan, but now Kane was ruining everything. "Kane, what are you doing?" I demanded.

"This doesn't concern you Ray, just stay out of it. Mr. Sanders, I won't ask again." Kane's anger is palpable. It consumes her and clouds her judgment. She blames Joey for everything, including the killing of Detective Marshall.

Desperately, I lean forward and try to reason with her. "Listen, Kane. It's not Joey. It's Frank Mulligan. He's setting up a meeting with me right now. I need Joey for this."

Her gaze shifted from Joey to me. I could see her brain working to process what I had just said. She rubbed her face with the palms of her hands, tightened her ponytail. "OK.... OK, it's Frank? How do you know this?"

"It doesn't matter how I know. But it means you don't have to take Joey. Right?"

She turned her focus back to Joey, a determined look on her face. "Wrong. Joey is a suspect in an unrelated murder case. He won't be helping you. And neither will you, Ray. You can tell me what you know, and we will handle the rest" she nodded to two officers nearby, who swiftly reached into my truck and hauled Joey out before cuffing him and leading him away. He didn't even have time to protest.

"What the fuck is that all about?" I demand, shocked by her sudden change in attitude.

"Forget about that," she snaps back. Now she is only focused on me. "What do you know?"

My mind races, Frank's warning still echoing in my head. I have to handle this delicately. If Kane charges in guns blazing, I may never see her again. "You have to understand, he has conditions. He told me to come alone."

"Well then, you don't need Joey, do you?" Kane retorts.

I nod, knowing there's nothing more I can do. I just need her to agree on a plan that will allow us to handle this quietly and safely.

Kane's eyes narrowed; she continued to focus her eyes on me. She was clearly torn between her duty as a cop and her desire to help me find Megan. After what felt like an eternity, she let out a heavy sigh.

"Fine. We'll do this your way, Ray. But I'm not letting you go in there alone. I'll be nearby, out of sight. You give me a signal if things go south."

I nodded, relief washing over me. "Okay, that works. But Kane, you have to promise me you won't do anything rash. Frank's dangerous, and he's holding all the cards right now."

CHAPTER 65 – IN THE CROSS-HAIRS

She holstered her gun and leaned against the truck; she was finally relaxing a little. "I get it. This isn't my first rodeo. So, what's the plan?"

I filled her in on Frank's details. The abandoned warehouse by the old freight yard. A one-hour deadline. I had to come alone and unarmed. As I spoke, Kane's expression grew more concerned.

"Ray, this has 'trap' written all over it. That place is like a deadly maze," she said, shaking her head. "I don't want this to be too harsh, but how do we even know Megan's even still alive?"

Just the words alone, the insinuation he may have already killed her, were enough to knock the wind out of me. I quickly recomposed myself. "I know she is; he made her speak to me just now."

Kane's eyes softened. She placed a hand on my shoulder, squeezing gently. "That sick bastard is using her to get into your head, to mess with your thinking. You cannot let him. You need to be prepared for anything in there."

I nodded, swallowing hard. "I know. I'm ready."

We had little time; I was already pushing it. Kane quickly advised me on her plan to maintain a safe distance, but ready when needed.

66

Chapter 66 – Checkpoint one

As I raced towards Langley's warehouse, I thought about Kane and her team waiting for me, just out of sight. It helped calm my anxiety some. They were my backup plan, Megan's lifeline. If anything was to go wrong.

I had to trust that Kane would keep them hidden. Frank had already shown how serious he was. I didn't need another demonstration, not if Megan was the subject.

With each passing mile, my heart pounded harder. A strange excitement grew at the thought of seeing Megan again, even under these awful circumstances. But I couldn't allow the excitement to takeover, I knew it wouldn't be as easy simply giving her a kiss and a cuddle and setting off home. I was prepared to risk myself to get her back to Alison.

As I got closer to the warehouse, I slowed my truck almost to a stop, trying to get a good look around, to spot any surprises Frank might have for me. I crawled to a complete stop and put the truck in park.

I took a deep breath to steady myself, to gather my courage, and jumped out. The warehouse looked as though it had sat

CHAPTER 66 – CHECKPOINT ONE

unattended for centuries, like it could crumble at the slamming of a door. I was uneasy at the thought of Megan being inside.

As I was about to make my way inside, my phone buzzed. A text from Kane: "In position. Be careful."

I nodded, thinking to myself that careful won't do me any good here, but I pressed on. My footsteps echoed as I approached the entrance, each step feeling heavier than the last.

There were any number of entry points, but I headed for what looked like the main entrance. The doors were huge and rusted, so heavy I had to lean my body weight against them to open up. The doors creaked loudly as I pushed through. Inside was even more depressing than outside. I looked around. All I could see were rusted pillars, broken, grimy glass windows, and holes in every wall. It was dark and hard to focus too far in front. Frank could be anywhere in here. But the place was deathly silent.

"Frank?" I called out, my voice sounding hollow. "Frank, I am here. I did as you told me to. Now show yourself."

There was no reply, only the sound of my own voice echoing around the empty warehouse. I moved on, slowly, deeper into the warehouse. Rubble from the broken walls and glass littered the floor. Joey and Kane had been right, this was place was a maze. There were corridors leading off in every direction.

"Frank!" I shouted again. But again, no response. I stopped and listened intently, wanting to hear him move so I could at least know which direction to expect him from. The silence was eerie. There was no movement anywhere, until suddenly, right next to me, something moved. I jumped back to give myself some room. I held my hands up to my face as a fucking pigeon flapped its wings over my head. "Damn it!" I cursed under my breath.

My impatience turns to seething anger as I realize I am still under his control. He was still pulling the fucking strings, wasn't he? He got me here and now he is making me wait on his every whim. The silence is shattered by the sharp ringing sound of a phone somewhere nearby. I stumbled around, following the obnoxiously loud sound until I found it. It was a burner phone, discreetly placed for me to find.

I answer the call, holding it to my ear, but I refuse to speak. "Well done, Ray. You made it to checkpoint number one." His voice sneers. My anger and frustration boiled over. "But you broke the fucking rules again, didn't you?"

"What the fuck are you talking about? I am standing here, alone, where you told me to be. Now where is she?" I demanded.

"Yes, you are standing there alone. But who is that I see backing you up?" he says "that wouldn't be Detective Kane, would it? Waiting to run in and save the day?"

My heart sinks as I realize I cannot hide anything from him. Even the highly trained detective backing me up cannot escape his attention. I cannot deny it. That will just piss him off more, he clearly knows.

"I am feeling generous Ray, I will give you one more chance. The first thing I want you to do is throw your phone, now. Hard enough to break it. Let me hear it."

I take my phone from my pocket, and I launch it at the nearest wall. I let out some of my anger in doing so. The phones crashes against the wall and scatters in pieces all over the floor. "There, done. Now what?" my tone is giving me away. I am letting him know he is getting to me, but I cannot control it anymore.

"Very good, Ray. See, you can follow instructions, can't

CHAPTER 66 – CHECKPOINT ONE

you?" he sounds like he is enjoying this, far too much.

"Cut the bullshit, Frank, you asshole. What now?"

He chuckles, an irritating sound that finds its way right under my skin. "Now, you get to checkpoint two. And this time, you come alone. There won't be any more warnings, Ray, I promise you that."

I clench my fists, fighting the urge to punch something... . or someone. Frank's smug tone grates on my last nerve. "Where's checkpoint two?" I ask through gritted teeth.

"So eager, Ray. The Pullman District, the old factory. We are waiting for your daddy, aren't we, sweetheart?" He has turned his attention to Megan. It makes my heart ache. "Keep the burner on, lose the tail. 30 minutes. Get going,"

The line goes dead and my hope fades further still. I scan the room, looking for an exit that Kane won't see. I pick my route, and I run fast as I can. The cool night air hits my face as I burst out of the back door, my feet pounding the pavement.

I look around, making sure Kane and the team cannot see me. The Pullman district isn't too far away. I can make it on foot in time, but I am going to do as told. I am going it alone. I sneak just far enough out of sight that I won't be seen when I break into a full sprint.

I take off; the wind whipping at my face. My heart pounds in my chest, a mix of adrenaline and fear. Megan's terrified face flashes in my mind, spurring me on, keeping my legs moving even when I feel I can't run any further. I am coming Megan; Daddy will be there soon.

67

Chapter 67 – Silent breach

Kane watched on from her surveillance point, her eyes locked on the warehouse. She hadn't moved in what felt like hours, staring as if looking away for even a moment would make her miss something critical. It was too quiet. Something felt off. Ray hadn't checked in, she just kept asking herself, what is going on in there?

She ran through her decision again in her mind. Letting Ray go in alone had been risky. She'd known it, but what choice had she really had? Now, that decision was weighing heavily on her. Her instincts, the same instincts that had gotten her where she was today, screamed that this wasn't right.

"We've given him enough time," Kane finally said into her radio. "Five more minutes, then we breach."

She raised her binoculars and scanned the warehouse, feeling more frustrated by the lack of any visual. The windows were blacked out. No movement, no sound. Just the wind whipping around the team and the faint hum of distant traffic.

Five minutes passed, too slowly for her liking. Kane exhaled, a small apology slipping from her lips. "Sorry, Ray, but it's

CHAPTER 67 - SILENT BREACH

now or never." She clicked her radio. "Okay, listen up. We're going in. No eyes inside, so take it slow. Innocent lives are at stake. We protect them at all costs."

"Copy that," came the clipped replies from her team.

Kane checked her weapon, the familiar weight doing nothing to steady her nerves. A glance at the officers nearest to her, a sharp nod exchanged, and they moved out.

The team approached the warehouse, moving low and quiet, splitting off to take separate entrances. Kane eased through a rusted side door, the creak cutting through the deadly silence. Inside, the air was stale, thick with dust. Flashlights flicked on almost in unison.

"Spread out," Kane ordered, her voice low but firm. The team moved with precision, boots crunching over debris.

Her eyes darted around, scanning for anything. A noise, a shadow, a sign of Ray. Then a voice called out, sharp and urgent. "Got something here!"

Kane sprinted toward the sound, her heart pounding. "What is it?" she asked.

The officer held up a shattered cell phone. "Looks like it was smashed recently. Certainly not being lying around her for long."

She didn't need to examine it, she already knew "That's Ray's phone" she muttered. The realization hit her like a punch to the gut. "This was a setup. God damn it!"

She turned to the team, her voice sharp. "Alright, listen up! We've been played. Ray's not here. Priority number one is finding him. How did he get out of here without us seeing him?"

An officer gestured toward the back of the warehouse. "Too many exits. They all lead toward the old industrial sites behind this one. If Frank's still moving him, that's the direction they'll take."

Kane's mind raced. It made sense. Frank wouldn't waste time dragging Ray too far. The abandoned factory spaces would give him plenty of places to hide and control the situation.

"Good work," she said, already moving. "Everyone, regroup. We're heading out back. Stay sharp. Frank could be watching."

The team moved quickly, following Kane's lead as they made their way through the warehouse and out into the night, the hunt for Ray and Megan pressing on.

68

Chapter 68 – A father's promise

As I close in on the factory, sweat pouring down my face, every breath now hard to come by, I realize I have made good time, better than expected. I stop and take a breather; I want to compose myself and go in there ready for anything.

I take out the burner phone, praying that it will allow me to make an outbound call. I wanted to call Alison, let her know what was happening, tell her I was doing all I can to get Megan home.

I punch Alison's number into the phone. That number has always been there in the back of mind, and right now I am so glad I have it. I press the call button and it rings. My heart pounds as I hope she will answer. One ring, two rings, three—

"Hello?" Alison's voice, tight with worry.

"Al, it's me," I whisper, glancing around to ensure I'm still alone. "I'm close. I think I've found where he is keeping Megan."

A sharp intake of breath. "Oh God, are you sure? Where are you?"

"It's an old factory out in the Pullman District. I'm about to go in." I swallow hard, steeling myself. "I just... I needed you to know. In case...."

"Don't," Alison cuts me off, her voice cracking. "Don't you dare say it! You hear me? You're bringing our daughter home."

I nod, forgetting she can't see me. "Yeah. Yeah, of course I am."

The call falls silent, almost as if we are in a moment of silent prayer together. Unspoken fears and desperate hope keep us on the line longer than we should be.

"Be careful Ray, please" Alison's voice is barely comprehensible above her tears.

"I will, I promise. And Al, I am sorry, I am truly sorry for everything. I love you both with all my heart," I am scared this is the last time I will speak with her; I want her to know I care.

I end the call before my emotions can consume me and put the phone back in my pocket. I take a few deep breaths and wipe the sweat away from my brow, and walk slowly, cautiously into the factory. Another dark, depressing place. It feels as though I am taking a tour inside Frank's mind with the places he is sending me.

I make my way through another broken-down, beaten-up hell hole, searching from room to room, corner to corner for Megan. A task made even more difficult by the darkness filling each room. The floors are again littered with crumpled parts of walls and pillars, glass and trash almost filling the entire floor space.

I pull out the burner phone, hoping that light from the screen will be enough to guide me through the debris. The small bit of light I am getting catches something, but it is just a shattered mirror. I catch a glimpse of myself in the broken pieces, my face looking more haggard as the seconds pass by.

CHAPTER 68 – A FATHER'S PROMISE

Another room full of silence, the only sound that of the broken debris under my feet. Every doorway feels like a potential threat, as though Frank could hide just inside with a gun pointed at my head.

I find myself in a room, looks like it must have been an office of some sort back when this place was up and running. There is a desk in the middle of the room, some paperwork on top, but the paper looks fresh. It is a blueprint, looks to be of this factory. I scan it and spot and X on the page. My heart jumps into my throat. Megan! That must be where he is keeping her. All my fear of any potential danger evaporates as I set off in that direction, determined to see her again.

Running through the factory was a bad idea. I was making too much noise. He could hear me coming from a mile off, but I didn't care. I was so close I could almost smell Megan's hair again. I had crossed the entire factory in what felt like seconds. I got to the room; the door was closed.

Reaching for the handle, I took a second to compose myself. I had to be prepared for whatever was on the other side of this door. I pushed the door open and there, tied to a little plastic chair, was my Megan. Her hair was ragged from where it had been hacked, she looked pale and thin. Her eyes were red, her face blotchy. She was still crying. "Daddy!" she screamed, more tears falling down her face. "Daddy, I knew you would come for me."

I crossed the room as quickly as I could, tearing at the ties and pulling her into my arms for a hug. I squeezed her so hard. I broke down in tears. I was sobbing uncontrollably. I tried to compose myself, but I was so happy to see her again, to hold her. "Oh Megan, I am so sorry I took so long. I love you so much, my baby girl," I say, wiping away the tears from her cheeks.

"I love you too, Daddy," she said, smiling back at me.

It felt as though the nightmare was finally over: salvation. But in the joy of seeing her again, I had forgotten I still had to get her out of here. I lifted her into my arms and stood "we gotta go sweetheart, let's go see mummy" but as I turned to head for the door, I see Frank standing there point a gun at us. My heart drops, Megan's sinks into my chest as though she is trying to hide from the bad man.

"Well, isn't this all very touching, Ray?" he sneers.

69

Chapter 69 – The face off

I pull Megan in closer to me, wanting to hide her from this continuing nightmare. I can feel her trembling against me as I hold her. I had always imagined her being so scared, but now that I could physically feel her fear, the anger burned up inside me. It took all of my self-control to stop myself from racing straight at him like a bull, looking to smash him into the nearest wall.

Looking around the room, I wanted to find an escape route, a way out without getting close to Frank. But we were trapped. He was blocking our only exit.

"Frank, you have had your fun. Now let her go," I pleaded with him. I just wanted him to let Megan go. If she was safe, I didn't care what happened to me.

He smiled, an evil smile that made my blood go cold. "Ray, my fun only begins now. Everything else was building to this moment. Now I get to play my game with you."

I hang my head; I just feel defeated. It is never ending and right now, even after how far I have come, he is still the one holding all the cards. He continues, "before we continue, how about you take that gun out and toss it over here."

I had forgotten I even had it. Kane had insisted I go in armed. I had to be able to protect myself should it come to.... Well, this, a standoff. But with Megan in my arms, I was too vulnerable. I wasn't about to open this out to a shoot-out. I gently removed the gun from my belt line and dropped in on the floor in front of me and kicked it over to him.

"Good, good. Continue following the rules and you may have as much fun as I am!"

"Why are you doing this, Frank? What could I have possibly done to you that justifies all of this?" I ask him, exasperated by it all. He wasn't one of the criminals I treated like shit over the years. I rarely interacted with him. It made no sense.

He stared me down, his expression hardening. "You really have no idea, do you, you clueless bastard?"

I just stared back, blank. I had nothing. He was right. I was clueless. I just shake my head, admitting I don't know.

"Mia Carter," he says, just the name and then he looks at me, watching me for a reaction.

"Who is that?" I ask, confused by the statement.

His anger picks up right away, his face twists as he tries to stop himself from letting it all out, but he snaps "you son of a bitch, you don't even remember her, do you? She really meant that little to you?"

I search my brain for the memory of the name. I dealt with so many people, but mostly men, this name should ring a bell. It should trigger something, but maybe the emotional trauma he has put me through recently has dulled all other damage. I just look at him, blank, unable to offer a response.

"Ray, you are pissing me off. You are disrespecting her, even after her death. You pushed her too far when you were you

CHAPTER 69 – THE FACE OFF

using her for information, and now.... Now you don't even remember her?!"

Suddenly it dawns on me, Mia. She was a sweet enough kid, for a drug addict, an informant with valuable information. One I didn't want to let go. I think back to my time dealing with her, not my proudest moments.

Around four years ago

I stood in the piss-stained alley way, waiting on my informant. She was young, 18 or 19 years old, sweet girl, but addicted to drugs. Was sad to see, really. I had learned a little about her, how she had fallen out with her parents when she had fallen in with a dangerous crowd. Drugs had become an escape for her, and now she had found herself intertwined with the criminal underworld of Chicago.

She was buying drugs when I first picked her up. At first, she offered me information in order to escape her own punishment. It was always good for a cop to find someone who has information and is more interested in self-preservation than the rest of the scum in their dirty little circles. I latched on like a leech, draining her of all the information. She was useful. Never let me down.

This one time she came to me; said she wanted out. She wanted to get her life back on track. So, she spoke with her parents. She told them she wanted to turn things around. But she was in deep. It was not just with the gangs she was running with, but with a cop. He was squeezing her for information. That cop was me.

"Mr. Gordon, I want to go home. I want to go back to school, make a life for myself. Can you help me get out of this?" she had pleaded with me.

I won't lie. It pulled at my heartstrings a little. I was a father.

I couldn't imagine my little girl out here going through life this way. But she wasn't my girl, and I was a selfish, power-hungry bastard. "Mia, you know it's not that simple. You have information I need; you have access, and you have committed crimes. I cannot just let you walk away."

She bowed her head, her voice cracking as she cried. "But I have done so much. Surely it is enough? It was just drugs."

"Just drugs?" I ask her, "You have continued to buy and take drugs this whole time, Mia."

She looks away from me. She is embarrassed. There is hope for her. She still has the capability to feel shame for what she has done with her life. I could sense her determination, and that scared me. Mia wasn't just saying she wanted out this time; she meant it. She was trying to escape, to claw her way back to some semblance of normalcy, and that didn't work for me. Not yet. I still needed her.

"You have been doing such good work. Think of the scum you have helped me take off the streets, Mia."

She snapped back at me, "I don't care, I just want my life back. I don't want to live like this anymore. I am scared all the time. Please Mr. Gordon, let me go."

This is bad for me. So, I think a little outside the box. I reach into my pocket, my fingers grasping the small bag I had taken from a bust a few days ago. I hesitate, considering if I really want to go this way, but eventually I pull it out.

I hold up the bag, the small white rocks clearly visible. Her eyes lock on it right away. I knew right then that she wouldn't be able to resist. Addicts rarely do. "You keep working for me, Mia, and this is yours. You can have it all."

"No... I can't.... I don't want to" she is trying to maintain her determination but the crack in her voice betrays her resolve.

CHAPTER 69 – THE FACE OFF

"Just one small hit and we can work this out together Mia," I say, stepping in closer and opening the bag.

Worked like a charm. She tells me what I need to know, and she takes the bag and off she goes. I can use her again when I need her.

Problem is, the next day Joey and I are called to another scene, an overdose victim. I wasn't quite prepared for this; the victim was Mia. She had taken the entire bag that night, used it all. And now here she was, just a kid, laying on the floor, dead.

"What a waste," Joey said. I simply nodded in agreement and then went on with my day. I hadn't even felt guilty at the time.

Back in the present

Frank was studying me as I was recalling it all. "You remember her now, don't you, you evil bastard!"

"It wasn't my fault," I say. "She was an addict before I met her. She was always going to end up that way."

"No!" he screams "No. Don't you do you that, don't you dare say that. You know she wanted out. She told her mother she wanted out, but you just couldn't let her, could you?"

I hold on tighter to Megan. I didn't want her hearing this about her father. I prayed she didn't understand any of it. The realization that there was no way he was going to let me out of here was setting in. I was just hoping that Kane was catching up.

"It didn't end there Ray, the pain continued to spread."

I look at him. I don't know where he is going with this "what do you mean?"

"You know she wanted out!" Frank's voice cracks, rage giving way to grief. "She begged you for her life, and you pushed her right back into that hole. Because of that, she died.

My niece, my sweet Mia, because of you." He chokes back a sob, his hands trembling as he grips the gun tighter. "And as if that weren't enough, my sister... she couldn't live with the guilt. You killed them both, Ray. You!"

My head was spinning. I felt as though the floor beneath me was moving and I rocked back and forth. I wasn't getting out of this. I had pushed him too far, without even knowing it.

"Now, send Megan over here, Ray. Come on."

I pull her closer to me again. "No fucking way Frank, you are not getting your hands on her again."

He firms up his stance, pointing the gun directly at Megan. "You can send her over or you can hold her lifeless body in your arms right now, your choice."

My mind raced. Could I trust him not to hurt her? Of course not. But what choice did I have? If I resisted, she'd die right here, in my arms.

"Sweetheart," I said, crouching to her level, my voice cracking. "I need you to be brave for Daddy, okay? Just... go to Frank. Trust me, baby. Trust me."

"No, Daddy! Please, no!" Her cries shattered what was left of me. She reaches for me, hoping I will take her back into my arms. But I guide in her in his direction. Every step she took toward Frank felt like a knife twisting in my chest.

Frank shifts his attention to Megan, maintaining his evil smile. "Come on now, come to Uncle Frank."

It is the opening I need. While he is looking away, I jump into action. I hit a full sprint as quick as I can, and I am past Megan in a heartbeat. Frank can't reposition his gun in time. I am belt line into him. My shoulder slams into his chest with all my force. The impact knocks us both to the ground.

"Run, Megan. Run, now get out of here!" I scream at the top

CHAPTER 69 – THE FACE OFF

of my voice.

She doesn't hesitate; she heads straight for the nearest exit. Good girl, I think to myself. I turn to see Frank stumbling to his feet. I take off running for the same exit. But I don't make it. There is a loud bang, then a searing pain in my right shoulder. It stops me in my tracks, then a second bang, another pain ripping through my lower back, and I crumple to the ground in an agonizing heap.

Through slightly blurry vision, I see Megan fleeing through the exit and just for a moment, relief washes over me. I knew I might never see her again. But at least she was safe, for now.

Frank stood over me, gun pointed at me as he became a blurry, dark shadow. "You didn't really think you could get out of this, did you, Ray?"

I felt myself slipping away. This was it for me.

70

Chapter 70 – Megan's cry

Kane and her team sprinted toward the factory, unaware of what was unfolding inside. She thought of all her decisions. The memory of Marshall's lifeless body flashed in her mind. She had allowed him to follow that lead alone. It was a brutal reminder of what can go wrong. And now she had allowed Ray to go in alone. She couldn't allow the same fate for him. Suddenly, some movement up ahead caught her eye, and she threw up her hand to halt the team.

"Hold up," she hissed into the radio. She crouched low, her hand hovering near her holstered weapon. She raised her binoculars and zoned in on the target. A tiny figure broke into view, running from the shadows of the factory. Her breath caught.

"It's the girl," she said, her voice not able to hide her relief. "Brown, go get her. Now."

Brown didn't hesitate. He bolted toward the girl, getting to her in no time at all. He scooped her up in his arms and was back to Kane within moments. Her small body was shaking, her face streaked with tears.

CHAPTER 70 – MEGAN'S CRY

He set her down in front of Kane, still sobbing. She cried "Daddy," over and over.

Kane kneeled down; her voice was soft but firm. "It's okay, sweetheart. You're safe now. We're here to help you, and we're going to take you home, I promise." She pulled Megan close, her arms wrapping around her trembling body.

Megan buried her face against Kane's shoulder, her words muffled, just about audible through the sobs. "The bad man... he's hurting my daddy... please... please help him." Megan's tiny hands clung to Kane's jacket. It was as if she didn't want to let her go. This gave Kane a strange, maternal urge to protect the girl with all she had.

Kane's body tightened, her heart twisting painfully at the desperation in Megan's voice. "We'll help him," she said, pulling back just enough to look Megan in the eye. "But I need you to stay here, okay? Stay with Officer Brown. He'll keep you safe."

Megan nodded, tears still streaming down her cheeks. Kane glanced at Brown. "Don't let her out of your sight."

She turned back to her team, her determination growing. "Let's move. Now."

Kane led the way, her team falling in line behind her. The factory was huge. It could take forever to find them. Kane's worry grew with Megan's words: "the bad man is hurting my daddy." She had to find Ray alive. There was no other option.

The team moved swiftly into the factory, their footsteps echoing off the walls. The air inside smelled of rust and damp concrete. The flashlights exposing the decaying features of the factory's walls and the exposed pipes.

Kane's eyes darted from shadow to shadow, her weapon drawn, ready to take Frank out at the first opportunity. But the place was empty. There was nothing to see. They did not know which way Megan had come from.

She listened intently, trying to hear anything other than the boots of her team scraping the floors. "Hold still," she whispered into the radio. The entire team halted in their tracks, obeying the command in unison.

The silence was deafening. It felt as though they were at another dead end, nothing but another abandoned building. But then, a small noise, the sound of someone gasping in pain, gave them a direction to follow. She pointed in that direction. The team moved on cue. Both experienced officers and rookies felt the same urgency. They were racing to save Ray's life.

71

Chapter 71 – Final breath

I lay on the floor, helpless to fight Frank off. The blood was draining from my body. Two gunshots well placed had completely disarmed me, and Frank knew it. He pressed his foot down on the gunshot wound on my shoulder, smiling as he looked me in the eye. He was enjoying watching the life drain out of me.

Everything inside me screamed don't let him know your pain, stay quiet, don't give him the satisfaction. But I couldn't hold out. The pain was too intense. It burned up from inside me and eventually I cried out in pain, which only made him smile more.

"This is what it has all been building up to Ray," he said while ensuring our eyes remained fixed on each other, "seeing you alone, helpless, in pain. Just like Mia, nobody is here to save you. Nobody will be here to protect your family when you are gone."

I felt like I was slipping between life and death. I summoned all my energy, determined to defy this monster. "Fuck you, Frank," I spat, blood leaving my mouth.

He just laughed. It grated on me that this was the last sound I would hear, the last face I would see. It didn't seem fair. But what more could I expect? I was a man who didn't care about anyone but himself for years. Maybe this was tragically poetic.

As my vision blurred, a sudden crash echoed through the room. Frank's head snapped in the direction of the noise, his foot lifting from my wound, causing as much as when he had pressed on it. I gasped and tried to suck in as much air as I could, but I was struggling to breathe. The blood had reached my lungs, and I felt as though I were being suffocated.

"What the...." Frank started, but was cut short as a team of police officers burst into the room.

I turned my head to see. My eyes struggled to focus, but I could just about make out the silhouette. It was Kane, her gun raised and steady, pointed directly at Frank. She didn't speak. She didn't give Frank a chance to speak. She just fired two sharp rounds and Frank hit the floor next to me, screaming out in pain. Despite everything I was feeling, I managed a slight smile at the sight, the sound of him crumpling in pain.

Kane left Frank to the other officers and attended to me. "Ray, can you hear me? Where are you hit?"

I looked her in the eye. I couldn't speak, I tried to, but all I could do was to gurgle on my own blood. I wanted to see her one last time, Megan's smile, her little arms around my neck. I wanted to tell Alison that I tried, that I fought with everything I had. But the words wouldn't come. My body had failed, but my heart burned with the love I couldn't speak.

I coughed once, twice.... And then Kane faded away. Everything went black. I was gone.

Kane leaned over Ray, listening for any signs of breathing. There were none. She felt for a pulse, but there was nothing.

CHAPTER 71 - FINAL BREATH

"Medic! Get me a medic in here now!" Kane shouted. Then she tried CPR on Ray's lifeless body. She pushed down on his chest, but knew it was too late. She knew this was another burden she would have to carry for the rest of her life.

The sound of Frank struggling against her fellow officer draws her attention. She wants to shoot him right between the eyes. But she resists. "I could have taken you out, Frank, but that's too easy for you. No, you are going to suffer for what you have done, you son of a bitch. Former cop like you in prison for the rest of your life. You are going to suffer for a long time."

Frank's eyes widened with a mixture of fear and rage. He spat blood on the floor and smiled back at Kane. "That bastard got what he deserved!"

Her hand twitched toward her holstered gun, her breath coming fast and shallow. Every fiber of her being screamed at her to end it now, to kill Frank, silence him so she never has to see that smug bastards face again. Instead, she turned away from him, tightened her grip on her emotions, and forced her anger down.

The room was filling with officers and paramedics, who had now taken over CPR on Ray, but she knew it was futile. It was too late to save him.

Her heart wrenched at the thought of seeing Megan again. How could she explain her father would not be coming back? That his sacrifice was the reason she was free.

72

Chapter 72 – A tribute

Alison sits next to Megan, holding her hand, a gentle but firm hold. She hasn't wanted to let go of her, not since she got her back. They have been here about 30 minutes already, talking to Ray. They are the only people here at the cemetery, so they talk with Ray freely.

The cool morning air carried the faint scent of freshly cut grass, the early morning sun warming their faces. It has been six months since Ray rescued Megan, giving his life to save hers. Alison has thanked him in her prayers every night since. She has cried every night since.

"Thank you. You kept your promise, Ray. You saved her. I just wish you were here to see how much she still needs you, how much we both do.... Megan talks about you every day," Alison says to the headstone before her. Ray's name etched into it. The dates show his life was too short.

"I miss you daddy; I hope you can hear me when I talk to you at bedtime," Megan cries, "I get so scared without you."

"He's here with you, sweetheart. In a way, he always will be." Alison squeezed Megan's hand tighter and pointed to her

CHAPTER 72 – A TRIBUTE

heart. "He'd be very proud of you right now."

Megan nods and smiles at that, wiping her tears with her free hand. "I drew you a picture, daddy."

Alison's heart aches at the sight of the picture, a crayon drawing of a stick figure man with a cape flowing behind him, a big smile on his face. "It is beautiful, baby; I am sure daddy loves it."

Megan stands up, places the picture on the grave and kisses Ray's headstone one last time before they get up and leave "my hero," she says.

Printed in Great Britain
by Amazon